ONE
GIRL
MISSING

BOOKS BY CARLA KOVACH

ONE GIRL MISSING

CARLA KOVACH

bookouture

Published by Bookouture in 2022

An imprint of Storyfire Ltd.
Carmelite House
50 Victoria Embankment
London EC4Y 0DZ

www.bookouture.com

ISBN: 9781-80314-155-8
eBook ISBN: 978-1-80314-154-1

I dedicate this book to teachers. The very people who impart knowledge onto our children, inspiring them to follow their dreams and aspirations. X

PROLOGUE

When you love someone so much you'd give your life for them, you know they're the one.

I know you're the one. It's rare that such love can be found. Now that I've found you, I can never let you go. I've waited long enough but a person can get impatient.

I wipe the blob of blue paint from my hand and pop the rag in my back pocket. Standing back, I admire my work. It's beautiful, just like you.

The time has come and I have a lot to do. You betrayed me once, but you will never get the chance to do that again. I'll make sure of it.

You do love me.

We love each other.

I love you.

ONE

SATURDAY, 2 APRIL

Annabel

As the door to the Angel Arms pub closes behind us, I hold on to Jen for dear life. When I look up, the starry April sky begins to spin. 'I shouldn't have had that last cocktail. Not only did it taste and look like swamp water, my head is swimming too.' I swiftly take my gaze away from the stars, which makes me lose my balance for a second. 'Never again.'

'Yeah, right.' The pub lights go out, leaving us in darkness. The woman who ran the place looked pleased that we'd left early so that she could close up. Jen takes my hand. 'Annie Bell, you always say that and every time you go that extra mile, but I wouldn't have you any other way.' Jen grabs my arm to steady me. Her long hair swings from side to side and it slaps my face with every step.

I drop my duster jacket and laugh. 'You still call me Annie Bell after all these years. I feel like we're still at primary school.'

She picks up my jacket and passes it back to me with a

giggle. 'You'll always be Annie Bell to me, my lovely. We best get you home.'

'Home, that word again.' I pause. I don't want to go home ever again but I suppose I have to confront the issue, confront him properly. Things are worse than ever and I can't live like I'm walking on eggshells for much longer. He's so angry and agitated lately. I don't even know if he's home. That's how much we talk. 'We haven't got a marriage anymore.' I've been telling Jen about it all night and I feel bad for going there yet again.

'You could stay at mine if your babysitter was up for some overtime.'

'My neighbour said to stay out as long as I wanted but I already texted to say that I was on my way back. I don't expect Grant will be there.' It wasn't likely anyway. He was never home. That giggly feeling has now totally gone. All that is left is a creeping emptiness that is threatening to topple me.

Jen leads me past the bus stop and along the high street. If Grant is home, he'll be tucked up in the spare room. If not, that's where he'll go when he gets home. Then, when I wake up, I'll be ready to confront him and his betrayal. 'We've had some good times, haven't we, Jen?'

'Of course we have.' Jen links her arm in mine and smiles.

'What were you going to tell me earlier?'

'Oh, it's nothing. I'll call you tomorrow.'

'Thanks for the chat earlier, at yours.' I owe her one. She's made me see what I need to do. I can't let Grant treat me this way. What I'm going to do will destroy Cally's heart in more ways than one, but I've had it with the lies.

'You're my best friend. I'm always here for you. If you need a place to stay when you've had it out with him, you and Cally are always welcome at mine.' Jen smiles at me but it's not her usual wide smile.

The lights of the high street are being left behind and I feel a chill on my arms. We take a right off the main road, the quickest way back to mine, and I almost topple in a pothole. Jen is sporting a serious look. I might be drunk but I know when my best friend has something on her mind. 'What is it, Jen?'

She shakes her head. 'I'm not in the mood to talk about it, really.'

'Jen's hiding something and I know it's important.' I'm using the sing-song voice I use with my little girl, Cally, and that makes Jen laugh. It's better than her frowning face.

'And I'm not telling you while you're hammered.'

I slip off the kerb, landing in the gutter. 'Help me up.'

Jen grabs my hands and makes a straining noise as she tries to pull me up, then she accidentally drops me back in the gutter where I lie, laughing like never before. I've had such a good night considering earlier today. I want to milk the last few minutes until I have to walk back into my problematic life again.

'You're so funny.' I'm dizzy as she pulls me up again, just in time as someone racing along the narrow road speeds past, lifting my hair in a sudden gust. I hear the engine revving as the car pulls away even faster. 'Dick,' I shout as I realise how close I just came to death.

'Idiot.' Jen sticks her finger up at the car, but it's too late. The driver has already gone. 'Those kids will kill someone one day.'

'Thanks for saving me, Jen.' I plant a kiss on her cheek and she continues to guide me to my house where she left her car.

'That was close. Feel my heart.' Jen grabs my hand and holds it over her chest and I feel it beating rapidly.

Soon we are passing a tired-looking community hall. 'That's where I used to take Cally for stay and play.'

'Do you miss those days?' Jen smiles as she looks across the mound of grass.

'I do. I miss them terribly. She was such a cute baby and then she was an even cuter toddler.'

'Cally is exceptionally cute. I'll give you that. It's those big brown eyes, just like her mama's.'

I cross my eyes and suck my cheeks in, and Jen laughs. That's when we leave the street lamps behind and keep trekking and staggering along the narrowing path. 'Can't fall over, can't fall over.' I repeat this over and over again as Jen dutifully keeps hold of me. 'I'm walking on that.'

'That?' Jen looks confused. I step down, now on the cycle path. She runs around to the other side of me. As she lets me go, I miss the stability of her petite but strong frame. Very soon, she's back by my side, standing between me and danger.

Headlights fill the road. The main beam blinds me and before I have time to react, I see the yellow of Jen's jacket flying over the bonnet, her dyed plum coloured hair splayed out midair before I hear a sickening thud. 'Jen.' I try to run around the car but my legs aren't responding. Leaning on the bonnet for support, I drag my way around the car and glance through the window as I pass the passenger side. The driver isn't in the car. There's a fold-up bike on the back seat. The driver must be tending to Jen.

Reality hits me. 'Jen,' I yell as tears flood my face. I fall but continue crawling along the cycle lane. My knees bleed as all my weight presses my skin onto the road. Jen's bag lies on the path, its contents strewn everywhere. The fancy cocktail sticks I asked her to save for me as a reminder of our night out. Her purse. Her car keys – everything. Then I see Jen and the blood makes me heave. With open lifeless eyes, she stares up at the moon. I shout but she still stares, not a flicker of movement.

Where's the driver? I glance around as I reach Jen. Hugging her close to me, I try to fish my phone out of my pocket. 'Please don't die.' I try to unlock it but my shaking fingers are like butter and my mind is fuzzy. Everything is so surreal, I think I might be dreaming. I feel a presence behind me; a waft of air as someone reaches over and snatches my phone. 'She needs an ambulance.' My phone is dropped to the floor and the driver stamps on it, cracking the screen. 'What are you doing? My friend needs help.' I'm distracted by the number plate. I recognise it but is the person in the balaclava him?

I see the shiny crowbar in the hands of a gloved person and I flinch as the searing white pain of the strike cracks my head. Blood trickles through my fingers and I can't see from one of my eyes for a few seconds. 'Please. What are you doing? Please just leave us.' The crunch of a fist hits my face and all I can think of is Cally. My little Cally. I want to be with her but I fear I will never see her again. I might not even see tomorrow. As he manhandles me, I grab anything, catching some material sticking out of his pocket. I let it go, whatever it was is of no use to me. The world is a blur and I feel rough material around me as he scrunches up my limbs to fit in the boot of the car. I cry out for Jen one more time but she can't hear. No one can hear. My nose fills up and my face is soaked with tears. I can't breathe. My heart – it's beating too fast. I gasp and fight my peppering vision as another blow meets my head. It's all over. This is how I'm going to die. 'Please,' I gasp between breaths, 'don't hurt me.'

That's when I hear the muffled voice through the balaclava. 'Why would I do that? This is just the beginning.' The figure strokes my matted hair. 'I have a surprise for you.'

Whatever it is, I'm never going to see it. I can't see and I'm sinking, losing myself and... I... can't... breathe...

TWO

Detective Inspector Gina Harte leaned over one of the desks in the incident room and stared at the boards. Another case closed. It had been a long day, as usual, and all she wanted to do was go home and snuggle with her cat. She removed the bobble from her hair and allowed her freshly dyed brown waves to fall over her shoulders. Tiredness had crept into every part of her body to the point that if she breathed any deeper, she'd be asleep with her eyes open.

'You heading home?' Detective Chief Inspector Chris Briggs walked through and grabbed his suit jacket, his thick fingers doing up the buttons after he'd pulled it over his shoulders. His hair flopped forward slightly as he reached for his bag under the table.

Gina wondered how, after they'd been so close these past few months, he could lie so easily to her face. 'Yes, just finishing up. I need a shower and my bed.' She yawned. Her gaze fixed on his for a moment longer than a glance, but he gave her no clues as to what he was thinking. He was the man she'd trusted with everything. He'd helped her to shut up the journalist who was trying to expose her secrets to the world. He also knew that she'd gone out of her way to make sure her ex-husband, Terry, died all those years ago after she helped him to fall down the stairs. All those skeletons were kept in the closet because he chose to keep the door locked and that was Gina's problem. She was losing him.

She'd seen him with some woman, coming out of a pub a couple of days ago on her way back from the supermarket. She swallowed, knowing that she could never give him the relationship he craved but now, tonight, wasn't the time to discuss it. Maybe this is how their secret relationship ended.

She sighed as she thought of the smart-looking, olive-skinned woman she'd seen him with. He'd looked happier and more carefree than he'd ever looked in Gina's company. If Briggs moved on, he would definitely leave a void in her life, especially as he was the only person on the planet who truly knew her.

Footsteps sounded down the corridor and Detective Sergeant Jacob Driscoll burst through the swinging door. Gina cleared her throat before looking away from Briggs. Jacob paced across the room before pulling out a chair, his ear fixed to his phone. He ended the call.

'You still here?' Gina pushed thoughts of Briggs from her mind. If you love a person, sometimes it's best to let them go. At least one of them could be happy. That's what she tried to tell herself. The churning in her stomach at the thought of him enjoying spending time with someone else, told another story.

Jacob nodded. 'Yes, I was just trying to get hold of Jennifer but she's not answering. I'll try again in a minute. I have a couple of things to do to wrap up the case but I need a drink. Anyone else want a cuppa?'

Gina watched as Jacob's foot bounced on the floor. It wasn't like him to be nervous, in fact, he was always the face of cool. Always neatly groomed, he was currently sporting the tidiest short back and sides she'd seen in a while. His late thirties were treating him much better than hers did. She unzipped her jacket. 'Yes, I'll have a coffee with you.'

Briggs smiled and stepped towards the door. 'I'll skip the drink. I'll catch you both tomorrow.' Jacob continued staring at his phone as Briggs waved as he headed towards the door. She glanced at him and forced a smile, knowing that he was probably going to be with her.

As Jacob tapped away on his phone, she glanced out of the window into the car park where she watched Briggs messaging someone before getting into his car. A couple of police cars pulled out and another arrived. Several drunken people sat on a wall smoking. There was always a crowd at the station on a Saturday night. She inhaled, taking in the smell of Detective Constable Harry O'Connor's cheeseburger from earlier and her stomach clenched in hunger. 'Are we getting this drink anytime today, Jacob? You could check to see if O'Connor left any of that chocolate volcano cake in the kitchen. Mrs O exceeded herself with that bake.' Yes, she needed a shower but with a coffee and a bit of cake being offered, she'd stay.

He bit his lip and rubbed the fine layer of the day's stubble. 'Yes, I'll just hit send on this message.' He stood in the middle of the room, staring at his phone. 'And it's gone.'

'You're not yourself.'

'That obvious, is it?'

'I'm afraid so. What's up?'

'I'm worried about Jennifer. She's out with her friend.'

'And that worries you?'

'No. Well, I don't know. I can't remember whether I said I'd pick her up and I can't get hold of her.'

'Maybe she got a taxi. I'm sure she's fine. She might even still be having fun with her friend.'

He pressed his lips together and nodded. 'You're right, that's probably all it is. I'll do that drink and head home. She's either having a brilliant night out or she's sparked out in bed. If she needed a lift or a pizza on my way home, she'd have called me.'

'Was she out anywhere nice?'

'Just a few drinks with one of her schoolmates at the Angel. I don't know if nice is the word.' He laughed and headed towards the kitchen.

Gina agreed. The new licensee had made it a much nicer pub than it had been in the past but it was still a bit rough around the edges. She went to grab her bag as her mobile began to buzz. 'DI Harte.'

'It's Jhanvi, we've just had a call-out to an incident and I'm there now. It's a hit-and-run.' PC Kapoor's signal began to crackle so she repeated the word hello a few times, the young Brummie police officer's accent as strong as ever.

'I'm still here, Jhanvi. How can we help with the hit-and-run?'

'It's the victim.'

'Okay. Do we know who it is?'

'It's one of our crime scene investigators, Jennifer. Jacob's girlfriend.'

'Damn.' She watched as Jacob returned with two cups of coffee.

'And there's more.'

'What is it?'

'There's another handbag at the scene belonging to someone else. We're working on the theory that there were two women and one is missing. The other is nowhere to be seen and we have searched the area. There is also blood at the scene.'

'And what about Jennifer? Is she okay?' Gina felt her stomach turn as Jacob stared at her.

'She's in a bad way. Paramedics are about to take her to Cleevesford General but it's not looking good. She wasn't conscious when we arrived.' PC Kapoor furnished her with more details of their crime scene investigator's injuries.

'I'm on my way. Cordon the scene off and call forensics. Get Bernard out to manage the crime scene. Can you message me the location?'

'Will do. See you shortly.'

Jacob swallowed and his hands began to shake. 'Something's happened to her, hasn't it?'

Gina took the cups from him before speaking. 'I'm really sorry, Jacob. Jennifer has been hit by a car and she's about to be taken to Cleevesford General.'

'I need to be there.'

'Just one thing, who was she out with?'

'Annabel Braddock, her best friend.' He took a couple of deep breaths. 'I need to get to the hospital. I'll call you in a bit.'

'Go.'

He charged out of the door, knocking O'Connor's heaped in tray as he left. Sheets of paper sashayed to the floor. Gina phoned Detective Constable Paula Wyre, prepping her to meet her at the location. Jacob needed to be with Jennifer and she needed to find the person who did this to one of their own. She swallowed the lump in her throat. She also needed to know what had happened to the other woman. Bag left at the scene. Blood too. Where had Annabel Braddock gone? Why was one girl missing?

THREE

SUNDAY, 3 APRIL

Gina pulled up alongside the police cars and spotted PC Smith tying cordon tape around the lamp post. At one in the morning, the usually desolate road would normally be quiet apart from the occasional fox. She glanced around, wondering if anyone would be close enough to witness what happened. There was a row of detached houses a short walk away, maybe someone heard something. The tall trees lining their houses told her that they probably hadn't. Beyond that, this narrowing road led to countryside. She imagined the perpetrator weaving in and out of the country roads to make their escape. Maybe they were drunk, maybe they were speeding, but where was Annabel Braddock? Stepping out, she headed over to PC Smith who filled out the login sheet and let her through. 'Alright, guv. Sad news.'

She shook her head. 'I can't believe this has happened to Jennifer. Jacob went straight to the hospital to be with her. Did the paramedics say anything?'

'It's bad, guv. She wasn't conscious. They mentioned possible swelling of the brain and they left with the blue lights on. We took some photos, then Bernard arrived with the forensics team. I forwarded them to him.' Smith shook his head.

'Any witnesses?'

'There doesn't seem to be.'

'How about the woman she was with? Jacob said she went out with her friend, Annabel Braddock. Any sign of her yet?'

He shook his head. 'Uniform have searched the area but there is no one else around. Her bag and belongings are marked out on the road. Some of the items are Jennifer's, like her purse.' A pile of parrot-topped cocktail sticks lay crushed flat on the road in a smear of blood. Amongst them, a keyring painted like a raspberry.

'Keep looking.' Gina turned to the other side of the road. Opposite the houses and just beyond the passing place was a dense copse full of mature trees and behind that an overgrown field. 'She may have stumbled off or crawled away from the scene, but who would leave their friend in the road in the state that Jennifer was in? Maybe she was hit too and is wandering around concussed. We need to knock on all the doors of these houses and check their gardens, maybe she passed out.'

'There is something, guv.'

'What?'

He fidgeted in his uniform, trying to loosen it a little. 'Her phone was found close to Jennifer. It's been smashed, like someone has stamped on it.'

'I don't like this at all. I best speak to Bernard, see if he and Keith have managed to find anything that might help.' She waved, catching Bernard's attention, then she took a crime scene suit and gloves from Smith. Before heading closer, she slipped it on over her trousers and shirt, then hurried towards Bernard Small. As she approached, he towered over her, half blocking out the light from one of the portable units. In the distance, Keith hunched over on the floor as he searched for further evidence of what had happened. The occasional groan about his bad back came from his mouth as he moved.

'Bernard.'

He wiped the beads of sweat from his forehead. His creased eyes held a sadness in them as he stared at the place Jennifer had been left. 'Whoever did this to her—' He clenched his gloved fist. Gina knew how he felt.

'We're going to find them and they will pay. I promise you that. What do we have?' She only hoped that she could make good on that promise.

'You can see that we've marked out Jennifer's outline. That's where we found her. There is a phone next to her but it doesn't belong to her as her phone was in her pocket. The other one must have belonged to her friend. Both phones have been logged into evidence as we didn't want any further damage to come to them. See the blood?'

Gina looked down. 'Yes.'

'It's not all Jennifer's. Her friend's blood drips for half a metre, then there are no more spots. The victim either covered up her wound before leaving the scene, or she was taken away from the scene. The trail ends there.'

Gina bit her bottom lip. 'Given that her phone is smashed and all her belongings have been left behind, it's looking like she was taken from the scene. Officers have been looking but she hasn't been found as yet. Jennifer was with a friend called Annabel Braddock.' She spotted PC Kapoor standing just outside the cordon. 'Jhanvi?'

'Yes, guv?'

'Can you call the station and get a dog team down here? That will confirm if the trail ends here or if she's lying out there somewhere, and we've missed her. We can't take any chances if that's happened.'

'I'll do it now.' Kapoor walked away to make the call.

Gina turned back to Bernard. 'What do you make of the accident?'

'The way she fell, it looked like she'd been thrown over the bonnet like a rag doll. I'd say the car came at her with speed.' He closed his eyes and took a deep breath.

'This is going to be tough on all of us but we need to do this for her.'

'I know.'

'Can I see the photos?'

Bernard unzipped his crime scene suit and pulled his phone from his pocket and held up a photo.

Gina exhaled sharply and looked away. Jennifer lay there, blood matted to her hair. Red smears on her yellow jacket. Her skinny jeans scuffed with dirt and her Doc Martens boots scratched and scuffed; her eyes closed and a deep cut under one of her eyes.

'An officer and a member of our team went with the ambulance. Her clothing will be bagged up. There may be traces of plastic or paintwork from the car.'

'We have a missing woman and one of our CSIs in hospital. Was this a random accident that led to someone mowing Jennifer down and taking Annabel or was it calculated? What's that?' Gina pointed to the item next to the yellow marker with a number eleven on it.

'A tiny piece of material that is now bagged. It has some sort of paint on it and a smear of blood.'

'Can I see it?'

Bernard headed over to the large box and pulled out the bag, passing it to Gina. She held it near a portable light and could see that it was about the size of a cloth handkerchief with rough edges. 'Is the paint or dye black or blue?'

'Not sure yet. It looks more like a deep blue but I'll tell you more when I've had a proper look. We might be able to get a paint match which might help.'

She passed the evidence bag back to Bernard.

'Guv,' Kapoor called. 'Dog team is on the way.'

'Thanks. Has anyone else been admitted to hospital displaying any injuries consistent with being attacked or run over?'

'We did check for that when we found the other woman's handbag, but no. Only Jennifer.' Kapoor paused then continued, 'A woman in one of the houses is awake and would like to talk to someone.'

Gina felt her heart rate pick up. 'Did she see anything?'

'She saw someone.'

'I'll catch you later, Bernard. Any updates, call me.'

'Will do.' The wiry man turned and joined his colleagues in bagging up the exhibits.

Gina glanced one more time into the darkness around them all. The epicentre of the hustle and bustle lit up in the nothingness around them. Officers had taken a look and found no one injured in a verge or behind a tree. Bernard had confirmed that there was a blood trail that wasn't from Jennifer's injuries that simply vanished. Deep down, Gina knew the dogs weren't going to find a thing. Annabel had been taken and the person who took her had left Jennifer in the road to die.

FOUR

A woman leaned against a huge tree in a grey hoodie and track bottoms. 'I'm DI Harte. You're?'

'Sybil. My baby is a bit fussy, can we go inside to talk while I feed him?'

'Of course.'

'That's why I was awake. I've been pacing the floor since early evening, back and forth, feed, cuddles, singing, rocking. It gets exhausting.'

It had been a long time since Gina had done all that for her grown-up daughter, Hannah, but she remembered the exhaustion well. She followed the young woman down the long drive and a stark light flickered on. Sybil's black hair fell straw-like over her shoulders and a patch of what looked like baby sick had absorbed into the shoulder of her top. She pushed open a huge door and led Gina into a Victorian tiled hallway, where a man rubbing his eyes met her. He passed the wrapped up bawling baby over to Sybil.

'Follow me.' She continued to a reception room where she sank back into a nursing chair. 'Have a seat.'

'Thanks.' Gina sat on the battered-looking couch opposite the huge open fireplace.

The woman unzipped her hoodie and opened her nursing top, allowing the very hungry baby to latch on and feed. 'That should keep him happy for a while.'

'Thank you for speaking to me. I know you're very tired and busy so I'll try to make this quick. Can you tell me what you saw or heard, and when?'

The baby guzzled away. 'It was probably between ten thirty and eleven thirty. Sorry to be vague but I didn't look at the clock. My boyfriend was asleep and has to be up early to travel for a meeting in London so I was trying to placate the little one. That's when I tuned into the noise of a humming engine. It's normally quiet around here so I was naturally curious. I saw a light flick on, like whoever was in the car had turned on the interior light.'

'Where was this car parked?'

'To the right of my drive which is mostly covered by trees.'

'Can you describe the person in the car?'

Sybil shook her head. 'I couldn't see a thing from right back here. I mean, our drives are pretty long. I began to swear under my breath because of the running engine, as you do. I was in half a mind as to whether to go out and ask them to turn it off while they waited. I thought that maybe it was a taxi picking up a visitor from a neighbour's house.'

'What happened after that?'

'Just as I was about to get my shoes on, the noise stopped. After that, I paced around with the little one. A while later, I heard a bang coming from the road. I'd have normally checked on something like that but with him crying his little eyes out, I had other things on my mind. Has someone been hurt?'

Gina nodded. 'Someone was run over and they've been taken to hospital. We also have a missing woman who may be injured from the incident.'

'I feel awful now. I should have gone out there or called the police. If I'd have known—'

'You couldn't have known. It isn't your fault but we do need to find the driver of the car. Do you have any CCTV or did you see the vehicle at all?'

'No to the CCTV, but the car... I can say that it was a car though, not a van and it didn't look big enough to be one of those huge four-wheel drives. Maybe it was a saloon or a hatchback. Not an SUV, something lower to the ground. It didn't sound sporty either. No exhaust growling, nothing like that. I hope that helps.'

'That's really helpful, thank you.'

The baby began to reject the woman's breast and started to cry again. She held him to her shoulder and began to pat his back.

'Have you seen or heard anyone since?'

She shook her head. 'I can't say that I have. The next thing I heard was you guys turning up. I did pop out to see what was going on and I spoke to one of the police officers. I really wish I could help more.'

'Thank you for your time. If you think of anything else after I've gone, please call me.' Gina placed a card on the coffee table.

'Will do. Can you let yourself out?'

Gina nodded and smiled as she stood.

'I hope the person who was hit is okay.'

'And me.' Gina bit back her sadness and left the house.

'Guv.' Kapoor met Gina halfway down the drive.

'What is it?'

'Dogs are here, nothing found so far and as suspected, no Annabel, so it does look more like she was taken from the scene. Also, Jacob said he tried to call you but you weren't answering so he called me.'

'Damn.' She pulled her phone from her pocket. 'Great, no signal.' She walked a few more steps and her phone beeped with a missed call. A message pinged up as a couple of bars returned. 'What did he say?'

'The bleeding on Jennifer's brain is bad. They've treated her in the emergency room and it looks like they'll be placing her on a ventilator. It's not looking good, guv.'

Gina swallowed as she thought of her colleague and what he was going through.

'Do we have Annabel's address?'

'Yes, she had a lot of ID in her bag.'

'I'll head to her house. Her family might be wondering what's happened and I think I need to speak to them in person, find out a little bit more about her. Has Wyre arrived?'

'Yes, she's talking to Smith.'

Gina glanced over and caught sight of Wyre's black ponytail. 'Great, we'll head over. What kind of evil mows down two women walking home, leaving one for dead and taking the other from the scene?' On reaching the end of the drive, she hit the tree bark and flinched as her little finger cracked a little. 'We have to find her. The perpetrator left Jennifer there to die, who knows what they will do to Annabel.'

FIVE

Gina pulled up behind Wyre at the back of the industrial park. Only five houses stood on the old road that eventually met the ultra-modern factory and office buildings. Close enough to walk to the high street, but far enough away from all the noise that came with it. The old detached farmers' cottages had been built in the eighteen hundreds and still looked quaint. She imagined Jennifer and Annabel at the Angel Arms. After having a drink, it looked like they'd begun walking back to Annabel's. Gina spotted Jennifer's Golf hatchback parked up on the road as she got out and walked over to Wyre. Only a few hours earlier, she'd left her friend's house for a night out and it had ended with her being placed on a ventilator.

Wyre stepped onto the kerb. 'Poor Jennifer. I was speaking to Smith and he filled me in.'

'It's hard to believe that someone would just leave her in the road like that. They left her to die.' Gina's brows furrowed as she contemplated the situation. 'We need to do a press release as soon as to appeal for witnesses but first, we have to tell her family what's happened.' Gina swallowed. 'I hate delivering this kind of news but I suppose we best get it done.'

She led the way, opening the waist-height gate and heading on the downward slope to the front door of the house where a warm glow came from behind the curtains. As they approached, a dog began to bark at the door. Ivy weaved up the stone wall and there were ceramic flower pots everywhere. She almost knocked her head on a hanging basket as she stepped back a little, waiting for whoever fumbled with the locks to open up.

'Wrong key, sorry. I'll find the right one in a minute,' the person behind the door shouted.

Gina glanced at Wyre. 'He's not Annabel's partner or husband.' The homeowner would know which key opened their own locks. She glanced at the neatly bordered cottage garden as she waited.

The key turned in the lock and a man stood holding a brindle lurcher by the collar. 'Hello.' His long nose and mound of brown hair stood out. The dog pulled. 'Milo, shush.' The dog continued barking and wagging its tail.

'I'm DI Harte and this is DC Wyre. May we come in?'

'Is everything okay?'

'It's best if we come in.' She didn't want to tell the man what had happened while standing on the doorstep. He stepped aside and they entered. As he closed the door, he released the dog who began to sniff at Gina's feet. She reached down and stroked its head. The carpeted hallway led to a wide galley-style kitchen. 'Are you related to Annabel Braddock?'

'No, I'm her neighbour.'

'Does she live alone?'

'No, she lives with her husband, Grant.'

'Where's Mr Braddock?'

The man shrugged his shoulders. 'I don't know. She didn't say.'

'And you're here because?' Gina smiled.

'I'm looking after their daughter. Their usual childminder has let them down and I know them well. Annabel knocked earlier to see if I could look after Cally. I've looked after her before. I know the family well, so I said yes. Something's happened, hasn't it? I've been trying to call Annabel as it's so late. I was expecting her to come back hours ago. Can we go into the lounge? I don't want to wake Cally. She took a while to go to sleep. That little girl has such an imagination on her.' He smiled.

'Of course.'

The man led them back into the hall and opened the lounge door. A huge open fireplace filled the main wall and the low dark beams made the room feel smaller still. Gina sat on the sofa opposite the fire.

The man grabbed the remote and muted an old film before closing the door. 'That's better.' In the lamplight, Gina could tell that he was probably in his late thirties, maybe early forties at a push.

'Could I take your name, please?'

'Sorry, yes, it's Evan Bryson.'

Wyre sat next to Gina and took out her notebook.

'Mr Bryson—'

'Evan, please.'

'Evan. What's your address?'

'Number two Stonewall Cottages.'

'Do you have a contact number for Mr Braddock?'

'Grant, yes.' He grabbed a piece of paper from next to the phone, scrolled through his mobile and wrote it down. 'Here.'

Gina passed it to Wyre. 'Have you seen Mrs Braddock at all this evening?'

He shook his head. 'No, she left about seven with her friend and I haven't seen her since. I tried to call her a few minutes ago and then tried Grant's number, but he didn't answer either.'

'There was an accident earlier. We found Mrs Braddock's friend but Mrs Braddock wasn't at the scene. We're trying to locate her.'

'Has she been hurt?'

'We think she may have been hit by a car so we really need to find her.'

The man began tapping his fingers on the back of his phone. 'I should get out there and help look for her. She can't be far. She must be hurt. Maybe she has concussion and has wandered off.' He stood and stopped. 'I can't leave Cally.'

'It might be best if you stay here until we locate Mr Braddock. Are you able to stay?'

He nodded and ran his fingers through his hair, messing it up. 'Yes, of course. I'm really worried now.'

'We are too but we have a lot of officers out there looking for her and conducting door-to-door questioning. We also have a dog team out there so we're doing all we can.'

He exhaled and sat back down.

'Can we try her husband?'

Wyre nodded and pressed the numbers into her phone, which went to voicemail. She left a message with her number and ended the call. 'Nothing.'

Gina turned her attention back to Evan who was now scratching his stubble. 'How well do you know Annabel?'

'As well as any neighbour would. She and her husband have been good neighbours. We get on well. I sometimes sit in their garden for a couple of beers when the weather is nice, as do the other neighbours. We're a close community on this row. We all get on. The Braddocks had a Christmas party last year and we all came. It was lovely.'

'So you're friends of both of them? Mr and Mrs Braddock.'

'Yes, and Grant's brother, Seth.'

'Do you live alone?'

He leaned back. 'Yes. I used to live with my father but he died a couple of years ago and I stayed in our family home.'

She smiled and continued. 'Can you tell me how Annabel was earlier this evening, before she left?'

'She seemed fine. Nothing unusual to report. She mentioned going out with her friend, Jennifer. Jennifer was already here when I arrived. I think Annabel had been to her house beforehand with Cally as Cally mentioned all the sweets that she'd been eating. Anyway, Annabel thanked me for looking after her and they left for the pub.' The man's brows furrowed and he shifted position in his chair and sighed. 'They went to the Angel Arms, I remember that much.'

'Did she say anything else?'

'No.'

'How are Annabel and her husband?' Gina had to explore why Annabel had been taken. It was possible that she knew the person who ran them over.

'There is something that concerns me, but it's nothing to do with me or you, or anyone. I know they've had problems. Annabel and Grant wouldn't be happy if I said anything as it really isn't any of my business. It's got nothing to do with tonight anyway. You said it was an accident.'

'We think it was an accident. Please, Evan. Go on.'

'They're going to hate me for telling you this.' He stared at Gina, then at Wyre. 'Okay.' He put his head in his hands and ruffled his hair again. 'They'd been arguing and I know he left with a bag earlier. The whole street could probably hear it.'

'What were they arguing about?'

'I wasn't eavesdropping but it was so loud, I couldn't not hear as I was in my garden feeding the rabbit. He'd been sleeping with someone else. She already knew he'd been playing her as he'd been previously banished to the spare room. Their relationship has been going down the pan for ages. The truth is, when she asked me to babysit, she was upset. The reason she didn't ask her usual childminder was because Grant had been sleeping with her. She must have found that out just then, which would explain the argument. I could see that she'd been crying but I didn't say anything. It wasn't my place. I just said yes, like a friend and neighbour would. As I already said, she left with her friend at about seven thirty and that was it.'

'Do you know the childminder?'

'Not well. I've spoken to her in passing and I've seen her around. Her name is Taylor. I gave her a lift home once when her car was being repaired at the garage so I have her location on maps.' He scrolled through his phone. 'It's seventeen Cherry Drive.'

He bit the inside of his cheek as he stared into the dark fireplace. 'Wait.'

'What is it?'

'No, it's silly. In fact, it's ridiculous.'

'It'll help if you tell us anyway then we can rule it out.' Gina felt her muscles tensing as she wondered what he was about to say.

'About nine this evening, the dog began to bark. Cally ran downstairs and said she'd had a nightmare. She'd only been asleep about twenty minutes. She said she heard someone in the back garden and then she thought there was a ghost in her wardrobe. I shouldn't have let her watch *Casper the Friendly Ghost*.'

'Did you check the garden?'

'Yes. There was no one there except a fox. I think that was what Milo was barking at. I then checked Cally's wardrobe and the rest of the house for this ghost and obviously we found nothing. I put her back to bed, read her a story and left her night light on. I checked on her about fifteen minutes later and she was fast asleep.'

'How old is she?'

'Five.'

'Are you sure there was no one in the garden?'

'Not that I could see. Do you think someone was outside, looking in? Has this got something to do with Annabel and Grant?'

'We're asking everything at the moment. We don't know where Annabel is and we need to speak to Grant. When he comes home, could you ask him to call us?' Gina pulled a card from her pocket and placed it on the table.

'Yes, of course. Would it be okay if I call Annabel's father? I think Cally would rather be with her grandad and I have things I need to do tomorrow.'

'Yes, could I take his number too?'

'She left me his number in case of an emergency.' He noted it down on another slip of paper and passed it to Wyre.

'We'd like to check the back garden if that's okay.'

He stood and reached for the bunch of keys that he'd used to open the front door and he led them through the kitchen. After testing five keys, he managed to find the one that opened the back door. 'There.' He pushed it open. 'She keeps a torch on the side.' He grabbed it and passed it to Gina.

Gina and Wyre stepped out into the damp night. A chilly breeze caught the back of her neck as she headed down the tiled path. She flashed the torch towards the back of the garden. A small hedge separated what belonged to the Braddocks from the field behind it. A detached garage stood at the end of a rubble path that led from the side of the house. She walked over and shone the torch on the padlock. It was firmly in place. She shone it on the ground, trying to look for footprints or any evidence of disturbance but she couldn't see anything. Maybe it was nothing more than a five-year-old imagining that she saw Casper the ghost. 'Do you have the key for the padlock?'

Evan stared at the bunch of keys before looking for one that would fit in the padlock. 'I can't see that any of these would fit.' Gina took the bunch and looked through the keys, trying a few of the smaller ones. None of them fitted. She handed them back to the man who wandered back into the kitchen.

'I can't see anything out here, guv.' Wyre stepped onto the grass.

Gina glanced back and a glint of something caught her eye. As she spotted the child looking out, the curtain dropped. 'Why don't we ask Cally what she saw?'

'That might help. Shall I call her grandad?'

Gina nodded. 'Yes, he'll need to be with Cally while we speak to her and he can take over from the neighbour.' She glanced up again and the little girl peered through the crack in the curtain and waved. Gina waved back, a sadness washing through her. That little girl's mother was missing and Gina knew she would do anything to reunite them.

SIX

Jacob paced under the strip light, listening to the sound of beds being wheeled, groans of pain, shouts of drunkenness and the beeping of machines. A doctor passed. 'Hey, give me an update on Jennifer? Sorry, Jennifer Bailey.' Sweat beads gathered at his hairline and his knees weakened to the point that they buckled slightly. He grabbed a plastic chair and sat.

'And you're—'

'Her partner. We live together. I spoke to another doctor a while back. I wondered what was happening next. She got brought in, it was an emergency and they took her into that room for some sort of emergency treatment because of a bleed to the brain.' His heart began to pound again, just like it had when he first came in. The words induced coma kept ringing through his head. He knew what that meant. It meant things were bad. He couldn't breathe. If anything happened to Jennifer, he didn't know what he'd do. He needed her more than he'd ever needed anyone.

'Just take a slow deep breath.' The doctor kneeled in front of him.

'I can't.'

'You can. Breathe with me. In through your nose, and out.'

'I can't lose her. Please find out what's happening.'

The doctor peered over his glasses. 'I'll go and have a word with the team who are looking after her and I'll find out what's happening.'

'Thank you.' His breathing had calmed a little. He wiped his brow with his sleeve. Why was it so hot? He pulled his coat from his back, almost tearing at the sleeves in frustration, then he threw it onto the chair next to him. He'd never loved anyone so much in his whole life. There had been girlfriends, in fact there had been many. Each relationship had barely lasted a few months, some only weeks. No one had understood the pressures of his job and what it meant to him; that was until he'd met Jennifer. She had her own ambitions and pressures in the forensics field. They were meant to be. It was like she'd waved a magic wand over him, completed him. Soon after he realised that he'd never felt like that before. It had to be love. He glanced up at the door and knew that Jennifer's life was in their hands and he waited.

He bit his nails. He tapped his feet, then he picked up his coat and threw it on the floor in frustration. The doctor came back out of the room. He hurried off the chair, almost slipping on his coat. 'Can I see her? I have to see her.' If nothing else, he could hold her hand and tell her how much he loves her and hope that she could somehow hear him.

'I'm afraid not, yet. She'll be taken to intensive care in a short while where you'll be able to sit with her.'

'How long will she be on that machine for?'

'I can't answer that yet. I'm really sorry.'

'I can't lose her. Please tell me she won't die.'

The doctor took a deep breath. 'Ah, that room is now free.' A woman came out with a doctor, crying as she was led up the corridor. Jacob wondered if that was the room they were taken into when they were told that their loved ones were going to die. His hands trembled uncontrollably, his arms shook and he knew if he spoke, his voice would quiver. The doctor was going to tell him that Jennifer would die.

SEVEN

Gina waited next to Wyre on the landing, listening to Cally's grandfather, Doug Latham, speak gently to the little girl. His clear voice successfully concealed his own worry so as not to worry his granddaughter. A few moments earlier, Evan had left and gone to his own house next door citing that he was there if they needed him. She peered around the door and saw that the man was lying on the bed over the covers with little Cally snuggled under his arm. 'Do you think you can tell the police what you saw in the garden earlier, darling? Gramps will be with you so you don't have to be worried?'

'Yes, Gramps. I'm not worried.' The little girl giggled. 'Can you read me a story after?'

'Of course, but no more ghost stories. What did we say?' His thick grey eyebrows raised as he spoke with a comforting smile.

Cally giggled. 'There are no such things as ghosts.'

'That's right, darling.' He kissed her head and waved Gina in. Wyre followed closely and stood in the corner of the room next to the plastic dressing table.

Gina smiled. 'Hello, Cally. My name is Gina and this is Paula.'

'Hello, Cally,' Wyre said in a gentle voice.

'This is a lovely bedroom. I have a granddaughter about your age. Her name is Gracie. I see you love Lego, just like her, and she loves Elsa from *Frozen* too.'

'My favourites are *Frozen* and *Moana*.' The brown-haired girl smiled and nestled shyly into her grandad's arms. 'Why are you here? It's night-time.'

'Well, your neighbour, Evan, told me that you told him that there was someone in the garden earlier and we just want to hear what you have to say.'

She gripped her snowman toy and pressed her lips together.

'What's your snowman called?' Gina knew the character but she wanted Cally to feel confident enough to speak.

'Olaf.'

'I love Olaf. Who is your favourite *Frozen* character?'

'Elsa. I have the dress.'

'How lovely.'

'Do you want to see it?' The little girl left her grandad's side and ran over to the chest in the corner of her room and rooted through the box until she pulled out a blue dress.

'That is beautiful.'

The little girl began to suck the ends of her brown hair.

'You said to Evan that you saw someone in the garden.'

'I thought it was a ghost. We were watching *Casper* cartoons earlier. Evan looked out the window and said it was a fox. He checked my wardrobe and under the bed, then he said I should go back to sleep because there was nothing there.'

'What did you see?'

Cally shrugged before running back towards the bed and almost diving onto her grandad. The man narrowly dodged a little knee in his groin and flinched. 'It wasn't a fox. It was a ghost, like a shadow.' She looked up at her grandad, her big brown eyes wide open.

'How tall?'

'He was tall like Daddy. That tall.' She held her arms out as wide as she could.

'Did you see his face or his clothes?'

'Ghosts don't have faces, except Casper because he's a cartoon.'

'Where did he go?'

The little girl scrunched her button nose and shrugged. 'I don't know. I hid on the floor and counted to ten. Then I looked out of the window again.'

'And what did you see?' Gina held her breath.

'Nothing, silly.' The little girl giggled. 'Ghosts go whoosh and you can't see them anymore. But I was scared so I screamed for Evan.' She frowned. 'Evan said it was a fox but it was a ghost.'

'You have been really helpful, Cally, so thank you very much.' Gina nodded to Doug. 'May we have a word downstairs?'

He nodded. 'Right, little Cally, I need you to stay in bed with Olaf and wait for me. I'll be up in a minute to read you a story. Do you want to watch *Frozen* on the iPad?'

The little girl nodded enthusiastically.

The man grabbed the device and began setting the film up.

'Where's Mummy?'

'She'll be home soon, darling.' He passed her the iPad and Cally snuggled under her blankets and began to watch *Frozen*. Doug led Gina and Wyre onto the landing. 'What am I going to tell her?' He scratched the grey hair on his head.

Gina didn't have an answer to that question. 'I wish I had answers for you. I'm really sorry but I'll need to ask you a few questions.'

The man nodded, his face washed out, eyes dark ringed with tiredness; the lines edging them, deep and creased. 'They're all I have, Annabel and Cally. Please find her.' He led them back downstairs and into the kitchen and closed the door.

'I'm sorry to tell you that it's looking likely that she was taken from the scene. Her friend, Jennifer Bailey, was left behind and has sustained some serious injuries.'

'Is Jen okay? I've known her since the two were at school. Best friends, they were. She was always stopping at our house.'

'She's being treated in hospital at the moment. I don't have all the details yet.'

'So, someone took Annabel? Is that what you're saying?'

'It's a line of enquiry that we're investigating, which is why we need to know a little more about her. Has she had any problems with anyone that you're aware of?'

The man slammed a hand onto the worktop, causing the mug tree to rattle. 'I can't lie. Grant has been a real arse. He's been having it away with their childminder. Annabel found out and they'd been arguing. I never liked him. The man has always been the same except Annabel has only just seen through him. I can sense his type from a mile away. I had friends like him in my younger days, never did approve of that kind of behaviour. People who cheat deserve all that comes to them and he didn't deserve my daughter. That man also said some things that were below the belt. Can you believe it? He's the one who couldn't keep his dick in his pants but he accused her of having an affair.'

Gina suddenly felt a little more alert. 'Who did he accuse her of having an affair with?'

'What does it matter? She wouldn't do that to her family.'

'We still need his name just so that we can eliminate him from our enquiries.'

He stared, tight-lipped.

'Please, Mr Latham, we just want to bring your daughter home and the more information we have, the better.'

'Some teacher at the school she works at. Annabel and I are close, she tells me things, speaks to me about her problems. We lost her mother when she was eight so I've been Mum and Dad throughout her life. She told me that he accused her of seeing someone else and that he works at the school, that's all she said. We both knew he only said that because he'd been cheating.'

'Do you have the name of the teacher?'

'No. I didn't ask and she didn't tell me. I got the impression that she was upset about something else but she didn't tell me what. I don't push her. If she's upset, she knows she can come to me, that's the way it's always been.'

'Which school does she work at?'

'Cleevesford High. She teaches maths. She's so clever and I'm incredibly proud of her.'

'Do you have a recent photo of Annabel?'

He began scrolling on his phone before turning it around to show Gina. 'This is a photo on her Facebook feed that she took a couple of weeks ago while out with Cally. No one else can see this as she keeps her profile locked and she calls herself Annie Bell. It stops the kids at school from finding her. That's why her profile photo is a picture of Milo.' The dog came running in on hearing his name mentioned. Doug pulled a treat from the cupboard and the dog almost snatched it from his hands.

'Can you email that to me?'

Doug nodded, taking the card that Gina held out and began to send the photo.

'We'll put out an appeal on the local news in a few hours. We're hoping that if someone saw anything, they'll come forward.'

'Gramps,' Cally called from her room.

'I should be with her. You need to find Grant. It's odd that he's not home but then again, he could be with his fancy woman. He's a nasty player, a liar and needs constant adoration. That's Grant in a nutshell. I despise people like him.'

'A liar?'

'Yes, like I said. He's had so many affairs and one-night stands and he's lied through his teeth each time. I've always seen it but Annabel didn't, until recently. It frustrated me badly, seeing the way he treated her. This time, Annabel had finally seen the light and told him she wanted a divorce. She thought it would be easy. He had someone else. He'd been sleeping in the spare room but he said he'd never leave his house or daughter. I told her to come and stay with me but she said she'd never leave the house either. There are going to be some battles ahead. As for the childminder, I don't know where she fits into his plan. Just like all the others, he was probably using her too.'

'How well do you know the childminder?'

'Not well at all. She's just a kid.'

'Kid?'

'Well, you know. Anyone under thirty is a kid to me. I think she's in her early twenties and still lives with her family.' Doug paused. 'Please find Annabel. Cally and I need her.'

Gina nodded sympathetically. 'If you think of anything else, please call me straight away. In the meantime, I'll organise a visit from forensics to check out the back garden, just in case there was an intruder.'

'Thank you.'

'Gramps. *Frozen* has stopped and I can't make it start again,' Cally called again.

'We'll call you later, Mr Latham.'

'And I'll call you if Grant comes back here. I don't think he'll be happy to see me in his house.'

'Has something happened between you and him?'

'No, but like I said, I see through his superficial charm and he hates it. He hates me because I always put Annabel first and I don't believe a word he says. In the past when he's been drunk he's told me that if I don't keep out of his business, he'll break my neck.' The man let out a snort. 'I'd like to see him try. I worked as a brickie all my life, kept me strong, and I'd definitely give him a surprise and he knows it. That type of threat gives you an indication of the type of man you're dealing with. I wouldn't be surprised if he knew where she was, followed her home and waited for his opportunity to hurt her. He hated it when she went out on her own with friends. It was okay for him but never her. For a dirty cheater, he was jealous. Yes, he probably saw her coming home and mowed her down.' He paused. 'Annabel told me once that he'd hit a man for looking at her. It was never reported. That's what he's like.'

Cally appeared at the door. 'Gramps, you promised you'd come up and I still can't make *Frozen* work.'

'I was just on my way, darling.' Doug smiled at the little girl and took her tiny hand in his. 'If you find him, you'll find her.'

EIGHT

Annabel

As I open my eyes, the pain is like nothing else. Searing white-hot pokers stabbing the back of my head. Then it radiates out before subsiding. Opening my eyes didn't help. I'm in complete darkness. I can't breathe. It's like there's something sitting on my chest, stopping me from inhaling. The cloth in my mouth tastes of oil, its dryness soaking up all moisture. Trying to let out a squeak is fruitless. There's no point and trying also makes my head hurt.

I want to see. The darkness is suffocating and all I hear is blood whooshing through my head. I'm scrunched up in the foetal position on a cold floor. What is outside this enclosure feels tinny and I can't work it out. The eggy sulphur smell is making my stomach turn and for a minute, I feel as though the space I'm occupying is spinning but again, the pitch-blackness won't let me see if what I feel is what is real. My sense of all that is has gone.

How did I get here?

Trying to wriggle out of the coarse rope binds is impossible. Someone has brought me here. It was him, the man in the balaclava – but why?

Another sharp pain flashes through my head and a damp tear seeps down the side of my face. Kick out. That will give me an indication of how much space I have. Maybe I'm in a room on the floor. No, when I make the slight squeaking noise again, I can tell I'm in a confined space, but it is quite large. Maybe I'm in a huge van or a compartment in a container, on the back of a lorry. I gasp for breath. I'm being people trafficked. Destined for another country, far away. Sold as a sex slave forever. I think of my daughter, my sweet little Cally and I can't fight the tears that slip down my face.

'Annie Bell,' the voice in my head calls.

Jen calls me that. It's her voice, guiding me back to reality. No, I remember the accident. This is all an accident, I've been hurt and I'm coming around from surgery. Any minute now, a kind nurse will smile and offer me a cup of tea.

I manage to shake my head, trying to properly wake up, trying to see light in the darkness but it's all encompassing and it's closing in on me. Total darkness is terrifying. Not like when it's night and you've just turned the light off. After a couple of minutes, eyes adjust and the room becomes a shadowy reflection of its daytime self. I'm trapped and lost. I'm bound and I'm gagged.

I try to spit the rag from my mouth by shifting my lips and trying to poke it with my tongue. That's when I feel the resistance. There is a piece of material holding it in place. I try to calm my breathing using only my nose. Slowly, my heart rate decreases.

Shifting about, I realise I'm so trussed up I can only half flop around like a dying fish out of water. I finally reach an edge and it's cold. Pressing my head against it, it feels grainy, like wood. I rub my cheek down it, looking for weakness in its structure but all I get is a splinter. Maybe I'm in a box in a trailer. The sound when I move suggests that. Outside is tinny, inside is wood. I roll over, trapping the skin of my arm under my body then I try to kick up and then to the other side. Again, I kick out.

Who brought me here? The argument I had with Grant flashes through my mind. *You will never leave me, ever. Do you understand? And, you will never take this house or my daughter or, I swear, you will just vanish one day. Do you know, on the Dark Web, I can get someone to dispose of you for just two thousand pounds? What a bargain.* Everyone knows he's a cheater, they tried to warn me but they don't know this side to him. He says these awful things when he's high and denies that he said them the next day.

Tears well up and my nose fills. Grant's words ring through my head. While I'd been thinking about the best ways to leave him, he'd been planning to kill me. He meant what he said. He said he'd never let me be the one to leave him and he's made good on that promise.

An image fills my head. Jen's body lying on the ground. Blood everywhere. He killed Jen and now he's going to kill me. I think of Cally and I weep. She idolises her father but she doesn't see what I see. To our daughter, he's perfect. I imagine her arms wrapped around him and Taylor taking my place in our home; a year, maybe two down the line, maybe Cally will even call her mummy.

I can't contain my emotion even though I know it might pain me more. I sob and shake. All I want is to be a mother to my daughter. If he comes to check on me, I will beg and I'll plead. I'll swear that I'll never leave him if that's what he wants. I'll do anything to see my daughter again. I try to think back to Jen and her lying on the ground. A car hit her. A silver car, like the old Merc that Grant keeps in the garage. My shoulders drop and I know that I won't get the chance to beg, plead or see my little girl. He's not even coming back for me. This is where I have been brought to die and I can't see a way out. No one is coming for me. No one will know I'm gone and no one will know where I am. I wonder if this is what he got for his two thousand pounds. I'm as good as dead.

NINE

Gina stood to the side of the podium as Briggs read out a statement for the press. The blown-up poster that had been pinned to a board showing a photo of Grant and Annabel Braddock together was on a slant, but you could clearly see them both. She had no doubts that the appeal for witnesses would be on the next local news bulletins. She spotted the journalist she hated the most, Pete Bloxwich. Since the last major case, he'd kept out of her way and she'd kept out of his.

As Briggs concluded a camera flashed. 'So, if you were driving or walking along Tennant Lane or you saw anything or anyone between ten and midnight last night, or if you have seen Annabel Braddock or her husband, Grant Braddock, both shown in the photo, call us. She might be injured, she might be concussed. It's important that she's reunited with her family. Any information is welcome, however unimportant or irrelevant you think it might be. If you saw anything, we want to hear from you. Thank you.'

'Is it true that she was having marital problems?' A reporter waited for an answer.

'It's not the time or the place for a question like that.' Briggs shook his head. Gina noticed how smart his suit was and he'd definitely bought a new shirt. She wondered if it was all for the benefit of the woman she'd seen him with.

Another reporter piped up. 'Where's her husband? Could he have taken Annabel if you're looking for him too?'

Briggs cleared his throat and took a sip of water. 'Any more questions, please forward them to the corporate communications department. This is an ongoing investigation. When we have any further news, we'll let you know. At the moment, we just need to speak to Mr Braddock and find Mrs Braddock.'

Gina checked her messages. Wyre was waiting for her so that they could go to Taylor, the childminder's house.

'Should the public be worried? One woman in hospital and another woman missing? Are we to believe that she was taken by the driver of the car?'

'We're still investigating. When I have any updates, I'll share them with you.' He grabbed his notes. 'That will be all for now, thank you.' He stepped out of the portable light beams and onto the main floor before swiftly heading towards the exit corridor, knowing that the reporters couldn't follow him through without a pass. The room filled with camera flashes and clicks. Gina hurried past a couple of reporters, hoping to catch up with Briggs before she had to head back out. That's when she spotted her sullen colleague, standing in the far corner of the room. She let go of the door and pushed through the crowd until she caught up with Jacob. His stubble and the musty smell coming from his clothes told her that he hadn't been home since leaving work to be with Jennifer, and she wasn't surprised. 'How is she?'

He went to talk but instead he swallowed and nervously looked down.

'You shouldn't be here? No one expects you to be at work.'

He walked out of the main door and she followed until they were standing alone by a wall.

'Jacob? Please talk to me.' Gina tilted her head slightly.

His usually neat hair was kinked to one side, like he'd half slept against a wall. 'She looks like she's dead on that machine and there's nothing I can do. I...' He took a deep breath. 'I might never get to speak to her again.' He paused. 'I couldn't stay there any longer, watching that... that thing pump and pump away. Watching monitors as they keep beeping. Watching as they feed her beige slop through a tube in her nose. I spoke to her and you know what? Nothing. That's what happened. She can't hear a word I say. All I wanted her to know was that I love her, and to fight. I need her.'

Gina placed a hand on his arm. 'Jacob, she knows you love her. You two are the most loving couple I know.'

He looked away. 'We had an argument yesterday. Our first argument, can you believe it?'

'Couples have arguments all the time but that doesn't mean she would have doubted how much you love her.'

'It was stupid really. We have our new house, our dream house, in fact. It's all white walls and plain, a blank canvas, new and fresh. We argued about the living room. She wants it to be a dark grey, I want it to stay white. She was so passionate about the grey, she said I was a total bore with the decor and it was her house too. She's right. I am a total bore. Right now, I wouldn't care if she wanted to paint the walls in pink with yellow polka dots as long as I could have her here, with me. As it stands, she got run over, she went to hospital, she's had some horrible things done to her, all after having a stupid little row with me. That's the last thing she'll remember.' He gasped.

'Jacob, it was a silly little argument. She'll remember the good times, all the lovely things you did together and how much she loves you. I doubt she'll be thinking about a disagreement over painting the living room wall and you can't think like that. She's not going to die.' Gina felt a lump forming in her throat. Who was she to tell Jacob that Jennifer wouldn't die? She had no idea if she would or wouldn't and she too knew that it wasn't looking good. Gina had called the hospital for an update. Jennifer had been seen by the neurosurgeon, then the trauma surgeon. She'd had various tests and an MRI scan. Her brain tissue was swollen and a bleed had been confirmed. All they could do was wait and see how she responded to treatment.

Jacob stepped from one foot to another, over and over as he rubbed his hair. 'She's not going to die. How can you say that? You don't know.'

'You're right. I'm truly sorry. I don't know.'

'What if I never see her again? I can't cope with that thought. I love her so much, more than anything. I should have said those words more.'

Gina sat on the wall and he sat next to her. The morning sun was just coming up and a few birds had lined up on a pylon above. Another message pinged through. It was Wyre hurrying her up. She placed her phone in her pocket. Wyre could wait another couple of minutes. 'We've all wished we'd said or done things differently but hindsight is a wonderful thing. No one could have predicted that this would happen. Jennifer knows you love her and that's all that matters. You have to be there for her now. Whatever happens, I'm here for you. You can call me or I can come over and we can talk any time of the day or night. We're all family here, you know that.' She swallowed.

'Thank you.' He puffed a couple of breaths out. 'Right, I have to stop wallowing in self-pity, we have a job to do.'

'What?'

'I'm on this case. I am going to help find out who did this to Jennifer and who took Annabel. It's the least I can do. If Jennifer could talk right now, she'd be telling me to catch the bastard who put her in a coma.' He brushed his creased clothes down.

'Jacob?'

'What?'

'You know the drill. You're too close to this case.'

'That hasn't stopped you in previous cases.'

'Touché.' Jacob was right and he'd assisted her at times when she should have stayed away from a case because it got personal. She owed him.

'I'm not going home and I'm not needed at the hospital. What use am I to her right now? Find me a role.'

Gina checked her phone. Wyre had tried to call. They had to hurry to Taylor's and she was losing precious time on the case. 'Okay. No groundwork, you're office based. We should start getting calls through soon. Sift through everything. Follow up by phone and interview any witnesses that come in.'

'Thrilling.' The sarcasm in his tone was something Gina had never experienced but she understood his frustration.

'But it's a job that needs doing and one that could lead to finding Annabel and catching the person who hurt Jennifer. What we do isn't all about busting down doors and getting into dangerous situations, you know that. Besides, if the hospital calls, you'll need to go straight away.'

He blinked and wiped his sleep-filled eyes. 'You're right. I'll catch up with you later at the briefing.'

Gina nodded. 'See you later.'

As Jacob made his way back to the station's main entrance, she grabbed her vibrating phone. 'Wyre, I'm on my way.'

'Guv, it's Annabel's phone. The tech team have taken a look.'

'What is it?'

'They're struggling to download everything from the broken phone but they have found a tracking app that was put there by her husband. It's even registered in his name. He would have known exactly where she was last night. There are a few text messages but nothing of any help to the case.'

'I'm on my way. Hopefully he'll be at the childminder's and we can bring him in for questioning.'

'I'll meet you at the car. Let's go get him.'

TEN

The satnav instructed Gina to take the next left and then they were there. This was meant to be where Taylor lived. 'Look out for number seventeen.'

Wyre nodded. 'As usual, no one has numbers on their houses. Wait, I think I see it. It's that one, there. The one with the extension.' Gina pulled up against the kerb. The house on the corner was just one of many on the pristine estate. Pruned hedges edged every garden and the ornate street lighting told her that it was an expensive place to buy.

'I'm impressed with Cherry Drive. So this is where Taylor lives. Do we have a surname?'

'No. We only know that she lives here. Look, guv. There are two front doors under the same number.'

'Looks like an annexe. We'll knock at the main door first.' Gina stepped out, putting her bag strap around her head before tucking the bag under her arm. She walked across the perfect block paving and grabbed the shiny pewter knocker.

A woman who looked to be about Gina's age answered. She was maybe fifty but had weathered much better. Her glossy aubergine coloured hair had neatly been pinned into a French pleat and her linen slacks fell effortlessly over her slim waist. 'Hello. You've come to collect the bench. I wasn't expecting you yet but that's not a problem, it's all ready for you to collect.'

'Sorry, I'm DI Harte, this is DC Wyre. We need to speak to Taylor.'

'Oh, right. Why would you want to speak to my niece?'

'We're investigating an incident and Taylor's name has come up.'

'What's this about?'

'I'm afraid we need to speak to Taylor. Is she in?'

The woman stepped out of the house in her slippers and charged over to the annexe. After banging hard, she waited for a reply. The neighbour opposite peered through the curtains. Taylor's aunt pasted on a smile and waved before turning back to the door and knocking again. 'I don't think she's in. That's odd. I'll get the key, check to see if she's okay. It is my house after all. She mentioned moving out soon to be with some boy she was in love with.' The woman rolled her eyes. 'It wouldn't surprise me if she's left and not said anything. One thing for sure is, she'll be back soon. As you can tell, we don't get on that well. We are in constant conflict over our wildly differing views of what cleanliness is.'

The woman hurried back into the main house and came out a few seconds later with a key.

'When did you last see her?'

'Friday, maybe. I don't go checking on her and I don't always hear her come and go. I think I saw her leaving the annexe for a jog on Friday evening though.' She turned the key in the lock and pushed the door open. 'As I suspected, the place stinks. This is why we don't get on.' Takeaway wrappers filled the bin next to the sofa and the kitchenette at the far end was covered in dirty dishes. 'She doesn't keep the place clean enough, I mean look; the kid she looks after has crayoned the carpet. She's my niece. I promised my sister I'd always look out for her when she died but this takes the biscuit. I don't charge her rent or ask her to do anything. All I asked is that she kept everything clean and tidy at all times. Well, as you can see, Taylor is obviously not in.'

'Could she be upstairs?'

'I'll check.' The woman looked as though she was gliding up the stairs, silently and elegantly.

As soon as she was out of sight, Gina bent over to take a photo of a girl and Cally that had been slotted in a colourful frame. The pink-haired girl looked younger than her years.

'She's not here, and the bed and bathroom are a complete mess too. Make-up everywhere. I can say with certainty that she hasn't moved out yet, well it doesn't look like she has. She's left all her wash stuff and her clothes are still in the drawers,' the woman called out as she hurried back down. 'Looks like I'll be spending my Sunday cleaning.' She picked up a tea towel, sniffed it with a grimace and threw it into the washing machine.

'Is that Taylor in the photo with Cally?'

'Yes, that pink hair is awful. I keep telling her that her blonde hair is much nicer.'

'Do you have a phone number for Taylor?'

'Yes, and you know what, I'm going to call her.' She pulled her mobile from her pocket and pressed Taylor's number. It rang and rang. She hung up when the answerphone message started. 'Probably with the boy.'

'Sorry, what's your name?' Gina nodded at Wyre who turned to a fresh page in her notebook. It was evident that they needed to track Taylor down.

'Sharon Acer. Why do you want to know who I am? I haven't done anything.'

Gina put most of her weight on her back foot. 'It's just

routine. We need to speak to Taylor with regards to an incident last night. Can you tell us a little more about her?'

'What do you want to know?'

'About her job, her boyfriend.'

'She looks after this adorable little girl called Cally. She's mostly based at their house but occasionally she's brought the girl here. I know she has a key to the house where she works because sometimes she cooks dinner and cleans when the owners are still at work. As far as I know, she loves her job. I'll give her that, she's good with children. It's probably because she's still quite childlike herself.'

'In what way?'

'She'll get down on the floor and play games in a totally immersive way. She really is like a big kid, hence how she lives. She's immature too, takes nothing seriously and spends all her money on clothes instead of saving.'

'Is her surname Acer?'

'No, it's Caldwell.'

'Does she work every day and during the holidays?'

'Let me see. She has the odd week off but that is normally in the school holidays. The woman she works for, Annabel, is a teacher so that makes sense. She works some of the holidays so that Annabel can get on with lesson planning for the next term and marking; things like that.'

Gina was getting a picture of Taylor's role. As a trusted keyholder, she'd be able to come and go as she pleased. Would Mr Braddock come home in the day to be with her while Annabel was delivering trigonometry lessons to teenagers? Had they come up with some intricate plan together to get rid of Annabel? Knowing that his wife was thinking about leaving him could be all he needed to formulate a plan and if Taylor was quite childlike and immature for her age, had she been easy to manipulate into helping him? There were so many questions running through her mind and only Grant and Taylor could answer them. 'How old is Taylor?'

'Twenty. It was her birthday last month.'

'How long has she worked for the Braddocks?'

'About a year. It's the longest she's stuck a job. Before that she worked in a child day care centre but that lasted about three months. She left for her current job. The pay wasn't brilliant but she said she wanted to look after one child not a room full of them.'

'Do you know who her boyfriend is?'

'Never seen him. I guess he's some layabout like the others. She normally picks boys who laze around all day, scratching their scrotums while playing computer games.'

'Has she ever mentioned a name?'

'Grant. That's his name but she hasn't told me anymore.'

'I noticed a car parked on the drive. Does it belong to her?'

'The Mercedes?' Sharon raised her eyebrows.

Gina guessed it wasn't but she had to ask. 'We know she has a car, where is it?'

'It's a right heap. I ask her to park it around the corner. It won't be there though as she's not here.'

Gina stepped over to the front door. 'Can you show me where she would normally park?' At the very least, she wanted to check to see if there were any dents on it that could suggest that her car mowed Jennifer down.

The woman stepped out onto the drive. Gina and Wyre followed her to the corner and she pointed. 'See that little parking place at the back of my garden, that's where she parks. That's her car, which is odd as she's not here. Someone must have picked her up.'

Gina hurried over to the small Hyundai and looked at the bonnet and bumper. The car was covered in dirt that hadn't been disturbed. She peered through the window and saw a photo of Annabel with scribble half-covering her face. As Wyre caught sight of it, she glanced up at Gina. Taylor's car hadn't been used to mow Jennifer down but the girl hated Annabel enough to deface a photograph. They needed to find her quick before a bit of vindictive scribble turned into an action that was far more sinister. Another piece of paper caught her attention. Creased at the corner on the back seat, the flyer for Clearview Cabins was in partial view. Luxury retreats at competitive prices. 'I know where we're heading next.'

ELEVEN

In the heart of the Evesham countryside sat a farm. On it, a small shop offered home-made jams and chutneys, fresh bread and newly laid eggs straight from the chickens on site.

'Is this it?' Wyre peered through the window.

'This is apparently where the Clearview Cabins are but I can't see a cabin anywhere.' As Gina pulled into a space, a woman exited from a side door, trudging in wellies while calling a collie to her side. Her straggly grey hair fell over her waxed jacket. 'Hello.' The woman didn't respond. 'Hello.' Gina got out and hurried over the muddy surface, calling the woman. As she turned, the woman let out a shriek and pulled her earphones out.

'You nearly gave me a heart attack.'

'Sorry.' Gina smiled and held her hands up. 'I'm DI Harte, Cleevesford Police. May we have a word with you?'

The woman checked her watch as Wyre stepped out of the car and joined them. 'Yes, it's nearly break time. Come on, Patch.' The dog followed her back into the rustic shop. The bell rang as they entered. Troughs full of dirty vegetables filled the room and the earthy smell was quite pleasant.

'What can I do for you?'

'We're looking for Clearview Cabins and this is the address we have.'

'Ah yes, they're hidden in the woodland for peace and tranquillity. That's what people come here for. They're also guaranteed privacy with their own hot tubs. I gather you've not come here to book a holiday?'

'However perfect that all sounds, you are right. We're looking for someone and we have reason to believe that she is staying here. Can I take your name, please?'

'Olive Flint. I run the place on my own since losing my husband several years ago. It's just me and Patch.'

'Sorry to hear that.'

'Thank you.' She grabbed her glasses and put them on. 'Okay, all the cabins are booked so who is it you're looking for?' She opened up a notebook.

'Taylor Caldwell.'

'No one by that name has checked in, I'm afraid.'

'How about Grant Braddock?'

'Now I know that name. Bear with me.' She flicked through a few pages in the diary and began to read. 'He booked cabin seven about a month ago. It's booked until four this afternoon. It was just him and his daughter.'

'How old was his daughter?'

'I'd say fourteen, fifteen maybe.'

It definitely wasn't five-year-old Cally that the woman was describing. Gina pulled out her phone and showed Olive the photo of Taylor. 'Was this her?'

'Yes, lovely girl. I gave her a packet of sweets.' The woman paused and scrunched her brows. 'Is that who you're looking for? He's not some sort of paedophile, is he?'

'No, Taylor is actually twenty.'

'Oh, I see. I had her down as about fourteen but maybe I'm

just bad at ageing people.' The dog settled at her feet and began to pant a little. 'Are they together?'

'As you can appreciate, this is part of an ongoing investigation and I can't disclose any details. I'd really appreciate it if you could give me a map of the site so that I can see if either of them are there so that we can talk to them.'

The woman pulled out a faded photocopy of a map and drew a circle around a cabin. 'It's this one. Am I going to get any trouble with them? This is a peaceful site. It's a relaxation haven.'

Gina smiled and shook her head. 'I'm not anticipating any trouble at all. Thank you for your help.' Gina and Wyre turned to leave.

'Can I interest you in any eggs, fresh this morning?'

'I'm fine, thank you, but I may pop back for some when I'm off duty.' As Gina went to open the car door, Olive ran out.

'Wait. I didn't want to say anything. It's stupid really but you're here for a reason.'

'What is it?'

'It wasn't *just* the girl's age. I thought she was his daughter because she looked like she'd been sulking. He dragged her in and she then stood in the corner of the room refusing to walk next to him. She didn't say anything, it was all in the body language. That's why I offered her some sweets. Thought it would cheer her up. I mean, she basically looked like a kid who had just been told off.'

'Thank you, you've been really helpful.'

'Great, I'll be hanging out here for a while. You know where to find me if you need anything.'

Gina got into the car and put the key in the ignition. 'Let's find this cabin. You navigate.' She passed Wyre the map. 'I want to know why Grant Braddock was dragging a sulking Taylor into a cabin in the woods. Something's not right.'

TWELVE

As they drove through a tunnel of trees along the thin windy road, Gina spotted a couple of cabins ahead.

'That's it, the one over there, guv.' Wyre pointed at the cabin on the right that backed out onto a valley of trees.

'Wow, it's amazing.' The small, panelled structure had a large wraparound porch. A rocking seat for two filled one end and the hot tub another. What Gina guessed was the main living space in the cabin peaked at the front like a chapel and the tinted huge windows and glass door allowed privacy for guests. All Gina could see was the woods reflected in them. A man came out of the next cabin, just a short walk away, and began placing bags into the boot of a car.

Gina pulled up outside number seven and they both stepped out. Ringing the doorbell, they waited, but there was no answer. Gina lifted the letter box and listened but no sound came from the cabin. 'Smells slightly smoky in there.'

'Breakfast or something else?' Wyre bent over to inhale.

'Don't know.' She knocked as hard as she could but again, there was no answer. Gina walked to one of the windows, pressed her nose against the glass and shielded her eyes from the light. She could see the outline of a huge settee and a kitchen island, but there was no one walking about. Several wine bottles lay on the floor, along with a pile of sweet wrappers and two dirty plates. 'I wonder if they're still in bed.'

'There's no car here, guv.'

Gina shook her head. 'Can't believe I didn't spot that. They must have gone out.' She hurried over to the man packing his boot. 'Hey, I wondered if you could help me. I'm looking for the people who are staying in this cabin. Have you seen them?'

'Have we seen them?' A young woman stepped out. 'We're cutting our break early because of them and I'll be complaining.'

Gina bit her bottom lip and hoped to learn more of what was going on. 'What happened?'

'That girl. That's what happened.'

'Can you tell me more?'

'This is meant to be a quiet break. I mean, the cabins don't even come with TVs but that bitch decided she was going to play club music most of the night. She was so drunk, and I don't mean a bit tipsy. She came out swigging from a bottle of wine, dancing all over the place. I asked her to keep it down but she came over to our porch around ten and basically told us to chill out. I mean, she could barely stand. Then she looked all weird for a few minutes and vomited on our porch. Totally out of it, she was. We were hoping to catch her father this morning but he must have gone out because his car isn't there, or maybe they left.'

The man slammed the boot. 'Who knows? All I know is that our weekend away was ruined and we won't be back. Tell that to your mother.'

'My mother?'

'She owns the place. Olive.'

'Sorry, she's not my mother. We're from Cleevesford Police,

DI Harte and DC Wyre. We're looking for the two people who were staying in this cabin.'

'Good, when you find them, do your worst. Horrible human beings. Deserve all they get,' the man said as he lit a cigarette and the woman sat on the bonnet.

'What time did you last see them both?'

The man exhaled a plume of smoke. 'As we said, ten last night. We closed everything up and went to bed. Soon after, the music stopped and we went to sleep.'

'Was the car outside the cabin at eleven?'

The man looked at the woman. 'I don't know. I didn't look.'

The woman shook her head. 'Sorry, me neither. The last time I saw her father was about seven in the evening. He was standing on the porch scrolling through his phone. I heard the hot tub bubbling at that point. She must have been using it.' The woman stopped talking and stared into the distance. 'Speak of the devil.'

Gina turned to see Taylor jogging through the trees, faded pink hair stuck to her face. 'DC Wyre, could you continue here while I head to number seven?'

Wyre nodded.

Leaving her colleague with the angry couple, Gina hurried over to the other cabin, trying not to trip over any of the mounds in the muddy path. 'Taylor Caldwell?' Gina held her identification up. 'I'm DI Harte. I need to speak to you.'

The girl pulled her hair from her damp face and twisted it into a low bun at the nape of her neck. Bending over, she took a few deep breaths and wiped her brow with her arm. Her Lycra shorts clung to her thighs and her sports crop top looked slightly too big. 'Sorry,' she said as she puffed and panted, 'just need to get my breath back. That run was insane.' Her high-pitched voice reminded Gina of a little girl's voice. She leaned against the door of the cabin and began circling her ankles.

'Happy that you ruined our break?' The woman from the opposite cabin stared.

Taylor stuck two fingers up and stormed into the cabin. Gina followed. 'Tell me all this isn't over me playing some music last night. I told that cow I was sorry about throwing up on the porch but she just kept going on at me. I turned the music off after that.'

Everyone was right about Taylor. She looked so young. Gina doubted she'd weigh seven stone if she was soaked through. Her face still bore the scars of acne and the braces in her mouth filled it. Her hair was badly dyed with chunks that looked unintentionally missed out and her nails were chewed down.

'It isn't about the music. I need to speak to you about something far more serious.'

Taylor grabbed a water bottle from the island and glugged down half of the water. 'I need some painkillers first.' She popped two paracetamols into her hand and swallowed them down. 'I thought the run would clear my head but it's banging.'

'Too much wine?'

The girl shrugged. 'S'pose so.'

'Are you alone?'

'Why?'

'There was an incident last night and we're speaking to everyone who knew the victims.'

'Is it my aunt?'

'No, it involves Mrs Braddock, your employer.'

The girl stared.

'Taylor.'

She snapped out of her thoughts and flicked the kettle on. 'What happened?'

'Her friend got run over in a hit-and-run and is now seriously ill in hospital. Annabel is missing.'

'Missing as in wandered off or kidnapped?'

'That's what we're trying to establish. There has been no sign of her since.'

'Is Cally okay?' A wash of genuine concern spread across Taylor's face.

'Cally's safe with her grandad. We're trying to locate Mr Braddock.'

She began picking at the label on the coffee jar. 'How would I know where he is?'

Wyre quietly stepped into the room and stood next to Gina. Gina nodded to her and they both sat on the stools at the island. 'We know that Mr Braddock booked the cabin and we know about your relationship.'

Taylor slammed the jar of coffee onto the worktop and began pacing around the small kitchen area. 'How? We didn't tell anyone. We were waiting for the right time. Does Annabel know?'

'Doesn't matter. What matters is that you tell us what you know.'

'I don't know why Mrs Braddock is missing or why someone ran over her friend.'

Gina leaned back and Wyre removed her notepad from her bag. 'Let's start at the beginning. What is your relationship with Grant Braddock?'

Biting the skin around her nails, Taylor stopped pacing. 'We're in love.'

'How long have you been having an affair with him?'

'Around three months. He said they were over, he just needed time to tell her and to work things out. He said he couldn't leave without Cally and he wouldn't lose the house so I had to wait. I didn't mind waiting because that's what you do when you love someone. I said that I'd look after Cally when Annabel left, like I already do. I know he wasn't making it up. He was sleeping in the spare room.'

'It must have hurt, seeing him with Annabel day in, day out.

I mean you are a huge part of their lives. Annabel must have trusted you implicitly if she left you with her daughter.'

'I knew you'd get judgy. You don't understand.' She pulled her shorts up over her navel.

'What don't I understand?'

'He has a kid. He couldn't just leave and I had a responsibility to look after Cally. Mrs Braddock was always out, doing things, leaving Cally with me and the neighbour. I told Grant that it was good. She was getting a life so that when he ended it, everything would be okay, that she'd want to leave. It's all going to come out now, isn't it?'

Gina nodded, hoping that the conversation would stay open. She thought of Taylor and the state the couple in cabin eight had said she was in. Gina wondered for a second if Taylor could have driven and Grant could have come along and helped to clean up her mess. 'Where were you between ten thirty and midnight, last night?'

'Here. I was so sick after the wine, I came in and went to bed. I couldn't even stand, let alone go out. I remember falling over in the hall and crawling to the bedroom. The room spinning and it felt weird. It's too quiet here. It was giving me the creeps, all those trees and foxes. I kept hearing noises.'

'Where was Grant?'

'Drinking on the settee. He kept saying that Annabel hates him having a good time and he was making the most of it.'

'Where is Grant, now?'

She shrugged. 'I don't know.' Gina spotted a heaped blanket on the floor and a couple of crumpled cushions at the one end of the settee. 'He slept there because he was in a mood which is why I got drunk.'

'Why was he in a mood?'

She shrugged. 'How would I know?'

'When did you last see him?'

'A bit after ten. He briefly popped into the bedroom. I don't know the exact time but I'd just got into bed. He came in and lay next to me but I told him I was too sick to do anything.'

'Do anything?'

'You know? Too out of it for sex. He then said that I must like someone else and that I was cheating on him. He says that a lot but I don't take any notice. He stomped around and then left me to it with the washing-up bowl next to the bed.'

Gina swallowed as she tried to picture Grant angry at not getting his way. Did he then look to see where his wife was on the locator app and leave in a temper? Maybe he'd hoped to talk to her, then saw that she was with Jennifer.

'You know Annabel was shagging someone else?'

'Who's that?'

'I don't know. Grant said she was and I said I was glad as she'd be happy when he left. He seemed angry about it though and told me to stop saying that all the time. I don't think he wanted another man to become Cally's father. That's all it was. He said I don't understand these things as I've never had a child.'

'Did you ever hear Annabel speaking to this person?'

'Nah. Look, I don't know anything. I'm only guilty of falling in love. He loves me. I love him. Annabel's obviously found out and run off in a strop.'

Gina felt her patience wearing thin. 'Taylor, a woman is seriously injured in hospital and she might die. Annabel is also missing and we can't find Grant. This isn't looking like a strop.'

Her cheeks reddened. 'What am I meant to do?' She drank a few more gulps of water.

'When did you and Grant get together?'

Taylor's cheeks puffed out and she exhaled slowly. 'Just after Christmas. I know Annabel and Grant had been arguing as I'd heard them. He went on about some party on a boat that she went to, but he won't talk to me about it. The party was just before Christmas, I think. I reckon he found out about this other man then. I didn't hear everything, it was just snippets when they'd both got home from work, while I was finishing up for the day or saying bye to Cally. Anyway, the one evening, she stormed out and said she needed some space and he was so upset. I stayed behind and ate their dinner with him. That's when he kissed me. He told me he'd liked me since I started working for them and I liked him, a lot. I felt sorry for him too. He's a really nice guy and she cheated on him. He deserved something more, someone loyal.'

'Like you.'

'Yes, like me. I wouldn't cheat on him. If you want to look into something, look into that party she went to. He said that something happened and that Annabel hadn't been the same since and he knew she'd been cheating. Maybe her boyfriend took her. Have you thought about that?'

'Your aunt said that you were moving out of her annexe.'

'Yes, Grant is finding us a place to rent.'

'Have you tried to contact Grant this morning?'

Taylor scratched her torso and nodded. 'I've called him over and over again but it keeps going to voicemail. I didn't worry too much. I just thought he was with Annabel and couldn't talk. Something's happened to him too, hasn't it?'

'We don't know that but as I said, we really need to locate him.'

'If he's not coming back, I'm stuck here. I don't want to be here on my own. Can you give me a lift back to my aunt's? I haven't got my car.'

Gina sighed. 'I can give you a lift back to Cleevesford Police Station where we'd appreciate a formal statement. We now have two missing people and we need to find them.'

She nodded rapidly and began to throw her things into a carrier bag. 'I'll do whatever. I want him found. You've got me worried now.'

'Taylor?'

The girl stopped packing. 'What?'

'Why do you have a photo of Annabel in your car, the one with her face scribbled out?'

She stared at Gina, then at Wyre and began to sob. 'I just want Grant to be mine. I told you. It must have something to do with Annabel's boyfriend. She's with him. Maybe they've run away.'

'Whoever took her nearly killed another woman. How much did you want Annabel out of the way?'

She held her head in her hands and sobbed. Maybe an interview at the station would reveal more. They had to put her under pressure. 'You're right. I did want her out of the way and I'm glad she's gone, but I didn't hurt her.'

Gina wondered if she could believe anything Taylor was saying. As they left, she turned to Wyre. 'Please call Olive while I get her in the car. Ask her if we can search the cabin before she cleans it.' Wyre nodded.

THIRTEEN

Gina entered the incident room and grabbed a croissant from the centre of the table. 'Just what I needed. I am so hungry, I feel as though my stomach is eating itself from the inside.' She bit into the pastry, enjoying the buttery sensation that woke her taste buds up.

O'Connor entered, his bald head shiny on top. He placed a tray of coffees down and smiled. 'I thought we could all do with some caffeine. Mrs O baked those croissants this morning so they're nice and fresh. Any news?'

Jacob removed his headset and stopped tapping away on his keyboard, and Wyre came in, retying her hair as she walked.

Gina took a coffee. 'This is most welcome, thank you. We know that Grant Braddock booked a cabin to stay with the childminder, Taylor, who he's been having an affair with for three months. Taylor can't remember seeing him after going to bed and according to the people in the next cabin, she was so drunk she could barely stand. I can't rule out that she's a brilliant actor, not yet, so don't eliminate her from the radar. We need Grant, we need to know where he is and what he did last night. His and Annabel's daughter, Cally, also said she saw someone lurking around in the garden. Bless her, she thinks it was a ghost but given what happened, I'm inclined to believe someone was loitering.'

'Could it have been Grant?' O'Connor took a bite of croissant and loosened his belt slightly.

'Not sure. The people in the other cabin saw him outside around seven so it's possible that he nipped back home later. All they heard was the sound of the hot tub whirring and they assumed that Grant and Taylor were using it. Maybe one of them was in the Braddocks's garden at the time Cally saw the intruder. O'Connor, I'll update you with everything first. Could you interview Taylor in a short while? We'll give her half an hour to stew on things.'

'Yup.'

'At the moment, it's a witness interview but try to draw her out. Right, onto Grant Braddock. Any sightings of him? Has he been home?'

Jacob shook his head. He reached for the stapler on his desk and began opening and closing it as he spoke. 'Not yet. His registration is out there. ANPR should hopefully pick him up soon if he's on the move.'

'We need him. What have you found out about him?'

Jacob brought up Grant's details on the system. 'Five ten, brown hair greying at the sides. Fit and slim. Father-in-law said he works out a lot at the gym. He works in facilities management at managerial level. He has a past record.'

Gina sat and undid her coat. 'Go on.'

'Drunken fighting mostly. He had a girlfriend when he was at college. Another man hit on her and he knocked him off his feet. There was no lasting damage and he got a suspended sentence and a fine.'

'A history of jealousy – interesting. There was talk of a work party that Annabel attended just before Christmas. From what Taylor said, Annabel was seeing someone and it stemmed from that party. The school is open tomorrow but we could do with speaking to someone sooner. Any luck with getting hold of the head teacher or at least the head of mathematics?'

'No, no luck at all with the school side.' Jacob spoke so low Gina struggled to hear him.

'Okay, O'Connor will interview Taylor. We all do everything we can to locate Grant. Jacob, keep going through the calls and delve into anything useful. Wyre and I are going to head back to the cabin. The woman who owns the site has given us permission to search it before she cleans it. There might just be some clue as to where he is or where he went. Jacob, could you also please keep trying to contact someone from the school. We need to know more about that party. If Annabel was seeing someone, they could be a person of interest too or they may know something. How's Jennifer?'

Biting the inside of his cheek, Jacob hunched over, his stubble now a slight brown mat over his chin. 'I called the hospital about an hour ago. No change.' His shaky hands told Gina not to push him for more information. 'Her clothes have been sent to the lab and swabs have been taken too. Everything is at the lab. She's still on the ventilator.'

'Do you need to be with her? You could head home to catch up on some sleep and come back later. If I hear anything at all, I will call you immediately, I promise.' Gina leaned forward and tilted her head. She wished that there was more she could do.

'No.' He pressed his lips together and shook his head vigorously. 'I am not leaving this building until we have caught the person who did this. We need to find Annabel. I can't do anything for Jennifer right now apart from wait for her to wake up. As for Annabel, they're the oldest of friends. I have to help find her. That's what Jennifer would want.' Jacob began scrolling through an email. 'Yes! Guv, we've had a response to the appeal. Someone has spotted Grant Braddock sitting outside the new sandwich shop on the high street. PC Kapoor is already on her way.'

Gina glanced up at Wyre. 'Let's go. We can't lose him.'

FOURTEEN

Pulling up alongside the road with a screech, Gina could see PC Kapoor standing outside the sandwich shop, talking into her radio. Then she sprinted down the path. Wyre and Gina hurried out of the car and followed her down the high street, turning right along a road lined with houses. In the distance, she could see a man turning towards the park and playing fields.

Kapoor called out as she ran. 'Police, stop.' The man ignored her.

Gina upped her pace but she was no match for Wyre who had almost caught up with Kapoor. Her heart banged and she struggled for breath as she pushed herself harder. She turned towards the park but couldn't see Wyre or Kapoor. She'd lost them, too slow to keep up. A grey cloud passed and the lunchtime sun had disappeared. She heard what sounded like a crashing bin coming from the estate that had been built in the sixties. Again, she picked up the pace, almost tripping over a Jack Russell as she took a shortcut across the field. The owner shouted something, she held a hand up in apology, not having time to stop.

Turning into the road, all she could see were rows of five-storey flats. She spotted the fallen bin. A woman came out, swearing under her breath as she began to pick up the spilled rubbish. 'Did you see a police officer come past?'

'She went that way, another woman was with her.'

'Thank you.' Gina ran down the road, dodging people with children and dogs, then she saw Kapoor down the next road, bent over and panting. 'Where did he go?'

Kapoor shook her head. 'Wyre is still chasing him. I guess I need to workout more. Come on, this way.'

'You and me both.'

'I've radioed Smith the location, he should have been here to back us up.' Kapoor held her side as she jogged past the convenience shop and down a tree-lined road.

Standing on the tarmac, hands in her hair, staring at the sky was Wyre. 'I lost him.' She kicked a tree and roared.

Fighting the stitch in her side, Gina caught up and Kapoor bent over to re-tie her laces. 'Which way did he go?'

'I thought it was this way but I can't see him anywhere. We told him we were police; we told him to stop but he ran. He might not have even come down this road. Damn.'

As they got their breath back, Smith pulled up in a car. 'Got here as fast as I could.'

'Too late, Smith. We lost him and we have no idea which way he went. One to Grant, nil to us.' Kapoor exhaled. 'I've never met anyone who can run so fast for so long, guv. He went like an Olympian chasing gold.'

'Let's head back to the sandwich shop. Is the person who called us still there? Maybe they can help us.'

Kapoor nodded. 'I asked her to stay put.'

They all got into the police car that PC Smith was driving. 'I'm really sorry I was late to the chase. There are roadworks ahead and cars were jammed in everywhere. I couldn't get through even with the blue lights on.'

Gina smiled. 'It's not your fault, really. He took us by

surprise.' She stared out of the window. 'Nothing screams guilt more than running away from the police. Catching him is our absolute priority. Annabel is depending on us doing just that.'

Smith dropped them all back on the high street. Gina hurried out, passing the chairs and tables on the path before entering the sandwich shop. The man at the counter smiled. 'What can I get you?'

'I'm DI Harte. Where is the woman who called us?'

'Ah yes, you're police. She said she had to leave or she'd be late for work. What was happening with that man?'

'We need to speak to him.'

'You might want this then.' He held up a sports bag. 'He left it under the chair outside.'

'Thank you. Do you have CCTV?'

'No, sorry. I don't leave anything on the premises overnight and we have metal shutters but no CCTV.'

'Did you serve him?'

The man nodded and removed his glasses. 'I did. He bought a sausage roll and a coffee.'

'How did he seem?'

'Agitated. He couldn't keep still while I put his sausage roll in a bag. He kept glancing around all over the place and then stared at the door. When he paid me, I dropped some of his money and I think he swore under his breath. He was stepping from one foot to the other, scratching his face, over-blinking. To be honest, I wanted him out of my shop. His stare gave me an uneasy feeling. Then the woman came in as he left. She said she was sure she'd seen an appeal on the news and the police wanted the public to call if they saw him or his wife, so she stayed inside and called while he sat on a chair outside. Your uniformed officer turned up and he made a run for it, leaving his bag.'

'Did he say anything to you?'

'Apart from effing at me for dropping his money, no.'

'Well, thanks for holding on to the bag.' Gina left the shop and joined Kapoor and Wyre on the path. 'He left this behind.' Gina unzipped it. 'A sweaty-smelling towel and T-shirt.' She reached in further and pulled out a gym pass. 'I think this is where he came from. Isn't Fit Gym just down the next street?'

Wyre nodded. 'I used to be a member there. Follow me.'

FIFTEEN

Annabel

I wake with a start but still I can't tell whether it's now day or night. My dream of Cally and me running away together all came back. It felt so real. My dad was helping me, saying that I had to get away from my toxic marriage. Then I remembered, I never told my dad everything. I wish I had now. My dad has always been there for me and he'd do anything to keep me safe. He's not perfect and he's done things he's not proud of, but haven't we all? What matters is that he loves me, he loves Cally, and he'll do anything for us.

I'm disappointed in myself. Had I confided in Dad, he'd have told the police about Grant's threats. As it stands, he knows nothing. He's never liked Grant and has often made it clear but right now, I imagine them being best buddies, working together to find me. I think of Grant's brother, Seth. He's away in the Netherlands working as far as I know. Dad liked him. He always said that I chose the wrong brother.

Did anyone find Jen? A tear drizzles down my face. I imagine the person who hit her left her in a ditch and no one knows where she is. Jen is strong though. I know she'll survive whatever injuries she has. Me, I've never been strong. I teach teenagers and they run rings around me. They don't do their homework and I lap up the excuses. I can't even hold my ground with fourteen-year-olds. There's one kid in my class who often stays behind to ask me more questions and he tells me of a girl he likes who doesn't notice him. I swallow, knowing that he has a crush on me. It wouldn't be him. Omar is a nice kid, one of the gentle souls in the class. The quiet, astute one who I know will get an A but why have I seen him hanging around my house? He thinks I don't notice him watching from behind the trees. I should have said more to my colleague, Kirsty. I will when I get out of this mess. Maybe she should teach him instead of me but he knows things about me and I don't want him blurting them out.

I'm lying in wet. I knew I wouldn't be able to hold myself much longer.

How long will he leave me here? Who is he? Is it Grant or a person he paid? If I can't get out of this, I wonder what Grant will do. He'll tell everyone that I have left them for the other man that he keeps accusing me of seeing. He loves attention and he'll lap up everyone's sympathy.

The way his mind works disgusts me. The other man. Yeah right. What happened at that party is my secret and I wasn't ready to talk but Grant could see that I was hiding something from him. Now I'm angry. I try to kick and nudge but nothing is happening. My anger has failed me and has resulted in nothing more than a slicing pain in my wrists.

Shivering, I try to ball up a little in the hope of preserving some body heat. Darkness. What can that mean? Maybe I'm underground. I thought I might be in some sort of container but underground is worse. That thought makes me try to swallow but the gag keeping my mouth open has dried me out. Every time I clench my teeth over the material, it makes me cringe. The arid feeling in my throat is like nothing I've ever experienced and I can't make it go away. I can't fight my way out. There is no one here to fight. I have no voice in which to plead with. My mind is awhirl and a creepy sensation prickles my neck. What if there is a night-vision camera on me and this sicko is keeping me here for his own pleasure, watching and filming? Panic fills my chest. Maybe they're making a snuff movie and I'm the star. Imagining that I'm being broadcast on the Dark Web, that people might be pleasuring themselves over, my misery sends adrenaline surging through me. I can't breathe again. Gasping, I wriggle but I truly am stuck.

Then, there's a bang. Someone is coming. My heart pounds again as I hear a thump against the side of whatever I'm in. The thought of not knowing what comes next is terrifying. I can't see and that's confusing. Another bang, then silence.

I know he's out there. He knows I'm in here. Bang! I'm scared to death by what I heard and I know he's watching and enjoying the show. That bang was too well timed.

Another bang. I jerk slightly then I hear a lock turn. Even with the door to my prison open, I can't see. We are still in darkness.

I try to mumble under the gag but no words escape. I want to plead for my release. There's a smell I recognise. It's Grant's deodorant, the same brand he's used since he was a teenager.

Fingers touch my hair and I want to scream loud but I remain still. I can't alarm him. I need him to let me go. Instead, I sink my head into his fingers and he strokes my hair. Then I feel a prick in my neck and the voice in my head starts to fade. I'm sinking down and down. I can't fight it.

SIXTEEN

Gina went up to the desk at the gym with Wyre following. PC Kapoor had left to take another emergency call. The young man behind the desk continued typing and putting files into a pile without looking up.

'Excuse me.' Gina glared over the desk.

'I'll be with you in a minute.' He opened a drawer and began fishing around for something.

She'd had enough of waiting and wasn't about to indulge the receptionist any longer. She had a missing woman to find and the woman's husband was a person of interest. 'Police, we need to speak to whoever's in charge.'

The man stopped fishing around and looked up. His polo shirt had a small logo of a weight and the name 'Fit Gym' written around it. His name badge told Gina that he was called Brad. 'Okay.' He grabbed the phone and asked for Phil to come to reception.

Within a minute a burly shaven-headed man appeared. His thick neck stood on an equally thick body. 'How can I help?'

'You have a member called Grant Braddock.'

The man nodded to Brad. 'I'm not good with names. Check the files, will you?'

Brad nodded and began tapping away on the computer. 'Yes, he was here this morning. I can see he used his pass to check in and out.'

Gina leaned against the counter. 'What time was that?'

'He arrived at ten fifteen and left at eleven. He comes at least four times a week. Times vary. Sometimes early in the morning, anytime at the weekend and occasional evenings.'

'Do you have CCTV?'

Brad smiled and pointed to the camera by the door. 'Yes. It covers reception and the main gym but it's not that clear.'

'May we take a look?'

Phil nodded and held out a hand, indicating that Gina and Wyre head to the room behind reception. 'This is the control room and office.'

Gina entered first. The stuffy room had fans and a couple of computers running. A large server flashed away in the corner.

'Take a seat in front of the screen.' He grabbed an extra chair for Wyre so that they could all sit. 'Brad,' he called out, 'go get three coffees, please. You want coffee, don't you?'

'Thank you.' Gina pulled her chair in. The desk light wasn't that bright and the main light had a whole strip out. Several protein drinks were stacked at the one end, along with several boxes of supplements.

'Right.' He began to click away until he came to the camera at reception. 'Let's just get to ten, see him coming in. There. Looks all normal. Gym bag over his shoulder.'

'Can we flick to the gym room?'

With another click, they were there. 'It's quite grainy, isn't it?'

''Fraid, so. You can see it's the man who came in at ten. He heads over to the weights. After a bit of a warm up, he gets going. Looks like he's heading to the treadmill now. I'll give him his due, he's good. I did see him as I passed through, about now. That's me there. He was giving it some. He seemed determined. Wait, he's stopped and holding a finger to his earbud. It's like he's listening to something.'

'We put out an appeal this morning, looking for him and his wife. It's possible that he heard it on the radio.'

Phil scratched his chin and acknowledged Brad as he placed the coffees on the desk. 'Cheers.' Brad left, closing the door behind him. 'So he hears something about himself on the radio and look at him go. I've never seen anyone leave so abruptly, he nearly knocked that woman over. Back to the other camera.' With a few clicks, they were looking at reception. 'And he bangs out of the door like the place is on fire.'

'Do you have a camera on the car park?'

'No, sorry.'

Gina took a swig of the tepid machine coffee. It wasn't pleasant but it was most welcome after the run she'd had. 'Can we go back to the main gym footage?'

He nodded and replayed.

'Don't you think he looks agitated?'

'Yes, he does. He's constantly moving, even while wiping the sweat from his brow. It's like he's hyper. I mean it's often like that in the gym but when I see him go on the treadmill, he's also running his hands through his hair, then biting his nails. He can't keep still. He stumbles a little here. Look, he's angry so he hits the equipment. Maybe he's on something.'

'You think he could be using drugs?'

'Well, I can't be sure but it's a possibility. I've seen it in people before and it's not something I approve of but people do it. They want to build more muscle, they want to be faster. They sometimes reach their limits and they can't accept that that's all they can manage, so they start looking for other ways to get better. It's an addiction. One I've suffered with but I'm proud to say, it's all in my distant past. He's disappointed with his performance, I can see that. I can also see that he's acting all too superhuman.'

'That would explain why we couldn't catch him.'

Phil nodded. 'Or, he might just be an agitated person, who can run really fast. Who really knows?'

Gina thought back to what the man in the café said. Also, the way that Grant lost Wyre and Kapoor, two of the fittest people she knew, the theory of him being on a drug to improve his performance seemed a distinct possibility and something she'd bear in mind when they caught up with him.

'Why are you after him? I haven't seen the news today.' Phil finished his coffee and leaned back with his arms folded.

'We're investigating an incident last night and we need to speak to him. Do you know if he has a car registered with his membership?'

'I'll check on that when we go back out there. Are we done here for now, as I have to get back to work?'

'Yes, could I please take a copy of the CCTV away? Apologies but I haven't brought a hard drive or memory stick.'

Phil began fishing in a drawer. 'You can borrow one of ours. I'll get Brad to put the footage on this for you.'

'Thank you, again.' Gina passed him a card as Wyre finished writing a few notes down. 'If he comes back or you think of anything else, please call me.'

'Will do. Brad, pop the footage from reception and the gym on this hard drive. Time, from ten up to eleven.' Phil looked up at Gina as Brad headed into the back room. 'I'll check his details, see if he has a car registered. Members can use the car park free but we have to have a registration number. Ah, there is Mr Braddock's. I'll write it down. It's a blue Volvo.'

'That's great.'

'If you want, you can head out to the car park and take a look. Brad will bring the hard drive out to you.' Gina nodded, noticing that Phil probably wanted the police out of his gym.

Two women entered, holding water bottles and Phil smiled and followed them towards the gym. 'I best get back to it. Break's over.'

Gina led the way to the car park. 'We need to hurry over to the cabin. I know the owner will want to clean it soon as Taylor has now left.' Stopping, Gina pointed at the Volvo. 'Looks like we've found his car. Call it in.' Gina glanced at the car. 'What if Annabel's in his boot?' She ran over and tapped on it. It was hollow. She shook her head. 'No damage to the car and nothing in the boot. This wasn't used in the hit-and-run. It's also dirty and there aren't any marks breaking up that dirt.' She paused in thought. 'One thing's for sure, he'll be back for it and when he does come back, we need to be waiting for him. We need a car parked up, ready to block him off when he gets into it, for at least the rest of the day. Two officers, and make sure they can run fast. Also, we need his gym bag swabbed. If he was on something, I want to know what. We need to know what we're dealing with. If he doesn't come back for it, have the car taken to the pound where he'll have to come to retrieve it or it may end up in evidence. He may not have used this car but he had opportunity and motive which means he's a suspect.'

SEVENTEEN

Omar

Mrs Braddock said I should consider A-level maths. She often says to me, '*Omar, you're really gifted in this subject and I know you love it, too.*' I don't have any trouble understanding anything she gives me but love it, no. I love her, not maths. I am gifted though. Quadratic equations – easy. Trig – easy. I try harder than anyone else because I know it's a subject Mrs Braddock is passionate about.

Some of the class struggle, which is why they're sometimes mean to me. They call me swot and I get picked on because they see the way I look at Mrs Braddock, or Annabel. In my head she's Annabel and sometimes I almost forget myself and call her that in class. On Facebook, she uses the name Annie Bell. Her profile picture is of her dog, a scraggy-looking lurcher. She doesn't friend pupils. I know that because I tried to add her and she rejected me and explained why the next day at school, like I was a dumb kid. *It's inappropriate.* That's her excuse. I'm not a kid though, not any more. One day, she will want me.

I search through her Facebook posts and going back a few months, I come across photos of him, her horrid husband. Pressing his photo on the screen, I imagine he's here and he's real and I'm squishing him like a spider. He even has his top off, showing off his abs. He doesn't deserve someone as nice as Annabel. Turning to the mirror, I catch a glimpse of myself. I need to be more like him and then she'll like me. My arms are thin and I wish my acne would clear. It's crusted along my hairline and there's nothing I can do to get rid of it. My chest and back are no better.

Some days, I stay behind at school and make up some rubbish to ask her. There's no way I needed her to explain something as simple as adding fractions up but I like being close to her. Sometimes I get that close I can smell her.

It seems like ages ago now I was riding my bike up towards the industrial estate on my way to visit Nan and I saw her with her little girl. I never imagined she'd live in a house like that. A semi-detached cottage in a row of cottages. It was small. Maybe her husband isn't as successful as he makes out on social media. All muscles, no brains, maybe. That's my edge. I have brains and Annabel is impressed by brains, and one day I'm going to be someone. The next Brian Cox, maybe. A part of me knows I'm destined for more than the average person. I feel myself harden as I think of her and I can't help it.

'Omar, sweetheart. Hurry up. I need some help with the shopping.'

'Mum, do I have to come?'

She bursts in, giving me no privacy at all. I drop my hoodie in my lap to cover up my thoughts of Annabel, then I shut the screen down. If Mum sees me looking at my teacher on Facebook with a hard-on, she'll never let me hear the end of it. She found one porno mag under my bed and she still bangs on about that. *It objectifies women. It's not real. They're all airbrushed.* She goes on and on and thinking about it is making my face redden. So, I'm a man now. I wanted to look at breasts. So what. I look on the internet now, instead. No more magazines for Mum to find. She's giving me a funny look as I wriggle in my chair. Trying to distract her eye from my lap area, I bring up TikTok and laugh as two girls dance on roller boots. Playfully, she swipes my thick black hair and kisses my head. 'Yes, you do have to come. Maybe when we've done the shopping, I'll treat you to a hot chocolate with marshmallows.' She looks at me and smiles. 'My boy, you're growing up so quickly.'

'Mum.' She's really embarrassing me now. I am growing up, she's right about that. I'm a man now and I'm man of the house. It's time for me to step up for her. 'I'll be down in a sec.' As she leaves, I get Annabel's Facebook back up then a new post she's tagged in appears on her wall.

If you see Annabel, please call the number below. Please be okay. We love you. Dad.

Attached is a missing person's poster that has been shared from Cleevesford Police. I've seen the photo they're using, she keeps it on her sideboard in the hall of her house. I think back to that day at school, when I saw and heard those private things. She begged me not to say anything. I would never betray her because I love her. Her secrets are all mine.

EIGHTEEN

'It's been an hour now and Grant still hasn't come back for his car,' Gina said as she and Wyre pulled on their crime scene suits. Gina acknowledged the police officer who had been guarding the cabin and she entered with Wyre close behind. Olive, the owner, had been briefed. They were looking for drugs and any sign of Grant having anything to do with the hit-and-run, and the abduction of his wife. Specifically, she was looking for something to link the scene of the crime to Grant.

'He knows we're after him and he must know we have his gym bag. He'll come back for it.' Wyre stepped into the kitchen area.

'Let's hope he doesn't spot Smith parked a couple of rows back. It's a good job Kapoor is with him. I can't see Smith running if he takes off.' Gina glanced down at the sweet wrappers.

'Do you need me for anything?' Olive popped her head through the door.

'No, we should be okay. A forensics van should arrive soon, could you please point them in our direction?'

'Of course.' She paused. 'I have more guests arriving soon. Will you be long?'

'We hope not but I can't make any promises.'

'It'll look bad, you lot here, dressed like CSI. People will think someone has been murdered.'

Gina bit her bottom lip as she thought of Jennifer in hospital. Her condition hadn't changed and if she didn't make it through, they could be investigating a murder. They were still no nearer to finding Annabel either. 'We're really sorry to put you through this.'

Olive dismissed her concern with a smile. 'It'll be what it will be. I hope you find what you're after. I'll be back at the shop if you need me.'

'Thanks.' The woman turned back and Gina left Wyre in the kitchen, rooting through the bin.

Heading to the one and only bedroom, she entered and the first thing that hit her was the smell. Taylor had been right about how drunk she'd been. There was a smear of vomit on the pillow and an emptied but soiled washing-up bowl by the side of the bed. The white sheets were mostly on the floor and an unopened pack of condoms were on the bedside table. Taylor's belongings had gone but Grant's remained; not that there was much. A polo shirt had been thrown on the floor and next to that, a pair of worn underpants. She kneeled down and checked under the bed – nothing. She opened the bedside table drawers – empty. Maybe forensics would find something by swabbing the surfaces. Large glass doors led to a small terrace. Gina slid the door open and instantly spotted the nub end. With gloved hands, she lifted it and sniffed. Weed. She pulled an evidence bag from her pocket and placed it inside before heading to the bathroom. There was nothing personal in there at all. Taylor must have been existing out of her holdall. She bagged the only thing she could find, a toothbrush that must belong to Grant. Leaning over, she checked the waste bin. It was empty.

Joining Wyre in the kitchen, she glanced around. What they really needed was to search Grant's house. He was now a person of interest after running from the police. 'Have you found anything?'

'No, guv. I've checked the cupboards and fridge. They haven't used the bin, it looks like they used the floor instead.'

'Have you been on the decked area?'

'Not yet.'

Gina sidled past the log burner and opened the bi-fold doors to a wooden patio area to a view of dense woodland that looked like it went on forever. She pulled back the hot tub cover and the smell of chlorine hit her. Birdsong filled the air. As she turned to go back in, she spotted a waste bin in the corner. Rifling through, she pulled out a wad of paper tissues with what looked to be smears of blood on them. 'Wyre, we have blood. Get this place properly cordoned off. No one can enter or leave now except for Bernard's team when they arrive. These need to go to the lab ASAP. We need to know whose blood this is. It should be a quick match if it's one of them.'

Gina's phone rang. 'Jacob, what have you got?'

'It's Grant's bag. After swabbing it, we found traces of amphetamine sulphate.'

She ended the call and turned to Wyre. 'At the very least, we will be bringing Grant in to discuss the traces of speed on his bag. At the most, if that blood turns out to be Jennifer's or Annabel's, we can put him at the scene. Best get those tissues to the lab now. Then let's head to his house. We need to call her father to make sure he can be there. I know he called the station earlier to say he was taking Cally to his house. Grant is in the middle of all this. Get a rush on that blood and organise a warrant to search his house.'

NINETEEN

Gina scoffed the packet sandwich they'd bought from the garage as she and Wyre waited for Annabel's father to arrive back at the house. He'd taken Cally to his a few hours ago. The taste of pickle hung in her throat. She glanced up. Jennifer's car was still parked on the road by their house, right where she left it. Gina took a mint from the centre console and popped it in her mouth.

'I wonder how long he'll be.' Wyre finished the last of her tuna salad.

'Hopefully not much longer. The lab are testing the blood sample now. We should get the results soon.' Gina checked her phone and no one had tried to call. They had all the samples at the lab, it was simply a matter of seeing if the blood on the tissues matched Jennifer's or Annabel's which were left at the scene of the hit-and-run. Gina wedged the empty wrapper in the side of the car as an email popped up from Bernard. 'Damn, I hoped for more. Nothing else of concern has been found at the cabin. The nub end was definitely weed. Swabs have been taken and will be processed at the lab. Great.' She stared out of the window. The sun was going down and it was past teatime for most people. A car pulled up behind them. She wound her window down.

Evan, the neighbour, got out and walked over. 'Have you found Annabel? I saw the appeal on the news.'

'No, sorry. Thank you for going to the station and giving a statement earlier.'

'No worries. I thought Doug would be here by now. He called me, asking if I'd look after Cally while he talks to you. Thought I'd take her to feed my rabbit. She loves Thumper. Would you like me to bring you both a drink, while you wait?'

Wyre shook her head and smiled as a car pulled in. Gina and Wyre met Doug and Cally on the pavement. Now that he had arrived, their work could begin.

'Cally, love, would you go with Evan for a few minutes while Gramps talks to the police officers?'

Evan smiled. 'Thumper is waiting for his dinner, Cally. I thought you could feed him.'

'Yay.' The little girl followed Evan into his house.

'I hope you don't mind. I didn't want Cally around asking questions, not yet.'

Gina followed him down the path and into the house. 'What have you told her?'

'I've just said that she's staying with me for a few days as Mummy and Daddy have had to work away. I didn't know what else to say and I don't think she believes me. None of this is normal and she knows it too. Is there any news?'

Gina stepped into the living room, out of the tiny hall. 'We had a sighting of Grant earlier. When we headed over to where he was, he saw us and ran.'

'I knew it. He's done something to her. How could he? I know they weren't getting on but she's the mother of his daughter.'

'As far as you are aware, do you know if Grant has ever taken drugs?'

The man fell into the chair. 'Yes. My daughter denied it but I know he does. You can tell. He's always fidgeting, doesn't sleep and that disturbing wide-eyed stare he does, it's creepy. One of the reasons he hates me too is that I caught him snorting something when I was over at Christmas. He didn't lock the door to the loo and I had no idea he was in there. I don't know what it was that he was snorting but he went for a long run afterwards. Cocaine, maybe. I did have a go at him, told him that Annabel was far too good for the likes of him and that it wasn't right that he did that in his home, around his daughter. Of course, I told Annabel and she told me she'd deal with it and asked me not to go on. I was worried about Cally, being around a man on drugs, but I didn't want to push Annabel away. I couldn't bear to not be in their lives. I thought maybe Grant had learned a lesson but it looks like he hasn't if you're asking me about drugs.'

'I know this is hard on you but with Annabel missing and Grant literally on the run from us, we have a warrant to search the house.' Gina placed it on the worktop, leaving it with Doug. Gina kept the news of the bloodied tissues to herself. It was too early to alarm the man with news like that.

'Look around for anything that might lead you to my daughter. I want her back. Cally is missing her and I don't know how much longer I can keep giving her excuses as to why Annabel isn't around.' The man leaned forwards and put his head in his hands. 'I can't be here right now. Is it okay to go next door with Cally and Evan while you do what you have to do?'

Gina nodded. 'We're so sorry for all you're going through. I'll knock when we've finished. Do you have the dog?'

'Yes. My neighbour is keeping an eye on him. You know where I'll be if you need me.'

'Thank you.' Gina watched him leave. 'Right.' She pulled a couple of crime scene suits from her bag and passed one to Wyre. 'Best not to contaminate anything, just in case.' They both pulled them over their shirts and trousers before snapping on some gloves. 'I'll head up to their bedroom, you see what you can find here. Give Smith a call. See if a couple of officers can relieve him and Kapoor of sentry duty. Someone else can take a turn in watching Grant's car. We're going to need their assistance.'

Wyre nodded. 'Will do, guv.'

Gina took the creaky stairs one by one. The wall was dotted with photos in a variety of frames, each one a different size and colour. There were lots of photos of Cally, some school photos and some that looked like they were taken in a studio. Then there was the family in happy times, together at the zoo, at a theme park, at the beach, riding horses. As she reached the top, she faced the bathroom. Peering in, she went straight for the medicine cabinet but all it contained was moisturisers, toothpaste and dispenser soaps, amongst a few bobbles that were entangled with hair. The bin was full of empty toilet rolls and that was it. She headed out and pushed a door open. She passed Cally's room then stopped outside the next bedroom. Pushing the door, it opened with a squeak.

The lack of personal belongings and an old desk at one end of the room told Gina that she was in the spare room, the room that Grant had been sleeping in. The quilt half lay on the floor exposing the single bed mattress. A pile of dirty clothes had been thrown into a corner of the room. If Grant was using drugs, Gina could guarantee that he wouldn't keep them in their shared bedroom. She glanced out of the window at the set-back garage and wondered if Annabel went in there often.

Kneeling, she began to lift the mattress and feel along it. She then bent down and saw that there was nothing under the bed. Then, she searched the drawers, the bedside table and the wardrobe and found no sign of drugs at all. Standing on a chair, she checked the top of the wardrobe. That's when she spotted the air vent with the missing screw. On the desk was a screwdriver. Hurrying, she grabbed it and stood back on the chair, stretching her arm over the top of the wardrobe before unscrewing the rest. The grill clanged onto the floor and she reached in, straining to feel if anything was in there. Her hand reached a bundle of cloth. She pulled the canvas bag out and took it over to the desk. As she unfolded it, about thirty baggies of white powder fell out. 'Wyre, I've found the drugs.'

Wyre began running up the stairs.

'We need to get these to the lab. Looks like Doug was right. Either Grant was dealing or he has a big problem with methamphetamine.' Gina glanced up at the recess. 'There's something else in there.' She stood on the chair again. 'I can't reach in. Can you pass me something? There's a ruler on the desk. That might help.'

'Here.' Wyre passed it up.

It took several attempts but Gina managed to drag the package out. She passed it to Wyre. 'Check that.'

'It's full of cash, guv. There has to be about five grand here.'

'We need to put out a warrant for his arrest. Looks like we've found ourselves a dealer. We need a forensics team here. Are Smith and Kapoor here yet?'

'No, Smith's on his way so he shouldn't be long.'

'We'll post him outside the door while we organise a forensics team to come over. I know they're stretched with the cabin but we can't afford to mess this up. For now, no one can enter the house. We need to find Annabel and this house might hold the clue to her whereabouts. I'm hoping that she hasn't been taken because Grant owes money to some drug lord. This discovery has thrown us in it, big time.'

Someone knocked on the front door. Wyre headed out of the bedroom. 'Must be Smith.'

Gina bagged up the evidence and began to fill out the details on the front.

'I need to tell you something.' It was Doug's voice.

Running out of the bedroom, Gina hurried down the stairs, almost slipping on the carpet in her shoe covers. She pulled the hood down and joined Wyre at the door.

'Mr Latham was just saying that he was in Evan's garden next door and he could see through the side window to the garage. Apparently, Grant's old silver Mercedes isn't in there.'

The man piped up. 'He's been working on it for a while. What work, I don't know. I think he mostly polishes it but it's not there. I know he hasn't sold it so he must be using it. I know it drives.' Doug held his hand over his mouth. 'He ran Annabel over with it and took her, didn't he? She's out there stuffed in his car.' He wobbled on his feet. Gina led him to the shoe bench by the door and he fell down on it. 'I just want her back.' He placed his head in his hands.

Gina turned away and closed her eyes. She could not leave Cally without a mother or Doug without a much-loved daughter. She remembered back to when she came to the house and spoke to Cally. There had been a padlock on the garage door and it was locked. Only someone with a key could have taken the car out. Maybe Grant's plan was to say that it had been stolen. It was time to talk to Taylor again. She checked her messages and there was one marked urgent from Bernard.

We have a match on the blood found on the tissues at the cabin. It's Jennifer's blood. We're relying on you to nail this bastard!

TWENTY

'What? Taylor's gone?' Gina barged into the incident room. Jacob turned around from his computer and O'Connor stood in front of her, his face even redder at having to tell her the news.

'She hadn't been arrested, guv. I told her that we needed a further interview and statement and she was cooperative.'

'I know. It's just... I thought you could have kept her here until I got back. Sorry.' She took a couple of deep breaths.

'When you called about the blood, she asked if she could have a cigarette break. I waited with her for a couple of minutes but then uniform brought someone drunk in. It all kicked off in reception so I helped. I left her for a minute at the most. When I turned back, she was gone.'

'Has someone headed over to her house?'

'Yes, she's not there and her aunt confirmed that she hadn't seen her. We've posted a car outside just in case she comes back. We figured she might need her car at some point.'

'She has to have met up with Grant. Did she have her phone?'

O'Connor nodded, sheepishly. 'She was on it constantly outside the station.'

'Have you checked the CCTV footage?'

He nodded again. 'As soon as I went in to assist, she darted off in the direction of the shops. She slipped through the alleyway between the houses. I ran over but she was long gone.' Gina remembered seeing Taylor running that morning. The lithe young woman would have had a huge advantage over O'Connor. They'd lost her, for now.

'Alert all units to be on the lookout for Grant and Taylor. They will turn up, I know it. I mean, how far can they get?' Gina furrowed her brows.

'Any news from the gym car park?'

'No, guv. Grant's Volvo is still where he left it.'

Gina turned to Jacob and Wyre. Briggs slipped in at the back of the room. 'Right, gather around.'

Jacob exhaled and sat back in his swivel chair.

Gina knew he had been told of the bloodied tissues. She stepped up to open the briefing. 'Grant is our number one suspect, right now. Wyre and I found bloodied tissues at the cabin and that blood is a match for Jennifer's. That puts him at the scene of the hit-and-run and he has motive for abducting his wife. They weren't getting on and he was having an affair. And now, Taylor is missing too. I believe that she has gone to meet Grant. While searching his house, we found out that Grant has another car, one he didn't use often but kept in their garage. That car is now gone so it might be safe to assume that's the car he's getting around in now. It's also possibly the car he used to run over Jennifer and take Annabel. All units are on alert so all we can do is hope that he turns up for his car or is spotted. He isn't using his contract phone either so we have nothing from that. We are likely to get a transcript of the messages and its content but that isn't coming straight away. Moving on to the appeal, Grant and Annabel's photos have featured heavily on local news today so a member of the public may even spot him and call in. For now, keep me updated with everything. Tomorrow, Wyre and I will head over to the school as soon as it opens, see if Annabel's colleagues can help. We know that Grant accused Annabel of having an affair. For now, go home and get some rest. You're going to need your energy.'

Wyre nodded and zipped up her bag and Briggs stared at the board on the back wall. O'Connor headed out with a couple of empty cups.

'Catch you first thing at the school, guv.' Wyre waved.

'Jacob.'

He flinched and looked up from his phone, his hands shaking so much, he placed it face down on the desk.

'Has something happened?'

Tapping his foot on the floor, he looked down as if avoiding Gina's eyes. Then he stood, grabbed his jacket and phone. 'I have to go.' Without another word he walked out, the door slamming as he left.

Briggs turned from the board. 'I can't even begin to imagine what he's going through.'

'Me neither. Something's happened. Have we had any more news on Jennifer?'

Briggs shook his head. 'I called the hospital about an hour ago and there was no change in her condition. It's still critical.'

'I hate that there's nothing we can do to help?'

'We can catch Grant and bring him in. He has to pay.' Briggs walked towards the door. 'I'll see you in the morning.'

'Wait.' Gina ran over. Briggs too was behaving strangely. If he was with someone else, she deserved to at least hear it from him. Yes, their relationship was casual but they also knew too much about each other for this not to matter. He owed her an explanation.

'I have to go. I'm going to be late.'

'Late for what?'

His gaze met hers and, for a second, she felt like she saw the Briggs she knew in there. The Briggs that would like to hold her and kiss her but within a second, that look had gone. 'See you tomorrow.' Just like Jacob had left, Briggs had too. She stood there alone in the middle of the incident room. It was just her and the board and her muddled thoughts.

She tried to call Jacob but he cut the call. Sitting in front of O'Connor's computer, she logged in as herself. There was no point going home to nothing. Unless... No, she couldn't. That was beyond wrong. What was she thinking?

TWENTY-ONE

Jacob hurried past the nurses' station, over to Jennifer's bed. A nurse was again pumping that beige liquid in through the nasal gastric feeding tube and Jennifer didn't even flinch. Her head had been shaved where the emergency team had treated her.

She was so deeply sedated, she wouldn't have any idea what was happening to her. He wondered what she was dreaming about or if she was even dreaming at all. He glanced up at her monitor, not that he understood what all the jaggedy lines meant. A nurse came over. 'How's she been?'

'She's had a stable couple of hours but we're still taking every hour as it comes.'

'That's good, right?'

'I can't say any more at the moment. We just hope she keeps responding to treatment.' The nurse finished up, noted down a few numbers from the monitor and smiled. 'I'll leave you alone with her. If you need anything, just come and find me.'

Jacob sat beside Jennifer and placed his hand over hers, being careful not to disturb the cannula. The hospital had called him in to discuss Jennifer's pregnancy. 'You should have told me about the baby. I know I said I didn't want to be a dad but' – he rubbed his eyes – 'people change. I've changed. Please keep fighting. I need you, I love you. Hell, I can't stop thinking about how we argued about what colour we should paint the lounge. I don't care anymore, Jennifer. I just want you to be safe. Fight this, please.'

'Can I get you anything from the tea cart?' A woman in a white cap smiled. 'A cuppa might help.'

A cuppa wouldn't solve a thing but he wanted one. 'Really sweet milky tea, please?'

'Coming up.' The woman grabbed a polystyrene cup and made the drink. Hot water splashed and spluttered from the canteen. 'Here you go.'

'Thank you. Do you think she'll be okay?'

The woman gave him a sympathetic smile. 'I just make the tea but the way I see it is she looks young and strong. I come in here every day and I like to have hope. She's in the best place.'

He took the tea and sipped. 'Thank you.' Almost as soon as she'd arrived, she'd left. He glanced up. The ward was full of distraught relatives speaking soothingly to really sick loved ones under dimmed light.

He placed his hand gently over Jennifer's slightly round stomach. She didn't look even remotely pregnant. He wondered how long gone she'd been. 'Why didn't you tell me?' A rush of thoughts went through his head. Maybe she didn't want to tell him or she didn't even want a baby. He removed his hand swiftly. During the short journey to the hospital, he'd dreamed of him and Jennifer with a little person. A child with a mixture of their features. Jennifer's thick hair and heart-shaped face. His nose. If he had to pick one of his best features, that would be it. The child would have brains, especially as Jennifer was a science buff. Those dreams were all for nothing. Jennifer was lying there and there was nothing he or anyone could do to help any further. It was a waiting game. Two hours of stability is what he would cling to. Given how bad things had been, that was good news and he'd cling to that.

He thought of Annabel. Maybe Jennifer had confided in her when they were out. He thought of the conversation they might have had. Jennifer may have asked her how she thought he might react to the news. She'd have told Annabel that he didn't want a child yet or maybe never. Her final conversations made their argument about what colour to paint the living room pale into insignificance. Then he thought again. Maybe the tiff was about much more. She may have been trying to find a way of striking up a conversation about the baby. His mind flashed back to that day. Their neighbour was holding her heavily pregnant stomach while loading the other three kids into her car and he'd made some jibe about how overpopulation was killing the environment. That's what started it.

'I've been a dick. I didn't mean to say what I did about our pregnant neighbour. No wonder you didn't want to tell me.' He held her hand again and stroked it like he often did. Maybe she could feel it under all the sedation and she'd take some comfort that he was there for her. 'Jennifer, I really love you and I'm sorry.' He paused. 'There's something I didn't tell you because... I don't know. We both think marriage is an outdated institution but I saw you crying when your sister got married last year. It's completely up to you but I want to know if you'd marry me? We don't have to have any stuffy old vows and we definitely don't have to change names. Or maybe if we don't get married, maybe we can have an "I love you" ceremony. I don't know what one of those is but we can be pioneers in its invention. I just want you to know how much I love you.' He felt her fingers for the slightest of movement but there was nothing.

Leaning over he kissed her pale forehead and tidied up the rest of her matted, dyed red hair. Gently, he lay his head on the pillow next to hers. He caught a whiff of some spilled beige food on the pillow and ignored it as he inched closer to her. His heart jumped slightly as he thought, what if this was the very last moment he would lie next to her? Every day, he'd taken her company for granted. Now he realised, every moment you spend with a person you love, could be the last. Ultimately, those moments will run out so each one should be treasured. He closed his eyes and he imagined that they were at home, in bed. Jennifer was asleep next to him. Everything was normal. He pressed his closed eyes together, not wanting to open them and spoil the illusion.

TWENTY-TWO

Gina pulled up in a parking bay opposite Briggs's cottage. His car was there and his kitchen light was on. If he caught her spying on him, she didn't know what he'd do but she had to find out what was going on. He'd dropped her like a stone and she deserved the truth. Being told allows a person to move on, being in limbo is confusing. Her bitten nails were testament to that fact.

Someone opened the front door but Gina couldn't see who was standing there. The bushes she'd parked behind had hidden her car well but they'd also blocked her view to the cottage door. Gina bit her lip as she opened her car door as quietly as possible. The interior light came on. She reached up and turned it off, hoping that whoever it was hadn't spotted it in the darkness. As she stood, she could see that a woman had stepped out with Briggs's dog, Jessie, and she was alone. Gina ducked as Briggs appeared at the door. He placed his hand on her shoulder and smiled warmly, then the woman left him and walked down the path with Jessie leading the way. The old dog waddled towards the edge of the nature walk that Gina had done with Briggs on many occasions.

Gina stood and watched as the woman waited for the dog to do its business, then just as she turned to come back, Gina ducked. That was the quickest walk ever. She imagined Briggs stirring the dinner while she took the dog out for the briefest of wees so that they could enjoy their evening of food, laughter and sex.

Cheeks burning, Gina remained in place. Her back was beginning to hurt. Slowly, she stretched up, just in time to see the woman stepping back into the house. Her long chestnut-coloured hair fell in the prettiest of waves. Was it Gina turning fifty that had done it for him? She was being silly. Her inability to commit to him had put the nail in that coffin. It was all her fault. She had lost the only good thing in her life. She had a daughter, she had a granddaughter but they weren't all that close. The kitchen light went out. She had to know what was happening.

She crunched across the gravelly car park and hurried to his end of terrace cottage. Scurrying alongside the house, she peered through the side window to see the lounge. At first she saw the log burner and the low lighting, then she spotted the mezze board with dips on the coffee table. Then, by the entrance to the room, she saw Briggs with his arm around the woman, her head buried in his chest. That's when she stiffened. A boy of about three or four years old ran in and Briggs lifted him up with a smile. That's the one thing she could never give him.

As she took a few deep breaths, he went to look up. She moved as fast as she could but caught a plant pot. It fell from the wall, onto the path. Without hesitating, she ran as fast as she could back to the car. As the front door opened, she ducked. Footsteps moved closer and closer, then stopped. She couldn't breathe. How would she explain to Briggs that she'd been at his house, spying on him? 'Gina?'

Slowly, she stood to reveal herself behind the car.

'I thought it was your car. What are you doing here?'

She ran to the driver's side pushing past him and got into the car. He held his hands up but there was no way she'd stop. A wash of total humiliation inched through every part of her body. She was meant to be at home working on the case, instead she'd been caught spying on her lover. Or was he her lover anymore? 'Idiot, idiot, idiot.'

TWENTY-THREE

MONDAY, 4 APRIL

Gina pulled up in the car park and turned off her engine. The school playgrounds were empty now, not like they had been several minutes ago. Groups of teenagers had been everywhere, but the bell had gone as had the crowd. Getting out, Gina inhaled the fresh Monday morning air. A damp grassy scent floated in the breeze. A group of kids came out of the sports block building carrying hockey sticks.

Her phone beeped.

Gina, why were you at mine last night?

She swallowed. Maybe she could tell him that she had some thoughts on the case so popped over. She saw the woman come out with the dog and realised he had company so left. But, she'd broken his plant pot and then hidden behind her car. Her cheeks burned with shame.

'Guv?'

'Wyre. Sorry, I was in a world of my own. I didn't even hear you pull up.'

'You okay?'

'Yes, I was just thinking about the case. There were no sightings of Grant or Taylor last night. Still, neither of their phones are turned on and his silver Mercedes hasn't flagged up but the Volvo has been taken away, for now. He's keeping a low profile. We really need a break. Maybe the school has something to offer.'

'Let's hope so. Any news from Jacob?'

'No, I tried to call him a couple of times but he didn't answer. In fact, he cut me off. I'd say he doesn't want to talk. I settled on sending him a message saying that I'm here for him should he need anything.'

'That's all you can do. I called the hospital.'

Gina grabbed her bag. 'And.'

'They mentioned Jennifer's pregnancy. I don't know if they should have told me that. Maybe they thought I was a relative. Jacob never said anything.'

'That's why Jacob must have rushed off the way he did. Something must be wrong. Did they say anything about that?'

Wyre shook her head. 'They did say that she's remained stable for a few hours now and some of the swelling has gone down.'

Gina smiled. 'That's good news.'

'They also said it's too early to say any more and that her condition was still critical.'

'I wish there was more I could do for Jacob.'

'The only thing we can do is what we all do best. Catch the person who did this to her and find Annabel.'

'You're right, Paula. Let's go and see what we can find out from her colleagues. If Annabel was in a relationship with someone she worked with, we need to find out who.'

As they entered the building a woman looked up from the computer. 'Can I help you?'

'Yes, we're here to talk to someone about Annabel Braddock. DI Harte and DC Wyre. A colleague called earlier from Cleevesford Police Station.'

'Oh yes. Ms Law is expecting you.'

'Who's Ms Law?'

'Head of mathematics. Annabel's manager.'

'Thank you.'

The woman hurried from behind the desk and beckoned them through the staffroom and back out. After a five-minute walk around the huge building, the woman gestured through a glass pane in a door that led to a class full of teenagers. The teacher said a few words to the pupils and came out. 'I've given them some exercises to do. Should keep them busy for half an hour. Can you sit with them?'

The woman nodded.

'Thanks, Miriam. Follow me. We can talk in the maths office.'

The tall woman's black hair stood an inch high. With her chin held up, she looked almost regal.

'Take a seat.' Gina and Wyre sat.

'Thank you for seeing us at such short notice, Ms Law.'

'Kirsty, please.' She fell into her leather chair at the other side of the desk, clasping her hands together in front of her. 'I just want to say how upset we are to hear of Annabel's disappearance. She is a remarkable teacher and much loved by her students and the other staff. Do you have any news that you can share with us?'

Gina clenched her teeth before speaking. 'I'm afraid not. She is still missing. Her husband is now missing too.'

'Is it looking like he did it?'

'I can't discuss the investigation, I'm afraid. I know you're busy but I'd like to ask you a few questions. We're just trying to get to know Annabel a bit better.' Gina gave her an apologetic smile.

Wyre opened up her notebook.

'Go ahead. I think we're all in agreement that we just want her home and back at work.' The woman placed her palms on the desk and leaned back a little.

'What does she do here?'

'She teaches maths.'

'How long has she worked at Cleevesford High?'

'She started just before me so that would be just over six years.'

'Do you know Annabel well?'

'I can't say that we're really close, like best friend close, but we do talk and have lunch together. I know she's married and has a little girl. She loves her job. I've been out with her to the pub a few times. We've had a few good nights out with a few of the other members of staff that have involved a lot of drinking and greasy food. We normally talk about work, films or music, that sort of thing. Normal things.'

'Does she confide in you?'

The woman swallowed. 'A couple of weeks ago she said she wasn't happy in her marriage but didn't know what to do. She said her husband had got them into a lot of debt. She also said he was sleeping with someone else.'

'Did she say anymore?'

'No. I just told her that she could do better.'

Gina's mind whirred away. She had found all that cash and the drugs in the spare bedroom. Had being in debt and having an addiction led Grant to drug dealing? Maybe both of them had felt stuck in their marriage and he saw that as his only way out. Or maybe it wasn't all happening fast enough and the only way to get a move on was to remove Annabel from the equation. The blood on the tissues put him at the scene and his Mercedes was missing, as was he. Where had he taken her? Gina wondered if she was even still alive. 'Do you know anything about a party on a boat, just before Christmas?'

'Oh that? Stupid idea but I guess when you don't want to be

involved in arranging staff Christmas parties, you settle for what others arranged. Miriam, who's now keeping an eye on my class, she organised that. It was cold, cramped and, frankly, after a couple of drinks, I started feeling a bit queasy. I don't like boats as you can tell. It was also a windy night, which didn't help. I remember Annabel saying that she was a bit scared of boats. Apparently her husband took her down the river in a storm ages ago and she's hated them since.'

'Tell me about the boat?'

'It was a barge, a really wide, long one. Maybe a Dutch barge. The type that do river cruises on sunny days. This one specialised in parties. A lot of the teachers loitered on the deck and the mooring. It was moored in a yard. The yard has a café and people visit at all times of the year. Anyway, the owners had set up a stall outside with a pizza van, too. It was part covered and surrounded by fairy lights. Miriam convinced us all that it would be fun with the stall outside, that it would be no different to when we all pile into the German Christmas Market, wrap up and enjoy winter. I beg to differ. It was wet and cold and I'd have preferred the usual disco in a hotel. Considering the storms we'd had only a few weeks earlier, I'm surprised it went ahead. Anyway, we all lived to tell the tale.'

'How was Annabel that night?'

'Annabel was Annabel. By that, I mean she was making the best of it. She doesn't get to go out much, what with having a young child. She had a thick coat on over her dress and she embraced it. I remember her knocking back a lot of tequila slammers.' Kirsty furrowed her brow.

'Did something happen?'

'I'm not sure. She said she needed to clear her head so she headed past the café and I saw her holding a tree and swaying. I thought that maybe she just felt sick and wanted a moment. I went back onto the boat and sat talking to one of the other teachers. After about forty-five minutes, I thought I should go and check on her. I wandered off, heading over to where I saw her last and that's when I found her crying. Mascara had smeared under her eyes. She asked me to call her a taxi, which I did. I tried to ask her what was wrong but she kept dismissing me. Anyway, I made sure she got into a taxi.'

'Do you know why she was crying?'

'She was slurring at this point and I wasn't catching her words.'

'Did anyone else see her that evening?'

'Actually, Miriam did. She was standing at the outdoor bar while I was inside the boat. I did ask her if she knew why Annabel had been crying. She said that the geography teacher, Mr Whittle, had come to the bar to buy Annabel a drink, then they both walked off together a few minutes later.'

Gina watched as Wyre caught up with her notes. 'How close is Annabel to Mr Whittle?' There had been talk of someone Annabel was having an affair with and Gina wondered if they'd found that person.

'Wait, are you saying—' Kirsty stopped talking.

'We're just looking into all of Annabel's friends, that's all, because we'll need to speak to them regarding the case.'

Kirsty eyed them up with suspicion. She knew that Gina was being vague with her. 'Mr Whittle?'

After pausing and thinking for a couple of minutes, Kirsty continued. 'They spoke in the staffroom but as far as I know, they weren't close. I think Annabel would have said something to me if they were. She did seem a bit off with him after the party and it showed more when we came back after the Christmas break. In fact, she's been a little quiet for a while. I should have spoken to her more but we've been really busy. Whenever we did get a break together, she kept mentioning her husband and how things were getting bad at home with the arguments. I've already mentioned that though.'

'Is Mr Whittle in today?'

'No, he's been on sick leave for a couple of weeks.'

'Sick leave?'

'Yes, depression and anxiety. All too common in this job. We burn out sometimes.'

'We will need his address before we leave.'

'Of course, I'm sure Miriam will be able to help you with that. She covers reception on Mondays until we're fully staffed again.'

'Is there anything else that you can think of, anything that might help us? We haven't spoken in too much detail about Annabel but we are working on the theory that she was taken at the hit-and-run scene. As you can appreciate, we need to find out as much as we can about her routine in the hope that we can bring her home.'

Placing her hand over her mouth, Kirsty grimaced and took a couple of deep breaths. 'You've got me wondering why Annabel was crying that night. I'll be honest with you. There has been a report by another member of staff about Mr Whittle, but it was only to me and off the record. In fact, it was withdrawn which is why I wasn't going to mention it. Mr Whittle claimed that she kissed him after she claimed that he assaulted her. Both of them decided to drop it in the end but it is odd that he was seen with Annabel just before she was crying. And Annabel wasn't the same since that night. I never really thought about all that until now.'

'Who was that member of staff?'

'Actually, it was Miriam. She claimed that he had kissed her just outside the ladies' toilets, the ones the staff use. I tried to speak with her more about the allegation but she said she didn't want to mention it again.'

Gina fished around in her pocket, shifting the pack of tissues and chocolate bar wrapper aside, eventually reaching deep enough to grab a card. 'If you think of anything else or you hear anything, please call me anytime.'

'She had so much going on in her life. I could have been there more and maybe I could have helped her, maybe offered to put her up so that she could leave her house. I shouldn't have let her wander alone when she was that drunk at the party. I have no idea what that man said to her but it obviously made an impact.'

'None of this is because of anything you didn't say or do. You've been really helpful and we don't want to keep you from your class. Would we be able to speak to Miriam next?'

'Of course.' The woman stood and nodded. 'I'll go and relieve her now.'

'Thank you.' As Kirsty left, Gina turned to Wyre. 'Looks like we have another suspect. Something happened at that party and I want to know what.'

TWENTY-FOUR

Omar

I have to keep up with everything and the only way I can do that is to watch Annabel's house. The police drive by now and again like they're on the lookout for someone but they can't see me when I stay back. There was a moment of excitement a few minutes ago when I spotted a figure sneaking around the back of the house. A clump of pink hair had escaped from her hood. I wanted to run over and confront the childminder. It's like she was waiting for the police to go. That girl and Annabel's husband have been making a fool of Annabel. That much I've seen from afar. Anyway, the girl soon went and now here I am, bored again. I'll be back later to watch and if the childminder comes back, I will confront her. No more hiding in the bushes, Annabel deserves better and I have to start becoming the man I want to be.

I hit a fly that lands on my arm then I play with my phone. Everyone is asking about Annabel. It's all over Facebook and

Twitter. Everyone's asking but no one has any answers. I select TikTok and watch a video of a dancing dog followed by those roller-skating girls again. I wonder if Annabel watches TikToks. She has a dog so maybe she too would watch the dancing dog video.

Not much more has been said on the news so it's down to me to fish for information. Mum thinks I'm at school. As I left this morning, it was all, *Omar, don't forget your lunch. I've popped in a pack of Gummy Bears because you're my little Gummy Bear.* I tried to get out of her embrace. She's weirdly clingy, like she can't accept I've grown up and it gets embarrassing when she's like that in public. It's since Dad died. She holds on to me like it will be the last time, every time I leave the house. I don't want her to put mini packs of sweets in my lunchbox. In fact, I don't even want my lunchbox. It's embarrassing. All the others at school go to the canteen and I have three pounds so it's going to be pizza for me.

As I wait, I try to work out the best way to sneak back into school. Going through the gym hall is always best. In through the back, past the shower blocks and straight into the back of block A. I can then simply turn up for my next lesson, which is maths. I bet Ms Law will be teaching me instead of Annabel. I don't really like her lessons. I'm bound to get a detention if I get busted, but it will have been worth it.

Pulling out the cheese and pickle sandwich my mother made, I remove the foil and throw it to the birds. If I tell her I don't want them, she'll be upset. She'll never know that I ditched them and had pizza. It's best this way.

I watch as a man delivers post to Annabel's house. Boring. Where's the husband and where's her dad? Maybe I should revise for my chemistry test. Pulling my workbook from my rucksack, I begin to scan my notes on metals and non-metals. It's no good, nothing is sinking in while I'm here. Instead, I stare at the house. Perhaps her husband chose that green front door.

He must have done because it doesn't look nice at all. More swamp than meadow. Annabel wouldn't lack that much taste. I've never seen her wearing a green this shade and she wears a lot of colourful dresses. I love her style and the way she moves and smiles. Her teeth are the brightest of whites and her skin smooth. I run a finger over my acne scars and scrunch my nose.

I watch as another man walks along the path. He seems to be gazing around as if he doesn't want to be seen so I duck behind the trees, trying not to catch my blazer on the low hanging branches. I wonder if he saw me. As I listen, I hear his footsteps stop. It's no good me hiding away. I need to get a better look at him, see who he is. It's all part of me knowing everything about Annabel. The more I know her, the closer we can get.

Creeping forward slightly, I peer between two branches. It's okay. He's pretending to look at his phone but I can see that it's too low and angled wrong. He's looking at her house. I duck as he turns. My heart starts to bang like someone is trying to punch their way out of my chest. If he saw me, I am in such big trouble.

What is he doing here?

Just as a car pulls up, he continues down the path. Annabel's dad and her little girl get out of the car and run to the door. That was close.

I check my phone and notice that I have a message.

You're in such big trouble, dickwad. Teachers know you're missing. Boo hoo! Mummy's going to be so upset with her little boy getting into trouble.

I'm never going to be popular but I am grateful of the warning. I throw my chemistry notes back into my rucksack and jump over the fence onto the footpath where I get straight on my bike. In a few measly minutes I'll have to face Ms Law and I'm dreading it. As I reach the high street, I wait for the traffic to subside before pulling onto the road. That's when my eye meets his. Does he know I saw him watching Annabel's house? The way he stares back, I'm sure he knows everything. It's like he's looking inside me.

As I turn back to the road, I swerve, narrowly missing the back of someone's car and half crash into a hedge. That was close. I pull a couple of leaves from my hair. Maybe next time, I won't be so lucky. Swallowing, I feel my muscles tense.

He saw me and he's dangerous. He's the secret Annabel wants me to keep. I must continue my work to protect her.

TWENTY-FIVE

As Wyre called the station to give Jacob and O'Connor an update, Gina checked her phone. Another message had appeared from Briggs.

Okay, so you're not talking to me now. That's mature.

She threw her phone into her pocket. If he wanted to be like that, then so be it. He had found someone new. He was in a relationship and he could save himself the bother of telling her it was over now.

The school office smelled a bit musty and she craved fresh air.

Wyre ended her call. 'I wonder how long we'll have to wait.'

Gina exhaled and leaned back on the chair. For once, she didn't mind waiting. After that message, she didn't want to go back to the station in a hurry.

'Sorry about that.' Miriam walked in, took her cardigan off and placed it behind the chair. She tucked a long brown curl behind her ear and sat down. Her flowery top bulged a little as she sat. Gina guessed she was in her early thirties. 'I would have been quicker but I caught one of the kids texting and he got a bit cheeky. Detention for him.' She smiled. 'Kirsty said you wanted to talk to me. She said it was about Annabel. We're all getting really worried. How can I help?'

'We'd just like to ask you a few questions. It shouldn't take long. Do you mind if we call you Miriam?'

'Definitely not. All I hear all day is Miss Dean this, Miss Dean that. Miriam is a blessed change.'

'Thanks, Miriam. Could you tell me a little about your relationship with Annabel?'

'I know her to say good morning to. Sometimes we talk about the latest *EastEnders* cliffhanger, but that's it really. We've never had what I'd call personal conversations.'

'Do you remember seeing her at the Christmas party on the barge?'

'Oh, that infamous night. She was so drunk and by drunk, I mean she was falling over everywhere. I helped her up once. It was like she'd been let out of a box.'

'A box?'

'You know? Pressures of a young family. Having a night off to let her hair down.'

'Later that night, she was seen crying. Did you see her?'

She scrunched her brow. 'Yes. It's vague as I was a bit hammered myself. She went off walking, alone. I was at the bar laughing and joking with some of our colleagues then I saw her with Tom Whittle.' Miriam's smile dropped and she paused.

'What did they do?'

'He came to the bar and bought her a drink. I think it was a bottle of something. Beer maybe. He went over to her and gave her the drink. They looked like they were talking for a minute or so, then she walked away from him with the beer. That's when I turned back to the people I was talking with and I didn't see her until she appeared back by the tree about half an hour later. Her hair had fallen from the pleat it was in and she was drunkenly shouting at Tom.'

'Did you hear what she said?'

'I wish I did but with it being a bit windy, I was wearing a scarf too that I'd hitched up over my ears. It was so cold. Anyway, I went to go over but he gave me a look.'

'A look?'

'As if to say, stay away and, frankly, I didn't want to go anywhere near him anyway.'

'You've had some sort of trouble with Mr Whittle?'

'You know, don't you?'

'Ms Law told us about the allegation that you reported, then withdrew.'

'I never want to talk about that again. She shouldn't have said anything. It was confidential.' Her cheeks reddened.

'It would really help us if you did. I know you don't want to but Ms Law was only trying to help Annabel.'

She swallowed and leaned back. 'You're right. This isn't about me. Maybe it's time to speak up and not let that man get to me. I know what happened.' Swinging around on the chair, she stared out of the window and began to speak. 'It was in November, last year. I'd just come out of the staff-only ladies. It was quiet as it was during lesson time. As I entered the corridor, I stopped to tie my hair back up, that's when I felt his slimy tongue on my neck. He turned me around and pressed me against the wall, telling me that he knew I wanted him. Anyway, I slapped him and pushed him away. I noticed how hard I'd hit him. His face was red. He said that if I said anything, he'd say I tried to kiss him and then slapped him when he said he didn't want me to touch him.'

'You told Ms Law.'

Miriam nodded. 'Yes, I had to. It was eating me up and I

couldn't face the man. It was horrible so I told her what happened. She questioned him, of course, and forwarded the complaint to the head. Literally, within hours, I'd had enough of the stares. Some of the staff thought I was making it up and others believed me but there was no proof and Tom was claiming that I assaulted him. Can you believe the nerve of the man? The thing is, he comes across as lovely and caring. They can't see what he's really like. I told Ms Law that I wanted to drop it and it had all been a misunderstanding. It seemed so trivial when I'd thought about it and I kept questioning whether something I said or did gave him the wrong impression. He also said he wanted to drop it. Since then, he's stayed away from me. He did do it though. I'm not lying. It was in no way my fault. That man is a snake.'

'Thank you for being so open, Miriam. It must be hard reliving that moment and if you want to formally report it so that we can investigate, our door is always open.'

'I don't want to. I really want it to go away. I don't want to be school gossip. I'm telling you so that I can help Annabel.'

Gina nodded, not wanting to upset Miriam. 'Did you ever see him approaching Annabel at school?'

'No, but I did see him and Annabel outside talking together and they seemed to be smiling and laughing. This was just before the party but I couldn't give you an exact date. I remember thinking she was mad letting him anywhere near her. I could see his hand on her lower back and she tilted her head. For a moment, I thought they might kiss, but they didn't. I think there was something going on. After seeing that, I kept away from her, too. Everyone knew what I'd accused him of but no one else saw that side of him. If you meet him, you'll know what I mean. It's also no secret that Annabel was in an unhappy marriage. She was vulnerable to his charm and attention.'

'When was the last time you saw him?'

'About two and a half weeks ago. Thinking about it now,

something did happen. A few days earlier, I saw Annabel whispering something to him in the gym block corridor. She looked really fed up. I've seen them loitering there to talk before.'

'Did you hear anything?'

She shook her head. 'No, but once she'd said whatever it was that she had to say, he gripped her arm and she cried out a little in pain. She then shook him off and walked away.'

'Where were you when all this was happening?'

'Just about to turn onto that corridor. When I have a free period, sometimes I use the gym equipment. When I saw them I stopped and waited. I didn't want him to see me. I'd spent so long avoiding him, it was like second nature. I peered around the corner and they were too busy in their own world to notice me. I don't go around spying on people. I came across them, that's all.'

'Do you know her husband?'

'No. I've only ever seen photos of him on Facebook.'

'Is there anything else you can tell us?'

Wyre scribbled away, filling the silent moment with pen scraping on paper.

'Only that something's definitely not right with Tom. If you want to look into someone, look into him. The way he treated me, I'm sure there will be others in his past. He shouldn't be working in a school.' She glanced at her watch. 'There will be no one manning reception in exactly five minutes. I'm really sorry but I have to get back.'

Gina stretched her legs under the table. They would visit Tom Whittle next.

As Miriam led them out, Gina stopped. 'Miriam, if you do hear anything or you think of anything else later, please call me.' She passed her card to the woman. 'It can sometimes be the smallest of things that lead to the biggest of breaks. Like you, all we want is to find Annabel and bring her home safely.'

Miriam took the card with a smile. 'I will do.' As they went to turn the corner, Miriam almost bumped into a pupil. 'Omar, you should be in class. Your absence in maths class has been noted. Where have you been?'

'I, err...' The dark-haired boy began to fiddle with the strap on his rucksack. Gina wondered how much he had heard.

'You were what? Didn't you think that I or Ms Law would notice your absence?'

He looked up at Gina, his mouth opening and closing as he struggled to answer Miriam.

'Omar.'

'Sorry, miss. I fell off my bike.'

Miriam looked him up and down. 'You look okay. Do you need to get checked out at the sickbay?'

'No, miss. It didn't hurt. Can I just head to maths?'

'Yes, I'm sure Ms Law will want a word with you. It's not the first time you've been late. Such a promising student. Don't ruin things. Okay?'

'Okay, miss. I won't. Thank you.'

'Now go on before you fall behind.'

The boy hurried past her. Gina turned to see that the boy was also looking over his shoulder at her, then he ran. His gaze, although brief, had been so intense that it made Gina shiver slightly. 'Who's that?'

'Omar Abidar. He's a good kid really, just bunks off here and there. He's one of Annabel's prize students – gifted and talented. She keeps saying he's destined for big things. If only he could knuckle down more and be on time. I'd hate for him to waste his potential.'

There was something in the way he looked at her that was still unnerving Gina now. Maybe he was worried around the police or maybe he knew something. He looked so skinny and childlike.

As they reached reception, Miriam smiled at the man behind the desk before he left her there.

'Could you please write down Mr Whittle's address?'

'Certainly. It will be my pleasure.' She tapped a few keys and noted down the address. 'Here you go. I know he'll have had something to do with her disappearance. Don't be fooled by him. He's an accomplished liar who takes what he wants.'

TWENTY-SIX

Omar

That was the police. Maybe they've been asking about me. Someone must have seen me hanging around by Annabel's house. I run to the toilets and lean over the sink and I imagine the police saying, *Omar, how well did you know Mrs Braddock? People have seen you hanging around her house and looking through her windows. And now she's missing. What have you done to her?*

The police are obviously talking to all the people who know Annabel so all I have to do is keep a low profile. It's only a matter of time before they get to me. My mum will go ape.

The man who lives next door to Annabel saw me staring through the front window one morning. I think he's called Evan. He thought I was probably going to play some teen prank so he told me to clear off. I've been careful since, only returning at night-time or hiding behind the trees. All I wanted to do was get to know her better and now look where that got me. I am in such big trouble. I should have kept away and not become so obsessed but it's harder said than done. It's true that love makes a person do crazy things. I've gone too far this time.

Splashing my face with a bit of cold water, I stare into my brown eyes. *Omar, just get back to class and let it go. You're making yourself look suspicious.* I know that police detective isn't worried about me. I'm one student out of many. She sees people every day, there's no way she'll think I know anything.

Tonight, I'll continue with my plan. I haven't been good lately. These past few weeks, I've been doing things that are totally out of character. I've started driving my mum's car. It's easy to take. She never goes out of an evening, which gives me a chance to take it. If only she knew what I've been doing. She'd never trust me again, and I've bumped her car. It's only a matter of time before she sees the damage to her bumper. I've been lucky that she leaves the house in a daze.

Everything I do is for Annabel. Love is deep. It's a powerful, all-encompassing emotion. Just thinking about it makes me feel as though my throat might close up.

The toilet door bursts open. 'Yo, dickwad.' Adam slaps me across the head and as usual I take it. If I hit him back, he'd floor me.

I sidle past him and he pushes me into a urinal. I get up and scurry out, running all the way to the maths department. Just as I dart around the last bend, I crash head first into Ms Law. 'Omar, my office. Now.'

'Yes, miss.' I know I'm in trouble for bunking but I don't know if she'll quiz me on other things. She's already had words with me about boundaries when it comes to Annabel and I can't make her think about that. If she mentions me to the police, they will definitely haul me in for questioning. I'll get accused, then blamed. I'll go to prison. My palms feel sticky as I take the long walk to her office. *Keep your mouth shut, Omar.*

TWENTY-SEVEN

Gina walked alongside Wyre in search of Tom Whittle's house. 'The car parking spaces are numbered.' Gina checked Whittle's address again. 'We're looking for number seventy.' She glanced up and down until she saw that his parking space was empty. 'I don't think he'll be in.'

'Let's find out.' Wyre stepped into the road in her heavy black shoes.

The seventies council estate was filled with a mixture of properties. Maisonettes, apartment blocks and terraced houses, all finished with a pebbledash render. 'The numbering is terrible on these houses.'

'Over here, guv. Number seventy's down here somewhere.'

Gina hurried and at last they spotted Whittle's house on the end of a row. Three storeys with water stains down the front. The wooden window frames looked rotten compared to the UPVC frames on the other houses. She knocked and the hallway echoed as if hollow. Bending over, she peered through the letter box. 'Whoa, the smell.' She recoiled and stood. 'I don't think he's in.'

'He's in alright.' A woman came out of the next house,

pushing a toddler on a red plastic tricycle. 'He just slammed his back door so loud, it woke my little boy up. You just need to knock harder.' The woman paused. 'He's a bit weird, having all those cats. I had to complain about them the other day, they keep coming in to my garden and crapping everywhere.'

'Thank you.' Gina smiled at the child and knocked again. The woman carried on down the path, pulling her hood up. A few specs of rain landed on Gina's nose.

'What?' A voice came from within.

'Mr Whittle? Police.'

He slid the chain and opened the door. As his vision met with daylight, he closed one eye. So far, Gina wasn't getting the superficial charm that people had described but then again, Kirsty Law had said that he was off with anxiety and depression. Without knowing his side of the story when it came to Miriam and Annabel, she tried to hold back any judgement. 'What?'

'May we come in?'

'Err, no.'

'You probably won't want to talk on the doorstep. We're investigating the disappearance of Annabel Braddock.'

'What's that got to do with me? She was a bit funny in the head. Probably just had enough of her husband.' He half huffed out a sneer. She had just told him that Annabel was missing and he'd probably seen the news too about the hit-and-run, yet he could stand there and sneer.

'Well, we've been speaking to your colleagues and unless you want to put your side to the story with your neighbours hearing, I suggest you let us in. I'm DI Harte, this is DC Wyre.' Gina held her identification up. 'Or maybe you'd like to come down to the station.'

A cat meowed and ran down the stairs. 'You best come in.' He let the door open and picked his cat up, before heading through the hallway into his living room.

Gina stepped in first. The pungent smell was cat urine. She spotted three dirty litter trays lined up against the wall. Grit peppered the tiles. As they stepped into the living room, it felt like they were entering another world. A newish-looking pillow backed settee faced a huge television and the wooden floor was fresh and clean.

Three cats hurried towards him. He sat on the chair and they jumped up on the arm. 'You going to sit or what?'

Gina sat first and Wyre followed. Wyre removed her notebook from her bag.

'Must be serious if you're going to write all this down. Do I need a solicitor?'

'We'd just like to ask a few questions. We've been to the school and spoken to your colleagues too. Do you feel you need a solicitor? If you do, we can take this down the station. I'm more than happy to do that.'

'Am I under arrest?' He stroked the huge ginger cat.

'No, as I said we'd like to conduct a voluntary interview. We need to ask you a few questions that relate to Annabel's disappearance.' Gina took a moment to take in his features. She tried to imagine how he'd look on a working day. He was taller than her, blue eyes and a full head of hair and smooth, lightly bronzed skin that was blemish free. His classically handsome looks, square jaw and stubble were attractive. Gina looked away. Although handsome, he was a mess. His old, stained lounge pants and sweater covered in cat hair told her that he was struggling with something.

'Go ahead, then. I don't want to go to the police station so fire away, ask me what you want. I don't need a solicitor as I haven't done anything. All I'm guilty of is not being able to cope at work. People don't realise how much pressure teachers are under.'

'I'm sorry to hear that.' Gina smiled. He was cooperating and she wanted it to stay that way.

'Yeah. Shit happens. Depression is a bitch.'

Gina spotted a box of Fluoxetine on the side. That confirmed that he was being treated for his condition. 'Could you please confirm your full name, age and job title?'

'Thomas George Whittle, forty, geography teacher. I prefer Tom.'

Wyre headed up her notebook with that information. A cat jumped up beside her. 'Hello.' She stroked its chin.

'That's Beryl, she's very friendly. I inherited her from yet another family that got a kitten and decided that they didn't want a cat. You can just call me Cleevesford Cat Rescue. This is where the unwanted cats get brought. People know I'm a soft touch.'

Gina was trying to picture this scruffy but handsome man surrounded by cats sexually assaulting Miriam. 'Where's your car, Mr Whittle?'

'Parked up, in my space.'

'We've just passed your space. It wasn't there.'

'What?'

'Your car isn't parked in its space.'

'I haven't used it for a week but it was there then. Wait.' He ran through the hall and came back five minutes later. 'I may have left the keys in it. I know I haven't been broken in to and I don't keep my car keys on the same ring as the house.'

'What makes you think you'd leave your keys in your car?'

'Because I've accidentally done it a few times. I realise I walk around in a fog. It's not healthy I know, which is why I went to the doctor a couple of weeks ago. That's when I called in sick at work.' He rubbed his hair and scrunched his brows. 'I'd like to report my car stolen. It's a good job you came.'

'We'll get onto that in a minute.' She took a moment to watch Tom. He began to tap the side of his head with his index finger, a confused look coming across his face. She also knew that most people who've committed a car-related crime try to dump their vehicles and say that they've been stolen. She wasn't convinced of his story.

'They're trying to frame me. You think I ran that woman over and took Annabel. Don't deny it, I can tell. I didn't do it. I've never hurt anyone in my life. I certainly wouldn't hit someone with my car and leave them. I'm not a monster. I mean look at me, I care for unwanted cats and teach children. I just wouldn't do that.'

Gina cleared her throat. She needed to get the interview back on track. 'Ms Law told me of a report that came to her attention, one that has been resolved but we'd like to talk to you about it.'

He shook his head and rolled his eyes. 'Miriam.'

'Yes.'

'She's got it in for me. The woman kept asking me out all the time and I kept saying no. She'd been harassing me. I told her I'd drop my allegation if she stopped lying and left me alone. I thought we'd got over this. We've been avoiding each other really well since.'

'Can you tell me in your own words what happened?' She hoped by starting with Miriam, she'd ease him in to talk about Annabel.

'I was on a free period so decided to set up in the staffroom. I like it there. It's by the coffee and food. I had a lot of marking to do so carried on. Miriam came in and sat opposite me. She leaned over the table and placed her hand over mine, and then she said that I should meet her in the toilets in five minutes. Just to clarify, she was asking if I wanted sex with her. This wasn't the first time. I found her overpowering so I told her to leave me alone or I'd report her. She then went on, saying that she knew I wanted her and I liked playing games. It got ridiculous. I know I was sharp but I said that I would never get involved with a crazy bitch like her. She got really mad and slapped me. I don't know where those words came from and if I could take them back, I

would. I was fed up with being harassed and it came to a head.'
He paused and stared at the cat winding around his leg.

'Go on.'

'Sorry. The very thought of her repulses me. I didn't want
sex with her, I never have done and I never will do. All I wanted
was for her to leave me alone. Next thing I get is Ms Law
demanding that I come to her office. That's when I found out
that she'd accused me of sexual assault. She'd been sexually
harassing me for months. No wonder I have to take these.' He
picked up the tablets.

Gina smiled sympathetically. She wasn't convinced by his
story but her personal thoughts on that weren't relevant. The
truth finds a way out. 'Thank you for sharing that with us. Can I
ask what your relationship with Annabel is?'

He sat again.

'There isn't one.' He paused. 'Oh, let me guess. Miriam has
been telling you stories. She's out to get me, I know she is.'

'Did you and Annabel ever meet by the gym block?'

'No, never. Why would I meet her there? I teach geography
and she teaches maths. I never go down to the gym block. Wait.'
He shook his head and smiled. 'I know someone who always
goes to the gym block. Miriam. She uses some of the equipment
in her breaks. I've heard her telling the other staff and she's
always walking around with a kitbag. If this carries on, I will be
reporting her for harassment. I can't take much more of this.' He
walked over to his tablets, popped one into his hand and swallowed it down without any water.

'Can you tell me about the night of the party, on the boat?'

'Really. It was just a staff party in the run up to Christmas.
Bloody stupid idea. It was cold and miserable and no amount
of fairy lights and beer could improve the evening. Everyone
thought it was a bad idea but they'd left Miriam to organise it.'
He shook his head. 'So, what can I tell you? Despite the cold,
there was a good turnout. I had a few drinks and I went home

about eleven after asking the taxi to stop at a chip shop. The driver waited and then dropped me home. I think I might still have the receipt as I haven't worn that thick coat since. Did something happen? Do I need to prove where I was that night?'

Gina leaned forwards a little. 'You were seen leaving the party and going for a walk with Annabel during the course of the evening. You bought her a drink?'

'I didn't. I wasn't that drunk that I'd forget buying her a drink. I didn't buy anyone a drink that night. Just saw to myself.' He sat on the arm of the chair and began patting a tortoiseshell cat that appeared from the kitchen. He pulled a small treat from his pocket and gave it to the animal.

'But you did go for a walk with Annabel?'

He looked at Gina, then at Wyre before his gaze settled at his feet. 'Yes, I did go for a walk with her.'

'What happened?'

'Nothing. We just talked.'

'About what?'

'Mostly school and some of the kids. That's what we do.'

'Annabel was seen looking upset after your walk.'

'I promised I wouldn't say anything.'

'Mr Whittle. Annabel is missing and another person is in a critical condition. It's important that you're not withholding information.'

He threw his head back and he swallowed. 'Okay, whatever. She was upset.'

'About what?' It felt like a long interview. Gina wished he would just talk without being constantly prompted.

'Her husband. She was upset with him and she didn't want to go home.'

'Go on.'

'Why don't you ask him the rest?'

'Because he too is missing.'

'Well there's your answer. He has her. He ran the other woman over and took his wife. Why are you bothering me?'

'Mr Whittle, we are investigating every avenue—'

'And because of what that woman said about me, you think I have something to do with it. Miriam is a liar and a drama queen. She thrives on attention. I don't know Annabel's husband. All I did was act as a sounding board when she was drunk.' He sighed and picked up the tortoiseshell cat, kissing it on the head. 'She said her husband was acting erratically and she'd caught him snorting something. When she confronted him, he got really angry and smashed a few things up in the house. I was concerned for her and because she was crying, I put my arm around her; that was all. I asked her if she was in any danger and she said that everything would be okay. We got on okay and I felt sorry for her; that's all. We got back from our walk and I could see Miriam staring at me. She is so jealous of Annabel... wait. Have you checked her out? After what she tried to do to me, who knows what she's capable of?'

Wyre caught up on her notes.

'Can we stick to that night please? We have a witness who claims that you and Annabel appeared to be arguing.'

'We weren't arguing. She was upset because of her husband and, yes, she was drunk and talking loud. I can see how it might look like that from afar. Seriously, you need to find her husband, oh, and my car. Shall I get the details so that you can look out for it?'

'We'll send a uniformed officer to take a statement. What is the make and model?'

'A Ford Fiesta.'

As Wyre wrote the information down Gina started to get to her feet.

'I don't know how important this is but I feel I should mention it?'

Gina sat back down and raised her eyebrows.

'There's a kid in Annabel's class who's absolutely obsessed with her. I've heard her joking about him always staying after class to ask her questions. Not in a mean way. She says he's a sweet kid and she wants to help him as he's so clever, but she was finding being around him a bit uncomfortable. I don't teach him but I know his name is Omar. There, you have three new leads. Jealous Miriam. Teacher's pet, Omar, and her druggie husband who likes to smash the house up. You're welcome.'

Gina glanced around his living room. His car being missing was a red flag. As soon as they left, they would need to put out an ANPR and get it found. Her gaze focused on the dark blue back door frame. She inhaled and could smell the slightest scent of paint in the air. 'When did you paint your door frame?'

'I don't think I want to answer that. Please leave.'

Her mind focused on the rag that was found at the scene of the hit-and-run. She pulled her phone out and logged on to the system. A few seconds later, she had found the evidence photo and that blue looked to be a match for the blue paint on the rag found at the scene. 'When?'

'About a week ago. Okay. Now leave.'

Gina thought about the blood at the scene and the tissues found in the waste bin at the cabin. Grant Braddock was there. He had to have been. But there was something about Whittle, something she couldn't put her finger on, that was until she saw the freshly painted door. Whittle had painted Grant in a bad light. That made the thought of them working together a possibility. Maybe they'd since fallen out. That was something Gina had to consider. She glanced at the paint again and back at her phone. There wasn't enough to arrest him on, not yet, and not with Grant being the main suspect.

They all stared up at the ceiling as they heard a thud. 'May we take a look around your house?' If he was keeping Annabel upstairs, Gina was going to find out.

He stood and folded his arms. 'You think I've taken her and

I have her here, don't you? Let me guess, I don't have to let you look at anything because, that's right, you don't have a search warrant. You know what, I'm a good citizen so yes. Be my guest. Go on.'

Gina nodded to Wyre and they stood. Tom swallowed like he was hoping that they'd backtrack and leave. A look around his house might just give them more than a painted door frame.

TWENTY-EIGHT

With Tom Whittle leading the way through to the kitchen, Gina glanced at the worktops. Several crusted over plates stank of cat food and a bowl of water with hairs floating on the skin, made her grimace. The kitchen was dirty but that was hardly a crime. His house was literally a haven for the cats.

'Can we get a move on, I'm tired.' He held his arms out, indicating that they should all move a bit quicker.

Gina nodded and followed him past the litter tray to the bottom of the stairs. With each creaky step, the smell of sweat and cat became unbearable. As she reached the top, Gina could see that there were three doors.

He pushed one open. 'Bathroom.'

She peered around. It was sparse except for a few bottles of squirty soap and body spray. The tiles had once been white but now they were mostly a stained buff colour, lacking shine.

Whittle opened the next door and a cat darted out and ran down the stairs. 'Spare room full of junk. Most of it is my dead mother's stuff. I still haven't sorted it.'

She glanced at the open boxes full of books and old orna-ments. Behind them an old Christmas tree with only several branches. An open shelving unit tilted to the left because of the missing leg and several folders had begun to expel old worksheets. Gina spotted something about volcanoes on one of them.

'My study.' A black cat darted from under the desk, straight past Gina and Wyre, then down the stairs. 'That's Danni, she hates people.'

Gina glanced into the last room on that floor. This room was cleaner and clutter free. So far there were no signs of Annabel or anything that suggested she'd once been upstairs. Her mind kept coming back to the paint. It might not even be a match in colour. A desk covered in paper and several geography text-books was the only piece of furniture in the box room. Books were also piled against the back wall, reaching Gina's height. On top of the desk sat an anglepoise lamp and a photo of a woman bent over a toddler. 'Who's that in the photo?'

'My sister with my niece when she was a baby.' He led them up the narrower steps to the top floor and flung open the door. 'This is my room. As you will see, Annabel isn't here, so that's it.'

He went to close the door again but Gina edged past and entered. A long-haired cat was scratching at the skirting board, snarling. Two bulky dark wooden wardrobes covered the one wall and the bed had been positioned under the dormer window. The old flowery wallpaper on the back wall stood out against the large vanity unit in front of it. An uncovered stained quilt had fallen off the bare mattress and the smell of urine hit her again. 'Do you have a litter tray up here?'

'No, the cats stay on the ground and first floor. I think I've proven that I'm not hiding anyone in my house. It's time you left. I'm a sick man and this is really getting me down now.'

'We're sorry to have bothered you.' Gina knew he was staring at her, willing her to turn around and leave the room.

'Right, I'll see you out then.'

The cat scratched again and a scraping sound came from behind the wall. 'I just heard something,' Wyre said.

'And me.' Gina walked over to the large vanity unit that stood against the back wall, and put her ear to the plaster. She flinched as she heard a tapping sound. It was a matter of preserving life. If Annabel was hidden in these walls, she had to find out. She allowed her finger to trail the outline of the wall-papered edge of a hidden door, which had almost blended into the wall from afar. 'Open this door now.'

'But, it's nothing. It's just loft space where I keep junk.' Whittle's forehead shone as he began to perspire. He could see that he wasn't going to get past Wyre. Gina's stomach dropped as Whittle pushed her colleague. All she saw was Wyre's hair coming loose from her clip before she disappeared down the stairs, backwards. Whittle was making a run for it. Gina heard a sickening thud and a yelp from Wyre moments before the front door slammed.

TWENTY-NINE

Jacob turned the key in the door, the same key that had filled Jennifer's eyes with so much happiness as they crossed the threshold into their new house. Neither had ever owned their own home and they'd chosen this new build semi together. He imagined walking in and seeing her there, kneeling on the floor maybe cuddling their baby, then he shook his head. She didn't want him to know about her pregnancy or she would have told him. He felt a stab of sadness as he thought about all that might have been and all he could think of was that he might never get to talk to Jennifer again. He might never get to ask about the baby, then he swallowed. What if she stayed in a coma? What if the baby survived and Jennifer died? He'd heard of that happening to other people. He leaned against the door, a dizzy spell almost taking him to the floor. The talk with the doctor came back to him. The baby was barely holding on. He'd been prepared for the worst news. He had to face it; he'd lose them both.

So many thoughts filled his head. Anger that she kept something so big from him. Sadness that he might never hold her again. Love – despite everything he loved her more than anything. Hope – the fact that her really awful condition hadn't got worse over the past few hours. He was reminded that all they could do was wait and see. Fear – all he could see was her pale face lying on a bed with a feeding tube down her nose. The thicker tube in her mouth filling her lungs with air, taped around the edge. Her moving chest and her lack of reaction when he held her or spoke. It was as if she was already gone.

With trembling fingers, he opened the door and entered the house. It was no longer a home. As he stepped into the tiled hall and cleared his throat, all he could hear were echoes. It was as if the soul of the house had left and all he saw was an empty shell. One he would have to stay in, alone. He hurried up to the bedroom. Lying on Jennifer's side of the unmade bed, he could still smell the sweetness of her body spray. The cream-coloured pillow had a slight red tinge where she'd lain on it after not washing her home hair dye out properly. He stood and walked over to her dressing table and picked up her perfume and sprayed it in the air. Closing his eyes, he momentarily hoped that the emptiness inside would go away but his mind couldn't be deceived that easily.

He closed the door on the bedroom and went back down to the kitchen, switching on the kettle. In the sink were three cups, two stained with lipstick around the rim. Annabel had come over earlier on the Saturday, bringing Cally with her. Jennifer couldn't wait to show them the house before planning their night out together. An open bag of sweets had been left on the worktop. He imagined Annabel and Jennifer excitedly talking about going out. Then maybe they all sat at the table or in the living room eating sweets and laughing. Then, he spotted a stuffed dog and he knew that Jennifer had bought it for Cally. She must have left it behind. He picked up the toy and clutched it to his chest. For the first time he knew that more than anything he wanted to be a dad. He was ready and it had taken such bad circumstances to make him realise. He wanted to experience playing football with his child, teaching them to ride a bike and swim; watch all his favourite childhood films. He wanted to feel that unconditional and overwhelming sense of love and he wanted to share that with Jennifer, then he came back to reality; one that was darker than he'd ever known.

He grabbed one of Jennifer's berry tea bags, the ones he said tasted like stagnant pond and popped it in his 'world's greatest lover' mug. Jennifer had given it to him for his last birthday and they'd both laughed as he'd pulled off the wrapping paper. He'd then carried her up to bed, both of them a little drunk and laughing as he dropped her onto the mattress.

He poured the drink and he sipped it. With a grimace, he removed the tea bag, not wanting it to stew any longer. It already tasted bad enough, not like his usual strong coffee or builder's tea. He went to throw it in the bin, then stopped. The tea bag dripped red onto the kitchen floor as he stared at the note in the bin. Those words sent a churning signal straight to his stomach. Snatching it up, he ran out of his house and headed straight back to the station. Everyone had to see this for themselves.

THIRTY

'Paula.' Gina ran out of Tom Whittle's bedroom and spotted Wyre in a heap at the bottom of the stairs. She almost slipped on the steps in her haste. 'Where are you hurt?'

Leaning to the side, Wyre allowed the blood to leak out of her nose. 'I'm okay. He kicked me in the face and I fell down the stairs. I wasn't expecting that, guv.' The woman slowly sat up and began to fiddle with the bridge of her nose.

For a second, all Gina could see was her ex-husband, Terry, lying in a heap at the bottom of their stairs, in the position where she left him to die all those years ago. She shook her head and took a deep breath. The only person who truly knew everything that she'd been through was Briggs and she'd lost him to some woman and child who seemed to have already moved in.

'Guv, can you help me? I'm wedged in?'

Snapping out of her thoughts, Gina nodded. 'I'm calling it in. We'll get you seen to. Don't move. You might have broken something.'

Wyre bled on her sleeve and pulled her phone out. 'I got this, guv. I haven't broken anything. I can still move. I'm just going to have some bad bruises and a sore nose. Don't let him get away. He went out the front. Without his car, he won't be able to get far. I'm okay, honestly.'

Gina stalled for a moment, not wanting to leave her bleeding colleague but as Wyre began to speak, she knew that help would be on its way. She hurried down the stairs and out the front door. Which way? She glanced back and forth, not having a clue where he went then she saw a flustered elderly man walking up the path. 'Are you okay?'

'Yes, love. People have no manners.' He shook his head.

'What happened?'

'The man who lives there was in so much of a rush, he crashed into me, knocking me off my feet and he didn't even stop to see how I was. I struggled to get up.'

Gina held up her identification. 'Can you tell me which direction he went in?'

'You're too late. He got into his car, back there and drove away.' The man pointed. 'He's always parking in other people's spaces. Drives them mad with anger. Loads of neighbours have complained. He's even used my space and I can't park too far away, can't do the walking I used to do.' The man paused. 'Has he done something?'

Gina knew she'd lost Whittle. He'd lied about his car being stolen and she now had no doubts that he'd lied about a lot of things. More than anything, she wanted to know what he was running from. 'We're investigating an incident. An ambulance should be here in a minute. Please get checked out when it arrives.'

He waved his hand. 'I'm okay. Just bruised.'

'What car was he driving?'

'A Fiesta.' The man used his stick to hobble away.

Gina ran back to the house and back up the stairs.

'They're on their way, guv. Did you catch up with him?'

'No, he's driven off in his car, it hasn't been stolen. He lied to us. Apparently he's known for using other people's parking spaces which is why we didn't spot it.' She held a hand out to Wyre. 'Are you able to get up?'

Wyre flinched as she allowed Gina to assist her. 'Everything hurts but, yes, I'm standing.' The bleeding from her nose had stemmed. She wiped the drying blood trail with the arm of her jacket sleeve. Slowly they took each step until they reached the bedroom.

Gina picked up the meowing cat and placed it on the landing before shutting it out. She began to pull at the vanity unit against the wall. The banging and scratching became more frequent. She and Wyre lifted it away, leaving a gap big enough to open the door. She thought the wobbly handle might come off in her hands but the hatch creaked open to reveal the storage room. 'I'm going in.' She turned on the torch on her phone and pointed it into the small attic. Boxes upon boxes filled it. She pointed the light to the walls and to a corkboard that had been stood on top of a box. Several photos of Miriam had been pinned to it. He'd written the word 'bitch' across her face. Then she spotted Annabel's face. There were other women, too. Gina didn't recognise them. Some of the photos looked old and worn. Another scratch came from behind the stack of boxes. 'Police, is that you Annabel?'

The noise stopped. Bending over, Gina headed deeper through the maze of boxes.

'Be careful, guv. The boards look rotten. Try to stay on the joists.'

Just as she crept around the boxes, she caught sight of a bushy tail and the squirrel darted out of a hole in the roof. Startled, Gina stepped back and before she could realise the mistake she'd made, she fell through the ceiling. With a thud, she landed on the desk. Breathless and winded, she grabbed her ringing phone and answered but she couldn't speak. Jacob's voice rang through her head.

'I've just arrived back at the station. You have to get back now. It's Taylor and Grant. They've done this to Jennifer and they've taken Annabel. I found a letter in our bin. Annabel must have brought it with her when she visited earlier on that Saturday. It's them, guv. We have to get them.'

She took a few deep breaths and ignored her aches as she managed to shift to a sitting position. Clawing at her face, she wanted the fibreglass specks to stop irritating her skin. Her back stiffened as she replied. 'We've just had an incident. We're at one of Annabel's colleague's house and we've found his little shrine to Annabel and several other women. This is only the beginning and the three people we need in custody have run. Wyre's called it in so all units are alerted.'

'What the hell is going on, guv?'

'We're just scratching the surface but thank goodness for squirrels.' She smiled through her croaky words.

'What?'

Gina shook her head. 'I have to go, uniform have just arrived along with an ambulance. We'll get Wyre checked out and head back.' She blew out, spitting the debris from her mouth as she brushed her face. With every move her body creaked and ached.

THIRTY-ONE

Gina rubbed the bottom of her back, where her tailbone had caught Whittle's desk. She flinched as she straightened out. 'Gather round. It appears we have a bit of a breakthrough, well, we have two and I can't as yet connect them. We have evidence that Tom Whittle, colleague of Annabel, had been obsessing over her and a teaching assistant called Miriam Dean. Wyre and I spoke to Miriam earlier today and she claimed that he'd sexually assaulted her, but dropped her complaint as he claimed it was her who assaulted and harassed him. We found this in Whittle's attic space.' She pointed to the photos of his corkboard and other items that had been found underneath. 'In this photo we can see that Miriam is wearing this peach coloured chiffon scarf. We found this scarf at the scene, kept with the board in his loft. We also found a pen with Annabel's name on it. It looks like he takes whatever of their possessions he can get hold of. There are photos of other women as you can see. We've yet to identify them.'

O'Connor opened up a lunchbox and a waft of lemon cut through the mustiness of the room. 'Help yourselves.'

Wyre reached in and took one, her other hand dabbing her

nose. Jacob stared into his hands, ignoring the update that Gina was delivering.

'There's more.'

Wyre nodded as she bit into the cake.

'We also found a box of random possessions that show his obsession with other women in the past. There are more scarves, a pair of knickers, tights and a lady's glove. This shows a pattern of behaviour. He was taking a more than healthy interest in these women and most recently, Miriam and Annabel. It looks like he gave up with Miriam after she reported him.' Gina pointed to the photo that had 'bitch' scrawled across it. 'He then started taking an interest in Annabel. He was seen with her at the Christmas bash on the boat. Miriam described seeing Whittle arguing with Annabel after they'd been walking together. Annabel was described as drunk. We don't know what was said or what happened. What do we know about Whittle?' Gina glanced at O'Connor who rubbed his hands of crumbs as he finished the cake in his mouth.

'I've checked him out, guv. No record at all. He's spent the last fifteen years working as a geography teacher. I did however find out that he worked at another school before Cleevesford High, one in Birmingham. I took the liberty of calling them.'

'And?'

'They say that he was a great teacher. I quizzed them about his relationships and the head did say that he was seeing the English teacher and things went sour. She said that things got uncomfortable and she left for another job. There were no complaints of harassment. He thought it was just a relationship that had turned sour.'

'Did you get a name?'

'The head of the school in Moseley is Mr Dunn and the English teacher was called Miss Teller. She now works in Redditch, so not too far. Apparently she keeps in touch with the secretary there so the head knows that she's still working in Redditch.'

'Great work. All units are on the lookout for him and his car. Forensics are attending his house as we speak to go through the items found in the loft and once they've finished, the house can be thoroughly searched. We need to find out if Annabel has been there. Whittle also recently painted his door frame blue and it looks to be like the blue paint found on the material at the scene of the hit-and-run. That will be taken to the lab and we'll soon know if there's a match. His computer will be brought in and hopefully that might reveal something helpful to the case. As far as I'm concerned, he's now a suspect. To get to know Whittle better, I think we should speak to Miss Teller. Right, onto the latest piece of evidence. The note found in your bin, Jacob.'

Clearing his throat, he looked up with glassy eyes, then he rubbed his dark stubble. 'Yes, I brought it in as soon as I saw it. I know this Whittle guy looks to be the one but there is a chance that he's simply run because he knows we've found out that he harasses women. This note directly implicates Taylor and Grant. They have motive for wanting Annabel out of the way. Grant didn't want her to keep the house and their daughter if Annabel left him.'

'And let's not forget that we found bloodied tissues in the cabin linking Grant to the scene.' Gina glanced at the photo of the tissues on the board. 'Go on.'

'That... there. It's disturbing, isn't it?' Jacob pointed to the photo of Annabel that was in the back of Taylor's car. 'I mean, she hated Annabel that much she's scrubbed her face out of the photo. With this letter...'

'Are you happy to read the letter out?' Gina tilted her head.

Jacob exhaled, staring at the bagged piece of scrunched up paper. 'No, I can't do it, guv.'

Gina gently took it from him and held it up. 'It's okay. The letter from Taylor to Grant. "*Grant. We have to deal with Annabel once and for all if we're to have a future. You need to do this for Cally and us. I can look after Cally, you know I can. Annabel doesn't deserve you, you said it yourself, and she's shagging someone so she doesn't care about you. We belong together. You said you loved me, now you have to prove it. I didn't use my phone like you asked. I know she reads your messages. I love it that you send me notes. It's so old-school and romantic. None of my other boyfriends have ever sent me love notes. Taytay. XXX*".'

An uncomfortable silence filled the incident room. Wyre broke it. 'Just what did Grant do to prove his love to Taylor?'

Gina piped up. 'That's what we need to find out. Are we still regularly going back to the Braddocks's house?'

O'Connor nodded. 'We've been back a few times but there has been no activity. The neighbour has spoken to us a couple of times. He said that no one has been back to the house except Annabel's father. There have been no sightings of Grant. We haven't located his silver Mercedes. As for Taylor, no one has seen her either since she ran from the station.'

Gina bit her bottom lip. 'We need Taylor. I want to question her about this note. She knows more than she led us to believe.' Gina checked her watch. 'I'm going to call the academy in Redditch to see if Miss Teller's in work today.'

'Already done it, guv.' O'Connor leaned back in the chair, arms folded. 'She's not in today as her mum was taken sick but she told her department head that she'd be back tomorrow. They're expecting one of us to be there, first thing.'

'Great stuff. Tomorrow morning, Wyre and I will go and speak to her.' Gina spotted Wyre rubbing her neck. 'Are you up to it?'

'Yes, I just ache a bit. The paramedic said I was okay, no major damage. Tomorrow morning sounds like a plan. I'll meet you there.' Wyre's usually pristine hair was tangled and fell over her shoulders. Gina pulled out a padded hairband and smiled as she passed it to Wyre. 'Thanks.' The woman scooped up her hair. It felt good to help, if only a little. Wyre was always the one with the hairbands and sympathy when Gina needed her.

'Given that Taylor is now a suspect too, I want her home thoroughly searched. Her aunt let us have a little look around but I want to know what she's hiding beneath the surface. We need to organise a warrant now that we have that letter. Jacob, can you do that?'

'Yes, guv.'

'Are you up to this? You know you can go and be with Jennifer or rest up at home.'

He shook his head. 'No. I'm no use to Jennifer and I'm no use at home. I want to be here. I'll sort the search warrant out.'

'Great. If you need anything, just say. We're all here to help and we want to support you in any way we can.'

Jacob forced a worried-looking smile and nodded.

'O'Connor, can you go with uniform and conduct the search of Taylor's house and car once that has gone through. A member of the forensics team will need to attend. I want to know if Annabel has ever been taken there or has been in her car.'

'Yep. Sounds good.'

'Right, we all know what we're doing. Any questions?' A hum of conversation began to fill the room. PC Kapoor entered. 'Jhanvi, can you work with O'Connor? He's going to need help with searching Taylor's residence when the warrant comes through.'

'Course, guv.' She headed over to O'Connor. Gina could see that PC Kapoor was delighted to help.

As everyone busied themselves with planning their next moves, Gina spotted Briggs entering at the back of the room. His stare met hers. Heart banging, Gina quickly left the room. She'd actually gone to his house and spied on him. Whatever excuse she gave, they both knew that's what she'd done and there was no way she could face him yet. Red heat crept up her neck. Had he told his new girlfriend about the mad ex that had been loitering? She hurried into the ladies, the one place where Briggs wouldn't follow her, and stood in front of the mirror fanning herself with her hands. The onset of menopause was playing havoc as were her emotions and her body. She blinked a couple of times. Her eyes red rimmed from rubbing fibreglass into them – how attractive. She ran a tap and began splashing cold water on her face, relieved that the hotness was subsiding. The door burst open and she flinched. 'Wyre, you okay?'

Wyre pulled a face as she moved her arm in a circular motion. 'I will be. I'm going to ache in the morning and I bet you are too. I mean, you fell through the ceiling.' She stared into Gina's eyes. 'You look like a demon, or something from a horror film.'

'Thanks, Paula.' She glanced at the bloodshot corner of her left eye. 'You're not wrong.'

Gina let out a small laugh, relieved that it was only Wyre that had followed her into the ladies. Things could have been much worse. 'I've never known a case with so many suspects on the run at the same time. I'm going to head home in a short while, take a shower. I'm itching like hell. I'll be working from home.'

'Yeah, me too.'

Gina paused and stared at her reflection. 'Annabel is out there somewhere, I just hope that "dealing with Annabel" doesn't mean killing her. What does Taylor mean in the note? Dealing with Annabel. We're going around in circles here. The more I think about it, the more it has to be Taylor and Grant. The forensics prove he was at the scene. They both wanted Annabel out the way. Then another part of me says Whittle had a mini shrine to her and other women hidden in his loft. That's as weird as it gets and we know he's a liar and he ran from us. I need to go home, go through everything we have and hope that the murkiness clears up. We need Whittle, Grant and Taylor brought in and it's like they've all disappeared.'

'They can't hide forever, guv. I'll see you in the morning unless they turn up in the meantime.'

'Yes, get some rest. It's going to be a long day. I can feel it in my bones.' She could feel more than tomorrow in her bones. She could feel the pounding of her body on that desk, the splinters of rotten wood she'd picked out of her side, and the itching. Whatever she did, she couldn't stop itching. What she needed was to get out of her clothes and have a shower before she clawed her skin open.

Wyre smiled and left. Gina closed her eyes and imagined the night of the hit-and-run. Annabel and Jennifer were walking back to Annabel's. Then a car hit Jennifer. Was it Grant's Mercedes that hit her, the one that should have been in his garage? Maybe he tried to mop up Jennifer's blood from the scene, which is why he had the soiled tissues. He would have known Annabel's location. He'd been tracking her phone and the woman with the baby, the one who lived by the scene, had heard a car. Had he then bundled Annabel into the Mercedes before driving her away. Gina tried to turn it all around. Maybe Whittle had followed Annabel from the pub. Maybe he hit Jennifer and Grant came to help her. If that was the case, why wouldn't he have intervened earlier? Or, was he too late to the scene? Both men still had opportunity. Then there was Cally. The little girl had reported hearing someone in the garden on the evening, the person she thought was a ghost. Was it her father getting his car out of the garage? He'd have a key to the padlock. Her mind flashed back to early Sunday morning at the scene. Fancy cocktail sticks on the floor, a fun raspberry keyring. A purse.

Gina dried her damp face on a paper towel and screwed it up, aiming for the bin but she missed. She bent over and picked it up. It was going to be a long night. They also left Taylor alone outside the station, smoking. Ultimately, they lost her.

She scrunched her brow. There was someone else to question, that's if Whittle could be believed. A student with a crush on Annabel. It was a long shot but she had to go back to Cleevesford High. Ms Law must know who this lovesick kid is.

THIRTY-TWO

Omar

The police have been outside Annabel's house again so I've hidden myself away, around the back this time. It's so easy with all the trees and far too risky being out the front without knowing when the police will turn up. Again, Mum asked where I was going but I can't say anything. I can't tell her that I love Annabel so I have to be here. She doesn't know that I will do anything for her – anything. Curiosity has the better of me. I saw both Mr Whittle and the Braddocks's childminder here earlier, and then I saw the police at school. I need to know who else is lurking and what they're up to. I owe it to Annabel.

The neighbour comes out of his house with a bag of what looks like animal feed. I peer through a gap in the fence as he bends over to retrieve a bowl, fills it, then puts it back in the hutch. I've seen him holding his rabbit before. I step back, cracking a branch underfoot and he stops. He stares over into the darkness and begins to walk down the path. That's when I dart back to my place in the bushes, where I'm sure no one can see me. I know it's a good hiding place because a man walked past with a dog earlier and he didn't notice that I was there, even when his dog came over for a sniff.

He opens his back gate and looks up and down. All I can see is his profile lit up by the moon. I hold my breath, hoping that he hurries back into his house. If he catches me here, I'll be in trouble and I can't keep still forever. He'll tell the police and they'll want to speak to me, especially when it becomes apparent that Annabel is my teacher. I also know I'm not supposed to tell, not just because Annabel asked me to keep a secret. I swallow, not wanting my mum to get hurt.

My heart bangs and I need to exhale. If I breathe, I'm sure he'll hear me and who knows what he'll do if he finds me here. My tense muscles begin to tremble. Just as I let my breath go, he heads back into his garden, locking his gate behind him. He'll think that I'm some intruder that might come back and burgle him later, which means he'll be on high alert. He's already seen me once before lurking around in the past, he can't catch me again. His back door slams. Phew. I got away with it.

Footsteps gather pace and get closer. Clop, clop, clop – then they stop. I stay back. Someone in a dark hoodie and black boots approaches Annabel's back gate. I can't work out who it is from their feet. I daren't peer too far around for fear of being seen. The figure enters through the back gate, that's when I come out of my recess. They duck under the washing line as I watch. That's when I recognise who it is. The intruder leans against the garage window, face pressed against the glass as if peering in. I hear them calling out in a hoarse whisper but no one answers. I can't make out what is being said. Up above, the neighbour closes their curtains.

I see the outline of a person nearing Annabel's kitchen

window. The intruder peers in and then creeps back down the path away from whoever is in the house. Annabel's husband must be back.

It's too risky being here. There are too many people around. I hurry back into my hiding space, nestled in the shrubs, my bike still tucked away. I wanted to use Mum's car but she had plans tonight. The intruder almost steps into my space and I keep as still as I can, hiding and holding my breath again. Then I change tack and jog along the path. There's a shortcut across this field. The intruder changed their mind and stayed on the path so I know where they're heading. Not many people walk through that field at night so I can't blame them for taking the longer and safer route. It's a creepy field.

Leaving my bike, I keep a safe distance but don't lose sight of the figure. I need to know what they know and the only way I can do that is to keep up and see where they're going, then I'll come back and see what Annabel's husband is up to.

There's a patch of grass to cross. I almost trip over the stile as I follow the figure. I realise I'm shaking. The bottom of the lane is in sight. There's a well-trodden break in the hedge where people cut through. That's when I hear the yelp and stay still. My blood goes cold and my feet barely work. That wasn't a normal cry, it was followed by a sickening wail. Stepping closer, I feel my legs threatening to give way.

Hiding, I sidle up along the hedge and peer through the gap. That's when I see the street lamp lighting up the intruder. I wait and catch my breath back. The sight of blood glistening almost makes me heave. I turn and go to run. I can't be here. Whoever just did that is still there. I feel a breeze behind me as if the killer is catching up and I trip over a verge. My heart is in my mouth. I close my eyes and cover my head, hoping that will be enough. If I die, I won't be able to protect Annabel. She needs me. I need to live. But, right now, that choice isn't mine. I wished I'd done as my mum said and stayed in while she visited Aunt Bet. She wanted to watch a film and eat popcorn when she got back but now I'll be in trouble for being so late. If only I'd have listened.

THIRTY-THREE

Omar

'Please don't hurt me. Please. I haven't done anything.' I can't look. If I see them, they'll definitely kill me. I've seen it in films. If I don't look, they'll think I can't identify them and they'll let me go.

'Hey, kid, are you okay?'

They're not hurting me. That doesn't sound like the voice of a killer. It's a sweet voice, a kind voice. They would have killed me by now. I prise open an eye and in the darkness, I can just about see hair piled up on a woman's head. I see Taylor behind her, lying there in pooling blood that looks black in the dark.

'Are you okay?' She asks me the same question again but speaks slower and louder.

I go to stand and realise I'm taller than her. She's shaking and that toy dog she's holding wouldn't be able to protect anything. I take a step closer to her, so that I can see her face.

'Please don't come any closer.'

'But—'

'Please. Just stay there and wait for the police. We can sort this out.' The woman's phone lights up her face. I recognise her. She runs the Angel Arms. As she steps away from Taylor's body, I can now see her Cupid's bow lips lined in blood-red lipstick, long faded. Her smoky eyes smudged. 'Police, please. Come quick, there's a dead woman and a boy in shock. Please hurry.'

She can't tell them any more about me. They'll think I killed Taylor. I lunge forward, knocking her phone from her hands, hoping that in the dark, she can't see me very well. Her poodle snaps at me but the phone lies on the ground and all I can hear is the operator asking if she's still there. She steps back from me, fear in her eyes. I didn't want to scare her, but I need her to stop talking while I make my getaway. I sprint through the gap, onto the field. I need to get back to my bike and back home, leaving this whole mess behind while I work out what to do.

Whoever killed Taylor is close by. They'll try to blame me, I know they will. They saw me but I have no idea who they are. As I take the shortcut across the field, I keep stumbling on the uneven earth below. In the distance, I hear a siren. The police are on their way. I need to keep off the roads, taking fields and the backs of estates to get home. Before I know it, I reach the back of Annabel's house and it's now in darkness. I hold my breath and I'm sure I hear a noise. It's getting closer. If I move, I'm next. I imagine my own head bust open on the floor; my mum's face as the police tell her they've found my body, and I think of Annabel. I have to remember that all I do is for her.

That noise again. I go to grab my bike but my hands don't work. Did I even hear a noise? I'm not sure if it's just the sound of my throbbing temples as blood pumps through my body. Annabel's neighbour's light comes on again and the man emerges barefoot, rubbing his eyes. I must have woken him somehow when I approached, running and falling all over the place. A fox darts out from under a tree and I scream.

'Who's there?' The man starts walking down the path.

I can't let him see me. I'm definitely going to get the blame for everything. The police are closer as the sirens are getting louder every second.

He opens his back gate. 'Don't I know you?' He squints and turns on his torch. As he goes to flash it in my face, I'm already on my bike, cycling as fast as I can up the path towards the industrial units, as far away from all the commotion as I can be. Don't look back. That's all I tell myself. I can only hope that he doesn't remember the time he saw me peering through Annabel's window.

I am in so much trouble.

Then I stop dead in the road and swallow. I know the killer saw me even if I didn't see them. I start to pedal again, as fast as I can, away from the sirens, away from the dead body and away from the murderer. I'm safe for now, but for how long? There is one person I know who is capable of doing this. I never did tell Annabel what he said to me, I never got the chance.

A police car turns into the road. I turn right, my tyres skidding behind a large biscuit factory sign and I close my eyes, hoping that the police didn't see. A tear begins to roll down my cheek. What have I got myself into? It's all my fault. If only I'd said something when it mattered. It's too late now. I've passed the point of no return and I have to play it cool and stay off the police and the murderer's radar. If I don't, I'm next.

THIRTY-FOUR

Gina ran down the lane, still trying to straighten out her jumper under her coat, wet hair stuck to the back of her neck. She'd been called out of the shower to attend a murder scene. She followed the blue lights of the stationary police car that had parked on the lane, that's when a woman she recognised came into focus. The licensee of the Angel Arms, Elouise Nichols. She was clutching a white toy poodle in her arms and it was fighting to be placed on the floor; legs flailing as it licked her face.

'DI Harte.' Gina had met Elouise while investigating a previous case so it wasn't surprising that the woman had remembered her name. A paramedic came over to her. 'I'm okay.'

The paramedic held his hands up and stepped back. 'If you're sure.'

'Elouise. You found the body?'

The woman nodded and rubbed her eyes. 'There was a boy here. At first I thought he was also hurt but then he started coming closer to me and I got scared. That was when I called the police. He knocked my phone out of my hands and ran away.'

'I'd like to speak with you but I just need to check in with my colleague.' She needed to confirm what she'd been told. Heading over to PC Smith who was guarding the outer cordon while forensics began to put a tent up, she stopped and glanced over. 'Is it definitely Taylor?'

'Yes, guv. She hasn't been formally identified but it's definitely her unless she has a twin sister. She has ID on her too.'

'Do we know how she died?' She peered over and spotted Bernard's lanky shadow elongated across the pavement. The portable light flickered as he shifted its position.

'I think Bernard would like to speak with you in a short while but it looks like a stab wound to the neck.'

Gina grimaced. 'Thank you. I'm going to take Elouise over there to sit on the bench. I'll take a statement from her. In the meantime, call a dog team and get some officers on foot searching the area. Any sign of the weapon?'

He nodded. 'A knife was found in the verge. It's been bagged and placed in evidence.'

'I'll speak to Bernard about that in a short while, thank you. Call in and arrange for door to doors on the bordering houses too. Wait, isn't Annabel's house just the other side of that field?'

'Yes.'

'Interview her neighbours. First Annabel going missing and now Taylor being murdered. This is no coincidence.'

'I'll get that all sorted, guv.'

'Thank you.' The sound of an owl hooting in the distance would have normally been something to enjoy but not tonight, not under the backdrop of a murder. 'Elouise, would you come over to the bench? We can sit there?' The woman followed her. 'First things, did you touch the body?'

Elouise sat under the lamplight and nodded, biting her bottom lip as if she'd done something wrong. She dipped her head. 'I know I shouldn't have but I thought she might still have been alive so I checked her pulse. I screwed up.'

'You didn't screw up. You did the right thing when you checked to see if she was still alive. But, I do have to ask if we can take your clothes and some swabs. Forensics will handle all that. Something from the murderer may have been transferred onto you when you helped.'

'This is my best coat.'

'Really sorry.' Gina tilted her head. 'We need to catch whoever has done this.'

'God, I don't know what I was thinking by saying that. Of course you do. What an idiot. Yes, I have other coats. I'm really messing this up.' Elouise began to shake.

'Bear with me.' Gina ran over to the paramedic and grabbed a foil blanket, then ran back. She placed it over the trembling woman's shoulders. 'I know this is hard but can you tell me what time you found the body?'

Elouise pulled the blanket close to her neck and scrunched it with her hands to stop the cold from getting in. 'I left my staff in charge of the pub to walk Bippy just before nine. He's my sister's dog. I'm looking after him while she's on holiday. I'd only been walking for about five minutes when I spotted something at the edge of the path. At first, I thought it might be a bin bag. I got angry because it wouldn't be the first time I'd found fly-tipped bags on the lane. When I got there, I saw that it was a body and what I thought was a bag, was dark clothing. Holding the dog under my arm, I kneeled over her. That's when I saw all the blood around the girl's head. I quickly checked for a pulse and then I stood. Then I saw a boy lying in the verge, staring like he was in shock. I asked him if he was okay but then he stood and started taking steps towards me. I thought he was going to attack me, that's when I called the police. He knocked my phone out of my hand then ran through the bushes, just by the body. I waited back here until police officers arrived and that's it.'

'Can you tell me what time you came across the boy and the body?'

'A little after nine.'

'Can you describe the boy?'

'That's going to be hard. It was so dark but I'll give it a go. He was about my height, so maybe five feet six inches. He was wearing a dark coat, like a raincoat, a sporty one, maybe. The pull strings were white so I could see them against the dark coloured material. Maybe he had jeans or cords on. Thin legs. I suppose I got a sense of his shape. He was quite skinny. Really dark hair, maybe black. As a bit of the light from my phone caught his profile, his hair shone. Really sleek hair, and thick. I didn't catch his features at all; just his dark eyes. Really sorry. It all happened within a matter of seconds.'

Gina noticed that the lane was on a slight slope and that Elouise would have been standing a little above the boy. She made a note that he could be a little taller than she had estimated. 'Did he say anything?'

'No, he just ran through the cut in the shrubs and trees and across the field. There was something else and maybe I'm imagining things. I mean, I could hardly hear with blood pumping all through my body but I'm sure I heard rustling from behind the trees as I arrived on the scene. There may have been someone else there. I did listen out for the noise again as I approached but I didn't hear anything. Maybe something or someone scarpered. I know there are a lot of foxes around here but I don't think it was a fox. Foxes don't sound like boots treading on twigs. Maybe the boy had a friend with him. Who knows?' Elouise paused.

'Are you okay?'

She shook her head and rubbed her eyes. 'No, what if whoever did this wants to hurt me now?' She glanced at the tent. 'I saw the body. I saw all the blood around her neck. Someone killed her, just like that and it could have been me if I'd been out walking Bippy just a little bit earlier.'

Gina looked into her lap, giving Elouise a moment. 'We're still investigating but I think this was a targeted attack and relates to an ongoing investigation. I know someone has spoken to you briefly about the hit-and-run and the missing woman.'

'Yes, an officer popped by to take a statement and a copy of our CCTV footage. It was Annabel and Jennifer. I know those two ladies. They've been in a few times. I mean, I don't know them well, just their names. Has this girl's murder got something to do with what happened to them?'

'Hopefully, we will have more information to release soon. Can you tell me how Jennifer and Annabel seemed that night, when they were at the Angel, drinking?'

'I've already been through this with one of your colleagues but, yes. Annabel was knocking them back, in fact she staggered out of the pub but Jennifer; she was on lemonade. I wondered how Jen was going to get her home. We joked a bit about that as they left. Earlier, they seemed to be having quite the serious conversation. Maybe Jennifer was comforting Annabel at one point but I couldn't be sure. They were sitting with their back to me most of the night facing the fireplace.'

'Did you see anyone approach or speak to them?'

'No, not at all. They were stuck in their little corner all night talking and drinking. There was something else.'

'Relating to that night?'

'No, another time.'

'How long ago was that?'

'A week or two ago. It wasn't in the pub. I saw that Annabel had parked up by the accountants to use the supermarket. The car park was quite full as it was about five when most people finish work. I saw a man with his hand on her arm and it looked like she was pushing him away. It wasn't her husband as she's been in the pub with him in the past. It looked like they were arguing. She seemed angry or upset.'

'What did he look like?'

'Quite tall. I only saw the back of him but he looked fit. Well proportioned, not in a workout with weights way but slightly broad. I do remember that he got into a silver Fiesta. That's all I have.'

'And can you remember the day?'

'No, I wish I could. At least a week ago, no more than two. Sorry to be so vague.'

Gina knew that Whittle drove a silver Fiesta. He was tall too. 'Thank you for this, you've been really helpful. Is there anything else that you can think of?'

'No. How do I give you my clothes?'

Gina nodded at a uniformed officer who was guarding the perimeter. 'I know this is a lot but I will need you to go to the station and give a formal statement? We can guide you through everything there.'

Elouise nodded. 'Yes. Of course I will.'

'Thank you. You already have my details if you need to contact me about anything.' Gina smiled at the PC. 'Would you take over?'

He nodded and went over to Elouise. Gina waved at Bernard.

'Gina, come over. I'm ready now.'

She swallowed as she thought about the girl who she'd met at the cabin and the thought of seeing her as a corpse wasn't sitting well. As she pulled on a forensics suit and got checked in by PC Smith, she glanced at the trees and shrubs. While Elouise was approaching and the boy was in the verge, there was someone else there, watching on. She shivered at the thought.

THIRTY-FIVE

'DI Harte. Stick to the stepping plates and come over.' Bernard gave a nod of his head and stepped into the entrance of the tent.

As Gina tried to keep to the plates, she nudged a light, almost knocking it over. A crime scene assistant caught it in time and repositioned it so that it shone brightly into the tent. The rustling of the hood seemed to distort Bernard's voice slightly. She peered in to where Bernard was standing hunched so that his head didn't touch the top of the canvas. Then, she allowed her gaze to settle on the body. The tiny woman was lying on her back, limbs bent a little and her face deathly pale. Thankfully, her eyes were closed. Gina swallowed as she saw the blood pooled around her head. If only they'd kept Taylor at the station. This wouldn't have happened. 'What do you know?'

'We'll obviously know more when we conduct a post-mortem but this is what we have so far. She was killed by a single knife wound to the neck. The carotid artery has been cut with the knife. She would have died quickly and, as you can see, she lost a lot of blood. Death could have happened within seconds.'

'So whoever did this knew what they were doing?' Gina

shrugged. 'Or maybe, it's just common knowledge. Anyone can find out anything on the internet. What else?'

'We have the weapon and I have briefly examined the wound. It looks to be a match and has blood on it too. Obviously, I can verify that when I get everything back to the lab.'

Gina looked away from the body. Taylor did not deserve this. She'd been foolish and she had betrayed Annabel's trust, but no one deserved this. 'Tell me about the knife you found?'

'It was in the verge, a metre away from the body. I measured it to be thirty centimetres long in total. It's a common make. They sell them everywhere as individual knives or as knife sets in a block. I know that as I have a set of them at home.'

'Anything else?'

'We have picked up a lot of debris. The usual. Cigarette butts. Rubbish. All this will be taken back to the lab. We do have a partial footprint, one of the only clear prints through the cut in the shrubs and we have a collection of prints just behind the tree line. It's quite a damp evening so we are making moulds. The footprint in the cut through looks to be different to the one in the field. I did notice that the trees could be easily parted for someone to slip through.'

'The witness I just spoke to said she heard someone behind the trees so that makes sense. We are looking for two people. The boy that she saw at the scene and another person. Do we have the shoe sizes?'

'Yes. The shoeprint at the cut through is a UK size ten, the same as the field print. The footprint in the field looks like it belongs to a person with a limp, not the same as the ones around the cut through. The right foot touches the ground in a lighter way. You'll see what I mean in the report.'

'Any prints detected on the knife?'

'No. Whoever did this was wearing gloves.'

'Anything else?'

'I'm afraid not. Not until I get everything back to the lab and the post-mortem happens. Will you be attending?'

Gina had so many interviews to get through and she needed to be there, to see the reactions of everyone she spoke to. 'I'll do my best but probably not. We have too many leads to follow up. I'll task DC O'Connor with that one. Will it be done tomorrow?'

Bernard looked down at the body. 'I spoke to the pathologist and he will do it tomorrow lunchtime. I'll get all the details to you as soon as.'

'I really appreciate you getting that organised quickly. Do you know the approximate time of death?'

He smiled. 'That I can help with. We know that she died from the stab wound. Given the temperature of her body and the state it's in, I'd say time of death was between eight thirty and nine. That might help with your timeline. I need to get on. Photos and video of the scene have been taken so I'll get all that emailed to you ASAP. We need her moved before rigor mortis sets in and that won't be long.'

'Thank you so much. Right, unless there's anything else you can tell me now, I'm going to see how things are going on the ground.' She caught the sound of an engine cutting followed by that of a van door opening. 'I bet that's the dog team.' That's when she heard a dog bark, confirming what she'd suspected.

As she left the tent, she caught sight of Wyre passing PC Smith's cordon. 'Guv.' She waved.

Gina hurried over and updated her colleague.

'Guv.' A PC ran up the lane and stopped in front of the two detectives while he got his breath back. 'We have a witness.'

THIRTY-SIX

Omar

'Where have you been?'

That's my mother's voice. I know I should have called her to say I was with a friend. I got scared of being seen by the police so I stayed behind that sign for ages. 'I... err, I was at Max's house.' She doesn't reply. She's doing that thing where she stares at her hands on the table, her brows arched in disappointment. 'Sorry, Mum.'

'You weren't answering your phone.' Still, she doesn't look up. Instead she picks up her phone as if to emphasise her point.

'Sorry. It needed charging. I should have taken my charger with me.' I wish she'd let me go to my room and not have to sit through a lecture. I haven't got time for this. My legs are shaking and I know if she looks at me, she'll see. I can't exactly tell her I saw someone get murdered and that the murderer might be after me now. I can't tell her about the secret, about Annabel, or about the threat I'm under. Everything is a big fat mess.

The woman who runs the pub looked at me but it was as if she was staring right at me at one point. I remember my mouth filling with spit and I couldn't swallow. I thought I could just say something, anything that might put her mind at ease that I wasn't a threat. I was going to tell her that I didn't kill Taylor but I couldn't speak. Instead, I stood there staring and that must have seemed menacing, then I hit her phone. Everything is out of control. I stuffed up. She'll definitely think I killed Taylor.

'I was worried.' My mother pauses and slaps her lips together, making a pop sound. 'I kept looking at Facebook, mostly your profile, and then I saw that there's been an incident on the lane at the back of the pub. Until you walked through that door, I thought it was you. I kept calling and calling you. I was so close to calling the police.' She trembles as she picks up a glass of water and sips. 'Don't you ever put me through that again. You're fourteen. You have to tell me where you are and keep your phone charged. I've never been so scared.' She stands and grips me close to her, almost squeezing the breath out of me. 'You're shaking.'

I can't deny that. My body is trembling like a road drill. 'You just scared me, Mum, when you said something has happened out there tonight. I promise I won't leave the house with an uncharged phone again.'

She lets me go. 'Sit.' Her worried tone is now serious. That, I wasn't expecting. I sit. 'There's something else we need to talk about and it's important that you tell the truth.'

For a minute, I hold my breath. Does she know everything? She's been through my things, my iPad or my wardrobe. She must have. She doesn't trust me. She knows I'm distracted and up to something. Why wouldn't she? She's my mum. She knows me better than anyone and I've let her down. 'Okay.' My voice is nothing more than a crackled whisper.

'You've driven my car again, haven't you?'

I shakily nod my head. Is that all she knows?

'I know we've been through some bad times. You lost your father a couple of years ago and things haven't been the same. I'm always at work. Maybe I don't give you enough of my time. I don't know whether you've got into a wrong crowd or what, but you promised you'd never drive my car again. Is it Max? Is he telling you to do all this? Staying out late and not answering your phone. Are you using drugs, out there drinking in parks?' She shakes her head. 'Tell me you weren't.' She doesn't wait for me to answer. 'You were always such a good boy, Omar. You're clever, sensitive, smart and loving. What you did wasn't you. Your father will be turning in his grave. I don't want you seeing this Max again. Okay?'

I nod. 'I wasn't taking drugs or drinking, I swear on my life. You can smell my breath if you want.' There is no Max, I made him up. I needed someone to blame when my mum saw me pulling back up in her car that one time. I wanted to drive it. I mean it's easy to drive with it being an automatic. She doesn't know that I've driven it many times, that's how I'd got so good at driving. I liked being able to go anywhere, quickly, and to race it around the country lanes when it was quiet. Recently, I needed it to watch Annabel. I didn't want to use my bike all the time. It's hard in the night and it's not like she notices it missing if I plan when I take it. 'Okay. I won't hang out with him. He's moving anyway.'

'Sometimes as a parent you have to do the right thing. If I keep letting you get away with breaking the law, you'll never know the consequences of your actions. You could kill someone. You don't have insurance and what you've being doing is stealing my car.'

'Please don't say anything, Mum. It might stop me getting into university or getting a job. Please?' I beg her. She can't tell on me. Not only that, the police will blame me for everything. I need to find out who killed Taylor, only then can everything fall apart underneath me.

She swallows and takes another sip of water. 'Okay, we can move on to my next question. Why is there a dent in my bumper?'

'I'm sorry, Mum. I promise I'll never go near your car again. Please, please, don't call anyone or say anything.' I'm actually crying, something I haven't really done for a few years but the enormity of everything is weighing heavily now. She has to keep quiet or my life is over.

'Go to bed. We'll talk more in the morning.' She crosses the kitchen, opens the fridge and pulls out a bottle of wine. I've driven my mum to drink.

'Please, Mum.' I need to know if she is going to call the police.

Slamming the bottle on the table she shouts, 'I said go to bed.'

Without wasting a second, I run up the stairs and slam my bedroom door. I've never seen my mum that angry and I don't want to see that side of her again. All I can do is wait until tomorrow to see what she decides to do. I walk over to my window, still in darkness, and peer out. I stare at the other houses, an intricate maze of buildings, some small, some tall, but all tightly packed around squares of grass. Cars are parked everywhere and I wonder if whoever killed Taylor is out there watching.

The house I'm interested in is the house in the distance of this rabbit warren. Mr Whittle's. He's evil. I know what he did and I wonder if he killed Taylor. I know she went to Cleevesford High and it wasn't that long ago really. I've been watching Mr Whittle when I can. I gulp and look around outside. Maybe it's the other way around. Maybe he's out there, watching me and was there tonight, killing Taylor. He's a dangerous man and he made sure I knew just how dangerous. The threat makes me shiver.

I stay dressed and get into bed, leaving my boots and coat on the floor, ready to put on as soon as Mum is asleep. Either I work everything out or I sit here and remain a target for a killer. I check my phone and scroll through Facebook. Everyone is talking in the *What's Up Cleevesford* Facebook group. Young woman murdered. Soon everyone will know it was Taylor when her face is plastered all over the internet. Why wait. The sooner everyone knows, the better. I type three words, under the post.

RIP Taylor Caldwell

For a second, I regret making that post. After all, I was there and I'm trying to keep a low profile but I need to tell the killer that I won't stay completely silent. A shiver runs through me. Maybe I've made a huge mistake. I don't even use my real name on my profile and it's new and the photo is of our old cat that died. I swallow. By breaking the news this fast, only the killer will know it's me. I go to delete my comment but everyone is commenting now. I've done what I set out to do so I go ahead and delete. I click onto Annie Bell's profile and look into her beautiful eyes. 'It's all for you.' I kiss her on my screen and wait. Waiting until Mum is asleep is all I can do right now.

THIRTY-SEVEN

TUESDAY, 5 APRIL

'Mr Bryson, may we come in?' Gina waited next to Wyre on the doorstep. The sound of morning birds just starting to tweet began to fill the air.

The barefooted man led Gina and Wyre into his living room. What was left of a fire simpered away in the hearth with a little crackle here and there. 'Please, it's Evan. Have a seat.'

'We're sorry to have to speak to you again, so soon. As you are aware, a woman was found dead on the lane a few hours ago. You told one of our officers that you saw someone.'

'Yes, it was a little before nine. I'd just woken up after falling asleep in front of a film and I heard something when I went to get a drink in the kitchen. I opened the door and heard a noise coming from the bushes. At first, I thought it might be a fox trying to get to my rabbit. It's been strange around here, lately. I keep hearing things. It's like someone is always lurking around. With what's happened to Annabel, I keep checking outside in the hope that she'll just turn up. It can get quite creepy living out here; road and trees at the front and trees and the field at the back. We are only a small row of houses and the industrial estate is quiet at night except for the odd lorry pulling in.'

'Are you sure it was a person?' Gina sat back on the wide settee, its cushions so soft they felt like they were hugging her.

'Yes. It was definitely footsteps I heard, not a fox or a badger. I saw him, and I recognised him. It took me a while but it was definitely the same person.'

'Same person?'

Wyre began making notes.

'Yes. A boy. I saw him a while ago, I can't even remember when. He was looking through Annabel and Grant's front window. I came out and he scarpered. Then I saw him again, last night. I'd heard someone loitering earlier too. I think it was him, he's always here.'

'Who is this boy?'

'I don't know his name. He must be about fourteen, fifteen maybe. Quite tall and gangly with black hair. Annabel teaches kids of that age, maybe he's one of her kids at school.'

Gina knew she had to make speaking to the school a priority. Ms Law had to know who this kid was. Even Tom Whittle had said there was a boy who had a crush on Annabel. With Elouise's description, it was now confirmed that the boy was a key witness. Gina swallowed. Or, maybe he was the murderer. Either way, she needed to catch up with him to find out what he either knew or did.

'It's too much of a coincidence, that boy being around, lurking and watching. I'm no child psychologist but that's weird behaviour.'

Gina had to agree with him.

'I also saw someone else a few moments before seeing him.'

'Who?' Gina was hoping that he had spotted Grant or even Whittle.

'Taylor. I'd definitely recognise her. I heard someone in the garden whispering Grant's name at first, I listened through the slight opening of the kitchen window. When I looked out, she was wearing black and looking through the garage window. Maybe she planned to meet Grant there.' He paused and looked between Gina and Wyre. 'Wait, the incident on the lane. It wasn't Taylor, was it? Did the boy follow her?'

'I'm afraid I can't confirm anything yet.' The last thing Gina wanted was word getting out before Taylor's aunt had received the news.

'Okay, I understand. Can I get you a drink?'

Gina shook her head. 'Have you seen anything of Mr Braddock?'

'No, I have your number. If I see him, I'll call you straight away. Are you any closer to finding Annabel?'

'We have leads to follow so we're getting closer.'

'I hope you find her soon. This is just horrible. Her father still hasn't managed to tell little Cally. I called him up to see if there was any news, earlier. The poor child thinks her mother is on a spa break and that her father is working away. She's such a good friend and neighbour and her little girl adores her. We all just want her home and safe.'

'As do we all.'

Evan paused and placed his hands in a prayer position in front of his mouth. He shook his head and removed them. 'I don't know if this is relevant but Grant was doing drugs. I know I should have said something earlier but I thought Annabel would come home and this would all be a mistake. The more I think about it, the more I feel it could be relevant. Grant was dealing in amphetamines and other things, but I can't remember what they were. I know that because he tried to sell me some. I'm not into drugs or anything like that. I really didn't think that what Grant was doing would have anything to do with what has happened to Annabel but I can't stop thinking about it. What if he owes a drug dealer and they're using Annabel to get to him? I haven't seen Grant either. He's missing too.' He shook his head. 'Maybe I've been watching too much TV.'

'Thank you for telling us. How well do you know Grant?' It wasn't news to them but it was news to know that they had a witness that could verify that Grant had tried to sell them drugs. They could definitely arrest him on those charges and further question him about his wife. If only they knew where he was. He hadn't come back for his car at the gym and his other car hadn't flagged up.

'As well as a neighbour would. I watch their home when they go on holiday and they do the same for me. I've looked after their dog, they do the same for my rabbit. You came over when I was babysitting for Cally. We're good neighbours, that's probably how I'd describe us. We've played golf together and been boating in the past, but he doesn't tell me his problems. We're not that close.'

Gina allowed her gaze to rove around the room and she stared at a photo on a shelf. 'Is that you and Grant on a boat?' The ancient-looking cabin cruiser was a relic from the sixties with its brown stripe running through the middle and its mustard-coloured curtains poking out of the one window.

'Ah yes. Grant bought that boat off me and I went out on it with him on many occasions. That was taken a couple of years ago.'

'Does he still have the boat?'

'Its days were numbered when I had it but I think Grant wanted a boat as his brother, Seth, had one. You can see how old it looks in the photo and I didn't maintain it well. I sold it to Grant for next to nothing because it wasn't worth anything. It was a bit of a fad on my part. Novelty soon wore off.'

'What's his brother's full name?'

'Seth Braddock. I've been friends with Seth for years but he works away a lot so you might not be able to catch him about.

He's a nice guy but I know he and Grant have had their differences.'

'What differences?'

'Sibling rivalry. Seth looks like Grant but he's that bit more handsome. He's successful, well respected, funny and fit. He's also free. I mean, without ties. No wife or kids.' Evan let out a chuckle. 'I shouldn't laugh but even I wish I was Seth. He's just one of those guys.'

'What does he do?'

'He's a well-respected professor. At the moment, he's contracted at a university in Amsterdam. He comes back during breaks. Maths and computer science, I think. I don't think he's in the country at the moment but then again, he doesn't have to check in with me, though he does normally call me when he's back to ask if I want a pint with him.'

Gina made a note of Grant Braddock's brother's name and details. 'Do you have Seth's phone number?'

'Yes.' Evan noted it down and passed it to Gina.

'Where is the boat that Grant owns now? What happened to it?'

'I think it got scrapped as Grant used it a few times then said it was too knackered to take out. Annabel and Cally got scared on it once. He took it out on the river in really bad weather. I remember Annabel saying never again. You might need to ask him what he did with it as he never told me. I'm assuming he scrapped it because that would be logical. Or maybe it's still at the boatyard, rotting away.'

'So, you didn't get another boat?'

'No. I'd never get one again. Too much work. Like I said, the novelty wore off.'

'What was the name of Grant's boat and where was it kept?'

'It was called *Freedom*. It would have been registered to Grant and last I knew it was kept at a boatyard in Bidford-on-Avon. That's where I kept it. He took over the storage payments when he bought the boat. I really don't know what he did with it after. I was glad to get rid of it. I told him it was in a state but he said it didn't matter.'

'What's the name of his brother's boat?'

'Erm...' He scrunched his brow. 'Something to do with fruit. Maybe a strawberry or raspberry.'

'Do you know where that is moored or stored?'

'No, sorry. I think it was at Evesham at one point but I know he moved it.'

'What type of boat is it?'

'A narrowboat.'

'Thank you. Could you please come down to the station and make a statement?'

'Yes. Of course.' He stood and grabbed his coat. 'I'm off work today so I'm all good for time.'

'What is it you do?'

'Admin for a chilled goods company, totally boring.'

As she turned, Gina glanced at his collection of fridge magnets. 'Pi is a pie.' She smiled at the magnet where the pi symbol had been turned into what looked like a fruit pie.

'Yes, Seth has a sense of humour. He gave me that. For some reason he thinks I collect fridge magnets because my father used to.'

'Well, thank you for your time.' Gina stood and followed the man to the door. 'We'll meet you at the station.'

He waved and got into his car. Gina faced Wyre over the top of her car, the orange lamplight from above catching the top of her head and reflecting off the car roof. Wyre cleared her throat. 'What did you make of that?'

'We need to speak to the kid, pronto. The school will be open soon. Let's hope the boy is the key to cracking the case. We should also check out Seth Braddock.' Gina scrunched her nose.

'You're thinking about the boat, aren't you?' Wyre tapped her nails on the car roof.

'Yes. Evan couldn't confirm that the boat had been scrapped. I dread to think where Annabel might be but we need to find out what happened to *Freedom*, if she was scrapped or where she might be stored or moored, starting with the boatyard in Bidford.'

THIRTY-EIGHT

Annabel

I gasp as I try to clear the fog. I'm still trapped and it's still dark and I'm alone. How long have I been asleep? Cally; I want my little girl. It's all a dream. It has to be. Jen and I got run over and I'm in some sort of coma. This box is a dream and when I find the strength to step out of it, I'll wake up. Isn't that how it works in films?

I chow down. The cloth is still in my mouth. I remember the smell of Grant's shower gel. He has a new life planned for me, one where he and I can never be apart. Staring into darkness, I feel like I'm suffocating. How can this be happening to me? I can never forgive him for this.

My head pounds like nothing I've ever felt before. All I need is a sip of water. My mind is going. This is what the journey to insanity must feel like. What's real is not. What's fake might be real. Reality isn't what we see every day. Reality isn't within. I am not real. What is real? I can't answer that question anymore as I cling to my version of reality. I can't feel any more. It's as if the pain has gone but the yearning for water is so strong, I'd literally kill for a drop.

Him. I can't bear to think his name. My mind is back to him and why I'm here. However elusive reality is, I must cling onto some semblance of it. I know I'm on the boat.

A memory flashes through my head. Grant had just bought this horrible old boat from Evan. I told him not to but he insisted on wasting our money, as he always did. When I saw the fees for the boatyard, I cried, telling him that there was no way we could afford it. I didn't want to go on the boat, not in that weather but he literally dragged me out of the house, high as usual and not taking no for an answer. It was a stormy day as I recall and the river water was thrashing dangerously. I hated him for putting us through that little trip. He could have killed us and he didn't care because he wanted a thrill. The rain fell down. Cally's cries could be heard from the cabin. She sat there, clinging on to the pull-out table in her little red lifejacket. I told her to stay there but Grant dragged her out onto the deck and it broke my heart. He forced her trembling hands on the soaking wheel, telling her that she was driving the boat. My little girl kept reaching for me. I went to grab her and he pushed me back. That was the first time he physically assaulted me, but not the last. I slipped, hitting my head on the back rail. Cally has never stepped on a boat since. He promised me he'd got rid of it. So much for *Freedom*. This boat has only ever represented my captivity and it has me again. I am not free and I don't know if I ever will be.

I knew he was on drugs then and he still is. The Grant I knew before he started using was the Grant I clung onto for so long. I thought I could help him, fix him. I thought all it would take was love and understanding and what does he do, he cheats on me, again. We are over.

A dizzy spell hits me and I feel like I'm whirling. I'm thirsty and hungry. Whatever new life is planned for me might not even happen. I'll probably die of dehydration first. I'm seeing things, not big things, and I can still reason with myself. The demon I see in the darkness isn't real. The only demon in existence is the very human demon that is torturing me. I wonder if I'll ever see Cally again. If I could tell her anything, what would it be?

'Mummy loves you more than anything, sweetheart. You are amazing and you can be anything you want. When you were a baby, I used to sit in my nursing chair stroking your soft hair while you fed from me. I'd smile and I couldn't stop kissing your head. You made me the happiest I've ever been and I want you to be happy. Know that you were loved...' I wish I could wipe the tears from my eyes. I think I'm still tied up but I can't even tell. Everything is numb. If I try to move even a little bit, it hurts so much when the feeling comes back. I'm best off numb. I'm numb that this has been done to me and I'm numb in the knowledge of who has done this to me. I'm numb because he said that you're next, Cally. If I could speak to you now, I'd say, 'Don't trust him. He'll be nice, really nice but he's not. You've never seen this side of him. Run as fast as you can.'

I begin to wriggle but it's no use. I've never felt this trapped. Knowing my child is at risk and there's nothing I can do sickens me. I let out a primal scream and it comes out muffled and crackly through my blocked nose. My stomach both churns and rumbles and now I see what isn't there. The demon is back. Whatever he's injecting me with is taking me to hell, one that I'm reliving over and over again with no end in sight. The demon looks real as it laughs, showing its little pincer teeth. Red eyes in the dark. I see anything but freedom. What hurts the most is I can't protect my child. A good mother would do something but I can't. The demon is here for me now and after, it's going for her.

THIRTY-NINE

The incident room was bustling. O'Connor entered with a cardboard tray of coffees from the all night McDonald's. Gina grabbed one and headed to the front of the room. 'I know you've all caught up on what happened. We know that Taylor was murdered between eight thirty and nine. Single stab wound to the neck, severing the carotid artery. We have two witnesses; one fled the scene. Wyre and I will head to the school as soon as it opens. We'll also go to the boatyard at Bidford. Any questions?'

'Do we have any idea who the boy is?' Jacob began peeling the promotional sticker from the side of the cup before rolling it up and throwing it in the bin.

'No.' Gina's thoughts were broken for a second. She remembered the boy who came into school late, the one Miriam was talking about. He had black hair and fit the height description. He'd looked back at her as he went off to join his lesson with Ms Law. 'Actually, I think I saw a boy who fits the description at the school when we went yesterday. I'm trying to remember what Miriam called him.' She snapped her fingers as if trying to recall his name and smiled. 'That's it. Omar. We don't know for sure that it's him we're looking for. It would be a long shot but I will mention him to Ms Law and Miriam when we are there.'

O'Connor slurped through the little opening from the plastic lid.

'Wyre and I spoke to Annabel's neighbour again, Evan. I know you just interviewed him, didn't you, O'Connor?'

He nodded.

'We need to track down a boat by the name of *Freedom*. Can you call up Bidford boatyard and make enquiries, Jacob, before we visit. Also, this is Grant's brother's number. His name is Seth and he's probably in the Netherlands at the moment. Could you call him too? We need to fill him in with what is happening and confirm his location.'

'Yes, guv.' He looked distantly at his cup.

'Has Taylor's aunt been informed of her murder?'

'Yes. PC Kapoor broke the news to her.'

'That's good, because I've noticed that the news has broken on social media already. This information hadn't been released to the public, yet they already know. The only way this could happen is if someone at the scene shared it. I've taken a look at the commenters. From the way the comments flow, it looks like one was deleted. Can you investigate those, Jacob?'

Jacob was staring at his coffee cup.

'Jacob? Are you okay?'

Jacob shrugged. Everyone in the room turned to face Jacob. He shook his head. 'No. I'm so not okay but I need to be here and I will call the boatyard and check out what's happening on social media. I'm not resting until whoever is behind all this has been found. Annabel is still missing and now a girl has been murdered. Jennifer is still lying in a hospital bed.'

Gina tilted her head and dropped her shoulders. 'Have you had any updates?'

He paused and slammed his cup on the desk. 'No, there's no change.'

Gina could tell that Jacob was holding something back. They'd worked closely for a long time and she knew him well. 'If you need anything, just ask. Ask any of us. We're here for you.'

Wyre and O'Connor nodded.

Briggs barged in through the door at the back. 'Right, that's the statement prepared. Just to give you all warning, the media are invited here at seven this morning so the news will break almost immediately after. Be prepared as I'll be appealing for witnesses. The phones will be red hot.' He paused and looked around as if taking in the silence in the room.

Gina cleared her throat and took a swig of coffee. 'Right, we all know what we have to do. Let's get to it. Thank you for the time you're putting in. I know you're tired and I know that we'd all love to go home, shower, have a sleep but there is a woman out there and we need to find her. There is a murderer on the loose and we need to bring that person in. We need to find out who put Jennifer in hospital and I for one will not stop to rest until we get results. I know we're on the edge of something, don't lose it. Are you all good to go?'

A wave of enthusiastic yeses filled the room as everyone left except Jacob who turned back to his computer and began scrolling through Facebook. Briggs waved her over so she followed him into the corridor. 'We need to talk.'

She shook her head so hard, her tied up hair began to slip out of the clip. 'We don't. What you do, who you're seeing, it's none of my business. I know that. I shouldn't have come to your house and I feel so embarrassed at my behaviour. Can we just forget it and move on?' She couldn't look at him and focused on his chest.

'I should explain.'

Gina paused, waiting for him to talk. He rubbed his eyes. As he went to open his mouth, Jacob popped his head around the corner. 'Sir, I've just had a call. The press are waiting.'

'This will have to wait. Damn,' Briggs called back, leaving the door swinging.

In her mind, Gina saw Briggs touching her, hugging her. Briggs simply wanted to be loved. This woman was filling a hole in his life that Gina never could. She hurried back into the incident room and saw Jacob sitting back in front of the computer, his head in his hands. 'Jacob.'

'She's losing the baby.'

Sitting beside him, Jacob gripped her arm and leaned his head on it. She placed an arm over him, offering all she could, the tiniest bit of comfort in a heartbreaking situation. She only hoped that the next bit of news wouldn't be that they were losing Jennifer too.

FORTY

Omar

'But, Mum. I'm sick.' I'm sick with nerves and so tired. After going to Whittle's house when Mum had fallen asleep, I spent the first hour waiting for the police officer to go. Just like Annabel's house, they kept coming all the time. I know they're looking for him. I'm looking for him too. If I find him, I will have the answers I need, but I'm scared. I look into my mum's blue eyes and I wonder if Mr Whittle would really follow through with his threats. What did he mean by my mum having an accident if I told the police or anyone what I'd seen? Annabel begged me to keep quiet about what I heard and Mr Whittle threatened me. I'm stuck. I look up at my mum as she picks up some of my washing, really taking her in and there's no way I could ever have anyone hurting her.

An accident, just like what happened to that woman in hospital. That's the type of thing he would do to my mum. It's all over the news. She's in a coma and will probably die. Will he run my mum over and leave her to die? Will he set fire to our house, taking care of me at the same time? He won't let me live, I know he won't, not after what he did to the childminder. It had to be him. Will he tamper with my mum's car? I don't know and I'm so confused.

'You don't look sick and you haven't got a temperature. You look tired and that's because you were out so late last night. I'm still not happy about that. I'm deciding how you should be punished. I have to get to work and you, my lad, you're going to school. You're not vomiting and you don't have a temperature, so get your butt out of that bed and get your uniform on.'

'Mum—'

'Don't Mum me. Up, now.' She threw my school shirt onto the bed and left the room.

There's no way I can go to school today but Mum is giving me no choice. I snatch my crumpled shirt and put it on while sitting in bed. Then, I check my phone. Notifications galore fill it. Taylor had made the news. Everyone knows that she's been murdered, but only I was there at the time. Gulping, I throw my phone onto the bed and step out into the chilly room.

Pulling my curtains back, I peer out of the window, wondering if the killer is out there. Maybe it wasn't a good idea to be at home alone. Another person knows I was there last night and I know they're coming for me. Soon I will have enough information to go to the police, when Mr Whittle turns up. If he can threaten to hurt my mum like he did, he's capable of hurting Annabel. I swallow. If I do tell the police, I have to tell them I've been watching Annabel and Whittle, and that I was there when Taylor got killed. They'll arrest me for stalking at the very least. People have seen me hanging around. Shaking, I realise I've done my buttons up wrong so I try to undo them. My fingers feel too fat to do it and I can't undo the top one. In frustration I pull it apart and the button pings off my laptop screen. I put my tie on to hide the missing button. The last thing I need is Ms Law on my back today.

'Are you nearly ready, Omar? Hurry up, I'll give you a lift.'

I throw my trousers on and gel my hair. I stink but I don't care. I literally have bigger things to worry about now I am being dropped off at school. 'I'm okay, Mum. I'll use my bike.' It's worth asking.

'No, you won't. I'm taking you to school.'

I kick the bedroom door and grab a tub of chewing gum. I wish she'd just leave me alone. Something big is happening and I'm on the cusp of it all. It's either me or the murderer and Mum is putting me at a disadvantage now. As I pass Mum in the hallway, I slip the spare key off the hook while she's putting her shoes on. It's a race against me solving everything or me being killed and I have no idea how this will go.

FORTY-ONE

'Ms Law, we're really sorry to interrupt your lessons again.' Gina smiled.

The apples of Kirsty Law's cheeks were a shimmery brown as she passed under the strip light and opened her office door. 'That's no problem at all. I've left Miriam with my class for now. How can I help you? Is there any news about Annabel? We're all really worried.' She pushed the door to her office open and they all sat in the same seats as the other day.

'I'm afraid not.'

Kirsty bit her bottom lip and exhaled. 'I know the girl who was murdered. I saw the news this morning. Taylor used to be a student of ours and I know she was Annabel's childminder. We're all really sad to hear what's happened and there is a lot of speculation that her murder is linked to Annabel's disappearance. It's too much of a coincidence, isn't it?'

'We are treating both incidents as linked. We're looking for a student of yours? Lad of about fourteen, maybe fifteen. Black hair. Described as thin and as having a crush on Annabel.'

Kirsty's nostrils flared as she inhaled. Eyes stark, she paused. 'Omar Abidar. He has the biggest crush on her and everyone knows it. He stays behind after her lessons and asks her question after question just to keep her in the room. You don't think he could be involved? I mean, he's just a kid.'

'We simply need to speak to him. We're considering him to be a witness at this stage.'

'Witness. This didn't happen at school. How could he witness anything? Wait, Annabel did mention once that she thought she saw him hanging around by her house and her neighbour saw a boy of his description looking through one of her windows. We didn't do enough, did we? Annabel wasn't worried so we never mentioned it again. She said she'd had a word with him and everything was now okay.' Kirsty slumped back in her chair. 'Do we have to worry about him?'

Gina unbuttoned her coat. It was getting stuffy in the little office. 'As I said, we need to speak to him. Could I please have his address and parents' phone number?'

'Parent. His father died a few years ago. It's just him and his mother now.' She tapped a few keys. 'He lives on Spool Close.' She stared at the screen. 'That's really close to where Mr Whittle lives.'

'Do you have his mother's number?' Gina made a mental note of the proximity to Whittle.

The woman began to write it down and passed the piece of paper over and Wyre took it.

'Is he in school today?'

'Let me check the registration records.' She clicked her mouse and scrolled before squinting. 'No, he's down as an unauthorised absence. It looks like we've tried to call his mother but she didn't answer her phone.'

Gina's heart rate picked up. As Omar didn't turn up at school it was looking more likely that he was at the scene of the murder. They needed to speak to him and they'd need his mother to be there. 'Where does his mother work?'

'At the post office on Cleevesford High Street.'

'How has he seemed lately?'

'Now that I think about it, he's seemed a bit odd. He's missed a few classes. He looks worried, like he has something on his mind and his classwork hasn't been neat. He gets bullied a little. Generally, he's keen, loves school and is very intelligent. As for his behaviour, it wouldn't be the first time a teen has had a bit of a crush on a teacher. They normally move on and start paying attention to kids their own age. It's not something I worried about with Annabel. She seemed to be handling it fine. Do you think he could have something to do with Annabel's disappearance?' She shook her head. 'No, it's just a silly crush. Omar is a lovely kid.'

Gina waited for Wyre to catch up on the note-taking. 'Thank you for all that you've given us, here.'

'Something else has come to light,' Kirsty Law said.

Leaning a little, Gina laid her hands on the desk and listened.

'Mr Whittle. Two more women have come forward since Annabel's disappearance. They claimed that he touched them inappropriately and they are convinced he has something to do with it. One is a lunchtime superintendent and the other is an evening cleaner. I was going to call you.'

'We'll need their names and contact details. We'll send someone to interview them.'

Ms Law nodded. 'I can't believe something like this has been happening right under my nose. It upsets me to know that the staff have been made to feel unsafe. I wish Miriam had formally reported him. Maybe she will now that the others have come forward.'

Gina smiled. 'Sometimes people need to find their own way through something like this. We will speak to her again, see if she wants to make a statement. It will add strength to the case, especially with the other two women.' She watched as Wyre noted down Whittle's name with sexual harassment and assault underneath. This case was getting ever bigger. They needed to arrest Grant Braddock on drugs charges and it looked likely, after speaking to the other women and seeing his shrine, they would be arresting Whittle.

As Gina followed Wyre across the car park, back to the car, she stopped and checked her phone. Still no contact had been made with the boatyard even though they'd called several times. No one was answering. 'We need to get to the post office and speak to Omar's mother, now.'

FORTY-TWO

Gina and Wyre waited behind a man with about ten small parcels in a bag. The woman with straggly brown hair processed each in turn. She took off her glasses and cleaned them before continuing. Gina checked her watch. They were losing time waiting in the queue.

'That'll be twenty-seven pounds sixty.' She spoke in a high voice. Gina guessed she was probably in her mid-thirties. The man tapped his card, took his receipt and left. 'How can I help you?' She smiled through the glass.

'Ms Abidar?'

Scrunching her brows, she glanced at Gina, then at Wyre.

'Who are you?'

'DI Harte and DC Wyre. We need to have a word with you. Is there somewhere we can speak in private?'

She hurried out of her chair and out of the booth. Gina watched as she spoke to the man behind the till at the other end of the shop. He nodded. She ran back. 'Follow me through to the back. Is my son okay? Please tell me Omar isn't hurt?'

'As far as we're aware your son is fine, but we do need to speak to you about him.'

'I knew it. I just knew it!'

'Knew what?' Gina tensed inside, wondering what Ms Abidar would say.

'You've found evidence of him using my car, haven't you? You have him on camera, driving somewhere. I told him what he was doing was wrong and he promised it wouldn't happen again. But it was too late, you already knew.'

Adrenaline began pumping through Gina's veins. Omar had illegally used his mother's car and knowing how obsessed with Annabel he'd been, she wondered if the boy was the person they'd been looking for all along. Maybe he hit Jennifer that night in his mother's car before taking Annabel. Maybe Taylor saw him lurking around the house while she was there looking for Grant. Omar may have felt threatened, giving him a motive to follow her and stab her in the neck.

'Is it about the car?'

Gina's attention snapped back to the woman. 'We'll need to take a look at your car.' Any sign of damage could be used as evidence.

'Of course.' She opened the back door and led Gina down a path full of cars. 'I'm just parked on the street back here. It's the closest I can get.' She glanced up and down and ran.

'Ms Abidar.'

'My car. It's gone. He's let me down, again.' The woman stopped dead in the street. A few drops of rain began to land on her nose. She reached into her pocket and pulled out her keys. 'He must have gone home to get my spare car keys. He was meant to be at school. I even dropped him off right outside the gates.'

'Do you have any idea where he might go?'

Wyre looked at the gap where the woman was standing, where her car would have been left and she grabbed her phone, making the call to the station. They were now on the lookout for another car.

'No, he's been secretive lately. He says he has a friend called Max but I don't know anything about him or where he lives. I've never met this kid and a part of me doubted if he's real. Is he in trouble?'

'I'm afraid so. Taking a car without consent is a serious charge. We really need to speak to your son. Is there anything you can think of that might help us find him?'

She shook her head.

'What's the make and model?'

'Silver Vauxhall Corsa.' She relayed the registration number and Wyre passed that on to the team. 'Please find him. I don't want anyone to get hurt.'

Neither did Gina. With one person in hospital, another missing and one murdered, she wanted nothing more than to find the boy in one piece. 'We'll need you to come down to the station.'

'Can I have a lift?'

'Of course.' Gina smiled sympathetically. She could see that Ms Abidar was scared of what might happen. If Omar was a killer, he was dangerous. If he was a witness, one known to the murderer, he was in as much danger as Taylor was. 'We'll put every resource we have into finding your son.'

FORTY-THREE

'Guv, that's all sorted. Officers are still driving by Whittle's and the Braddocks's house. I wish we weren't so understaffed, we could keep someone posted there all day but given the staffing and overtime funding issues we have at the moment, it's not possible. They have Omar's description so are on the lookout and his mother is giving a statement now.' Wyre put her hair into a ponytail, low at the nape of her neck.

Gina turned into Redditch High School, parking in the tight visitor space. 'Great. The boy has to turn up soon. As long as we're keeping an eye on Annabel's house, we can hope that he turns up there or our officer spots the car. Right, let's speak to Miss Teller. See if we can find out more about Whittle, then we have to get to the boatyard.'

As they entered the high school reception a woman smiled. 'You must be from the police. I'll give Miss Teller a call.'

'Thank you.' Gina sat next to Wyre on one of the padded seats that had been lined up next to a window. She gazed out at the gaggle of teenage girls all dressed in netball bibs, carrying balls.

'Hi,' the petite blonde woman said as she entered. 'I'm Anita Teller.'

'Can we go somewhere more private?' The receptionist was peering over the desk.

'Of course.' Anita Teller led them both to an empty class-room. 'Here should be fine. Take a seat.'

Gina smiled. 'May we call you Anita?'

'Please do.' The woman pressed her lips together and grimaced. 'It's been a long time since I had anything to do with Tom.' Anita nervously ran her hands over her skirt.

'I know this is hard for you—'

'Look, I really wanted to forget him and move on. I'm with someone now and I have three children. I love my family and I really don't want to dredge up the past. I've never mentioned Tom to my partner, let alone told him what happened. All I wanted to do was start again when I left the school in Moseley. I wanted to forget everything and move on. It's not like I could win against a man like him.'

'A man like him?' Gina wanted to press her further.

'Yes. He's all round nasty. He really is. To think that I once thought I loved him.' She shook her head and placed her hands neatly in her lap where she began to twiddle her fingers.

'There have been other accusations against Tom Whittle. Your testimony would really help those women. We are also investigating the disappearance of another woman and Tom is on the run. You could help us bring this woman home to her daughter, who loves and misses her. She's a mother, like you. Her little girl is five.'

Anita expelled a breath. 'He's kidnapped someone?'

'At the moment we're saying our victim is missing and Tom's name has come up in our enquiries. We have evidence to prove that he was involved with her somehow. I know this is hard, but we really need your help.'

'I've been watching the news. It's Annabel Braddock, isn't

it? Before you ask, I don't know her. I saw she was a teacher so we've all been talking about her at the school. Was Tom working there too?'

Gina nodded. 'I'd appreciate it if you didn't discuss the case as we're dealing with sensitive information and we don't want to jeopardise the investigation. Our primary aim is to find Tom Whittle in the hope that he leads us to Annabel, or helps us to obtain information about her whereabouts.'

Anita sat back and the plastic chair creaked.

'Can you tell us how you know Tom Whittle, how you met him and what happened?' Wyre said as she smiled sympatheti-cally and started to make notes.

'I was twenty-three and a newly qualified teacher. He'd already been teaching for two terms at Moseley before I started. He was handsome and likeable. Within weeks he'd asked me out on a date and I really enjoyed his company. He was fun, funny even. He loved animals and he really loved his job and working with the kids. I think that's why I was drawn to him. Soon things got more serious and he wanted us to move in together but I wasn't ready. I'd barely lived on my own and I was enjoying my own space but he wasn't happy, saying that if I loved him, I'd want to be with him all the time. In the end, I moved into his and gave up the tenancy on my apartment even though it just felt wrong.' Anita stared at the wall behind Gina.

'What happened after that?'

She looked back at Gina and Wyre. 'It was all fine for a while but then, nothing I ever did was good enough. Slowly all his little jibes about how I was too messy or I didn't clean up properly, eroded my confidence. I could see what he was doing. Suddenly, I was no longer going out with friends or even seeing my parents or my sister. It was all about him or he got angry. Anyway, I had enough and left him but we worked at the same school so I had to see him every day.'

'Did you tell anyone?'

'No, I didn't want to make a fuss. I thought he'd soon get over me. We hadn't been together for too long. Time passed and I dated another guy this once. We met in a pub. Tom must have been watching as I got bombarded with texts asking me who he was and calling me a slut. That's when I realised he'd been watching me. I'd go home and close my curtains so he couldn't see in. I'd double-check that I'd locked my place up. I became scared to go out at night, just in case he was around and watching. It might sound like I was being a bit extreme but he had an intensity about him that scared me. He's obsessive and controlling. He did it in a way that I barely noticed, starting off small with things like, "Your friends have let you down. I don't know why you give them the time of day. They don't really like you that much or they wouldn't have cancelled. I love you, not like them." It was the little things. Like I said, I could see it but it was of no comfort after I moved into my own place.'

'What happened after that?'

'There was an incident. He locked us both in the changing rooms when they weren't being used. He pushed me up against the wall, saying that we were meant to be together and that I was his. Before I knew it, he had my skirt up and he...' Anita fanned her face and wiped a tear away.

'I know this is hard for you.' Gina pressed her lips together.

'It is.' She pulled a bottle of water from her bag and took a sip. 'I've tried so hard to forget, to move on. I don't want to share this with my husband and I never want my children to know.' She put the cap back on the water bottle. 'He raped me and I didn't stop it. I was stunned and it happened quickly. He kissed me after and laughed about us getting caught and having to clean up quickly. He made out it was nothing and that I'd been party to what happened. I remember being terrified and asking what he'd done to me.' She ran her fingers through her hair. 'Then he said that we should go out for dinner later that night or to the cinema, now that we were dating again. I couldn't speak. He was denying what had just happened between us and assuming that we were a couple again. I did not consent but then again, no one spoke about consent fifteen years ago like they do now. It was bizarre, it really was.'

'I'm so sorry you're having to relive all this now.' Gina could see that Anita was struggling but now they had a good picture of the man they were looking for and, in Gina's mind, he was more than capable of taking Annabel. Maybe he had charmed her at the beginning but soon after, everything went stale and maybe he had her trapped somewhere, keeping her because she no longer wanted him. Tom Whittle was sounding like a man that wouldn't take no for an answer.

Anita cleared her throat and wiped her nose. 'I confronted him, after the rape. As soon as we got out of that gym block, I told him that I'd report him. He calmly said that I'd asked him to meet there and that I'd told him how much I wanted him and that we'd made love in the changing rooms. He said that they'd sack us both for being unprofessional. Then he went on and on about how I was falsely accusing him and that everyone would know it. He'd tell them all that I'd been cornering him in the corridors asking for us to get back together, that I'd shown him my breasts on the school premises. I thought long and hard about everything. I had no bruises or scars and all I could see was my name getting tarnished. My biggest fear was that I wouldn't be believed and I'd never get another job in teaching. That was my first job and the last thing I needed was a question mark hanging over my head so I left to work here and I've never looked back. For years I hated him, I hated myself but then I met my partner and he's nothing like Tom.' She shrugged. 'That's what happened. That's everything. Am I going to have to make a statement?'

'Anita.' Gina leaned forward. 'You don't have to do anything you don't want to but another two women have come forward with accusations, another might, and another woman is missing.

If you do make a statement, it will really help us to build a case against him and stop what happened to you from happening to other women in the future.'

She opened her mouth and stared out of the window. 'I have to do this, don't I? I mean, it's the right thing to do.' Pausing, she pulled her sleeve over her hand and began picking at a loose bit of thread. 'I'll make a statement. I've kept this secret for too long. I'm ready to speak but I want to tell my partner first.'

'Of course. Would you be able to come to Cleevesford Police Station later?'

Anita nodded. 'I'll be there about seven.'

'Thank you. Can we offer you any support?'

'No. I just want to get it over with.' She stopped pulling the loose thread. 'He's a dangerous man. It's about time he got punished for what he did to me and the others. I wouldn't be one bit surprised if he had Annabel because she turned him down or dumped him. For the safety of all women, you have to find him.'

Gina tilted her head and nodded. Anita was far braver than she was in confronting her past. Gina had hidden the abuse she'd been on the receiving end of, finding it utterly humiliating to talk about. She knew just how much guts it took to do what Anita had just done.

FORTY-FOUR

Omar

Several messages flash up on my phone. Mum is livid.

Omar, the police are questioning me. They know you have my car. Please bring it back.

Where are you?

Pick up your phone!!!

Why aren't you answering???

You are in such big trouble.

Omar, are you in trouble?

I'm worried. Please call me. X

I'm in such big trouble. No way can I call her yet. I'll end up going home or worse, she'll insist on getting a taxi here to take the car or she might bring the police. I stay at the back of Annabel's house. I remain as I am, hidden.

Grant has to come back at some point. That's why Taylor was here last night. She was looking for him. I heard her calling his name. That is why I have to be here even though I'm sick of the smell of damp earth and even worse, I'm fed up that my bottom is damp from sitting on grass. When he arrives, I will confront him. I'll do it for Annabel. He is a bad person, a bad father and a bad husband. She deserves better and I want to know where she is. I can't trust the police to do a good job. From what I see, they drive past the front every half an hour or so and do stuff all apart from take a quick glance out the window.

I hear a car door slam out the front and I wonder if it's Grant. The police have only just done their rounds. If he's watching too, he'll know the coast was clear for a short while. Keeping back, I remain hidden out the back in the bushes, holding my breath as a man comes into view. I exhale as I watch as Annabel's father appears in the kitchen. The light from the cooker clock glints off the one side of his face. He stops and stares out, almost meeting my gaze. I duck and take a few deep breaths, wondering if he saw me. I lift up my head and peer back at the window and he's no longer looking out. Instead, he's grabbing a couple of toys that must belong to Cally. Soon after he vanishes out of view. Maybe he's in the hall. He'll be gone soon.

Turning my head, I glance across the field, wondering if the person who murdered Taylor is watching me. It's a dull day. The sky is one flat shade of grey with the threat of rain. I'm taken back to a moment when my mum sang a song about April showers while washing up and smiling at me. I think I must have been about five or six. Then I remember my dad joining in and it hits me for a second, how much I miss him. My loving, wonderful dad. Shivering that thought away, I stare back at the house and I can't see Annabel's dad. It looks like he's gone but then I spot his car through the side entrance. He walks down the path, towards the garage at the back of the garden.

I tread on a twig and he stops. Heart pounding, I retreat behind a tree and hold my breath. I hear him opening the garage door and clattering around. He's up to something but I don't know what as I'm stuck behind this tree. In my mind, I picture Annabel. Her kind smile lights up her face. She always has time for me and talks to me. Everyone else at the school is mean. I'm sick of the kids picking on me because my father wasn't born in this country, because my mother is poor and I don't have branded trainers, because I'm good at maths. The list goes on. They just love to pick on me. That's why I have this burning need to prove myself. I need to find Annabel, rescue her from her horrible husband and be the person to bring her home. I need people to see that I care, that I'm kind, that I'm a good person. Maybe they'll leave me alone then. More than anything, I love Annabel and I need her to see that I care.

Swallowing, I close my eyes. She could never love a kid she teaches. I understand the law and I understand who I am and who she is, but I care. I will help her because I love her, then I will leave her alone and simply work hard at school.

I think of my mum talking to the police. Everything is a mess. They will know that I have her car and they'll be on the lookout for it. Snatching my phone out of my pocket, I turn it off and remove the battery. This is what they do in films, then they stamp on their phones or throw them in the river. I won't do that, though. I need this phone and my mum can't afford another.

Annabel's father continues to rummage. I place the phone and battery in my bag. No one can trace me. I am not giving myself up or going home until I find Annabel. I need everyone to know that I didn't hurt Taylor and that I had nothing to do with taking Annabel or running over the other woman. Now my mum will be talking to the police and they will know I use her car, they'll think it was me.

The noise in the garage has stopped and I wonder if Annabel's dad has gone. Peering around the tree, I look around but I can't see him. The car is still there but he is no longer in the garden. He's not in the kitchen. My gaze moves up. He's not in Cally's bedroom or the bathroom. Where is he? For a second, I think I spot a person by his car alongside the house but I might be mistaken. It is more of a shadow.

White-hot pain flashes through the back of my head and my vision blurs. I go to turn around to see who has just attacked me but it's too late. The metal bar comes down again and the sky above begins to whirl until I fall to the ground with a sickening thud.

I failed to save Annabel and now I'm going to die.

FORTY-FIVE

As Gina drove to the boatyard, she listened to Wyre discussing their progress on the phone with O'Connor and she ended the call. The afternoon dullness left a chill in the air. 'Have they conducted the post-mortem on Taylor?'

Wyre nodded. 'Yes, O'Connor attended. It was confirmed that the stab wound to her neck killed her and the time at which she died was around nine. All that has done is confirm what we were told last night. They also found a trace of amphetamine on her clothing. We won't know until all the tests come back if she was using. We know how long the tox report can take.'

Gina rolled her eyes. 'Weeks. Too long to help us right now but it's a link to Grant. Either she'd been using or had been close to him recently. It still puts him in the frame for her murder. He was her lover, he's on the run and he had opportunity to take Annabel and run over Jennifer. Whittle was Taylor's teacher when she was at Cleevesford High. Given his track record, there's an association there. Then we have the missing boy, Omar Abidar. No sign of him and he wasn't answering his phone. That's three suspects and we can't find any of them with all the resources we have.' She swallowed. 'It's odd that Grant hasn't turned up at all. His car should have shown up somewhere by now.'

'Totally.'

'I'm hoping that we get a leg-up on the investigation from the boatyard. We need to find *Freedom*. It's still Grant's boat. Whoever owns the boatyard would know what had happened to it.'

'Here we are.'

Gina indicated and pulled into the boatyard. There looked to be about fifty boats on stands, all out of the water, covered in thick tarpaulin. 'We'll never spot *Freedom* here. They're all covered up.' She drove towards the river. Several weeping willows lined the road, that's when she spotted a man with a jet wash, hosing down a huge luxurious looking cruiser. Earphones in, he didn't even look in their direction. Gina stepped out of the car, closely followed by Wyre. 'Excuse me,' she called but the man carried on washing the boat and humming to whatever he was listening to. His long grey hair bounced as he danced. She also knew exactly why he hadn't been answering the phone. Gina tapped him on the shoulder and he snatched his earphones, pulling them down and letting the buds dangle.

'You scared the life out of me.'

'Sorry.' Gina smiled and stepped back out of the puddle. 'I tried to call you but—'

'Yeah, my fault.' He pointed to his earphones and smiled. 'What can I do for you?'

'I'm DI Harte and this is DC Wyre. We need to speak to you about one of the boats that you store here.'

He scrunched up his red nose. 'Why would you want to speak to me? I haven't seen any unusual activity. Which boat do you want to know about?'

'It's called *Freedom*?' Gina watched as the man paused in thought.

'Oh, that old thing. I keep calling the owner as it's on its last legs. Damn thing is falling apart through neglect. I keep it in the next field along with the rest of the old scrap that people keep paying me to house. The guy didn't even want it cleaned properly but he kept paying me to keep it here so that's what I did.' He paused and placed the jet wash on the tarmac. 'What do the police want with that old boat? I know it's not in the water as the owners normally ask me to get the boats in the river for them, besides it's trapped in by other boats. They wouldn't be able to just come here and take it.'

'We have reason to believe that it may have been involved in a crime. Can you show it to us?'

'I don't like doing this. Should I call the owner?'

'The owner, Grant Braddock, is missing and we were told he has a boat. We are concerned for his and his wife's welfare.'

'In that case, follow me.' He lit up a cigarette as he led them past the riverside house and onto a field. The smoke he puffed out trailed under Gina's nose as she followed him. 'This is the premium area. Tarmacked, watched by CCTV.' He sucked on the cigarette.

'*Freedom* is over here?' Wyre scrunched her brow.

The man laughed. 'You're going to wish you wore your wellies. *Freedom* is on the field. That's the budget section. There is no CCTV. It has a dirt track entrance and although it is in a fenced area, I can't guarantee the safety of the boats and I charge accordingly. *Freedom* had been left on tarmac but the owner stopped paying, saying he couldn't afford it any more so I moved it until he paid his debt. He's behind with his payments by about three months. He said he was coming into some money, that he'd have his boat cleaned and restored soon. I guess that's not happening now.'

Gina stepped into the sludgy field, the coldness of the mud splashing her ankles and dirtying the hem of her trousers. Before they proceeded any further, she and Wyre bent over and rolled theirs up. The man didn't seem to care about muddying his.

'Told you. See in the far corner, by the trees.'

Gina looked up and continued squelching on. 'Yes.'

'That is *Freedom*. Wait.' He stared at the boat. 'The tarpaulin has been removed. Someone's been here.'

Gina began to run as she heard a bang coming from the old boat. Grant had to be keeping Annabel there, it made sense. All this time he'd kept her on a boat. Just beyond the trees, she saw a silver Mercedes, Grant's other car. 'Stand back, sir,' she called to the man. 'Call for backup.'

Wyre nodded.

The last thing Gina wanted was a hostage situation. She imagined Grant, desperate on drugs, terrorising his wife.

FORTY-SIX

Omar

I press my fingers against the sore on my head and it's sticky. If only I'd answered the phone when my mum had called. The police would have come to get me and I'd be at the station trying to explain everything. That sounds bad, but nothing is as bad as where I am now, except death.

I'm trapped in a sloped cupboard. The door is wooden but appears to be locked and I can't see a thing. I bang and bang against the door.

My head throbs and I don't know how long I've been here. Reaching down, I feel the sores on my arms, long and stinging, like I've been dragged across a rough path. Have I been in a car? I try to recall the moments before my attack. Everything went dark and it was fast. I remember falling to the ground and the searing pain as I was hit. Next thing I know, I'm here. I didn't see who did it. All I saw was the glint on the crowbar.

I saw Annabel's dad. It had to be him. He must have hit me

and brought me to this place as there was no one else around. Why would he do this to me? I bang again but I have no strength. The sound is dull. I think he's put something heavy against the door so that I can't get out. I'm not tied up which I'm thankful for. I've been ditched here.

Panic fills me and my chest tightens. What if he's leaving the door closed until I die? I stare around but for what I can see, my eyes may as well be shut. This nothingness is the last thing I'm going to see before I perish.

I don't want to die. I want to prove to my mum and everyone that I am good. I want to redeem myself in her eyes. This wasn't supposed to happen. I was supposed to find Annabel and bring her home to her daughter. My face was going to be on the news for all the right reasons when I became the hero. All those kids who pick on me, they were going to like me and see how brave I was. My mum has always loved me but I wanted her to see that I could be the man that Dad was. Dad was fearless; he fought fires for a living. It doesn't get more heroic but that's what killed him. He was loved by all and my mother worshipped the ground he walked on. He was the same with her. He loved her. Now, all I am is a loser; a loser who was about to die in the shadow of my hero father.

All I wanted was for people to love me, to be proud of me, to want to be my friend or girlfriend. Sad? Maybe. But, this tiny dark room is sadder. This is where my story ends. I wish I'd got to explain to my mum why I'd taken her car. I wasn't joyriding this time, I was trying to save Annabel. I needed it.

I flinch as I hear a bang. Someone is running above me. I'm under a flight of stairs. I bang and shout, that's when my captor speaks.

'No one is coming for you.' That's all he says.

FORTY-SEVEN

Half-slipping in the mud, half-running, Gina reached the boat.

'Guv, we should wait for backup to arrive?'

A spec of rain landed on Gina's nose as she turned back to Wyre. 'What if he has Annabel in there?'

'He might hurt her.'

'I know, I know. Because of that, it might be best if we try to coax him out without the cavalry being here.' If Gina could get her feet out of the sludge easily, she'd have paced while she contemplated her next move. Go in or wait for help? Go in. She stepped closer, holding her index finger to her lips, and whispered to the boatyard man to stay far back. 'Grant, Annabel, are you in there?'

She flinched as one loud bang came from inside. 'Annabel?'

No response. The only sound they could hear were the magpies squawking in a line on a branch above.

A short stepladder led up to the boat. Gina stepped onto the bottom rung and began her ascent. As the boat's living quarters came into view, she could see that the brown and yellow curtains were closed. Moss and slime coated the bottom of the boat and there were footprints. It looked like someone had been pulled through the mess, leaving green and brown lines behind. Gina went to open the door but it was locked. She pushed slightly and it rattled. She knew if she slammed into it, it would open.

'Guv, can you see anything?' Wyre's head appeared over the side.

'I'm going to have to try smashing it down.' She leaned against the door. 'Police, open up.'

The person inside banged again.

'Someone's trapped in there.' Gina stepped back and with all her weight, she pounded the door. Without too much effort, the ancient door flew open to reveal the living quarters. Several dirty pans and plates lay on the tiny bit of Formica worktop. 'Police.' Another bang came from the knocked together box in front of her. It was almost as tall as she was and it was made of rough, heavy, wooden sheets that had been carelessly nailed together. Several slide locks had been fixed to the door, keeping whoever was in there contained. She gritted her teeth as she moved the heavy weights from in front of it and slid all the locks in turn. She almost fell back when she saw the man bound and gagged, the stench of bodily fluids almost knocking her sick. His eyes, starkly staring at her in fear, were red rimmed and bruised. 'It's okay, police.' She edged into the small space slowly and untied his wrists. 'Grant.'

He was trying to speak. She untied the gag and he spat a hunk of dirty blood splattered material onto the wood.

'Where's Annabel?' she asked him.

He scrunched his eyes as he adjusted to the light streaming through the door. 'I don't know. I had a message from her to meet me and the next thing I knew I woke up here.' He opened his mouth, further breaking the tender skin at the corners of his mouth.

'No messages were sent to your phone.' She knew they'd

requested ongoing data from his phone and nothing of any help had been found.

'I have a burner phone.'

Gina thought of the drugs that they'd found at his house. Of course he had a burner phone. People like him always did. The man leaned forward and began untying himself. 'Can you call an ambulance? We need to get him checked out.' Wyre nodded and pulled her phone out.

As he moved, his knees cracked and crunched. He let out a little cry of pain. 'I don't need an ambulance. I'm okay. I just need to get out of this hellhole and walk around for a few minutes.' He swayed a little as he tried to shuffle out of the box, grabbing onto the worktop to pull himself up. His hand slipped and he almost landed nose first into the door. 'Woah.' He held his head and traced the dried blood down his cheek. 'Someone whacked me over the head and I think I was drugged.'

'Do you know who would do this to you?'

'No.'

'Grant Braddock, I'm arresting you for possession with intent to supply a class B drug. You do not have to say anything, but it may harm your defence if you do not mention when questioned something which you later rely on in court. Anything you do say may be given in evidence.' She looked at him; weak, thirsty and dazed. She didn't even go for her handcuffs. He wouldn't get bail either, after running from them.

'What, I'm the victim here. Someone hit me, drugged me and locked me up. You should be arresting them.' He held his head and flinched.

'After you've been checked out, if you get the all clear, we'll head back to the station where we will question you about that.' Gina heard the sirens in the distance. Assistance was on its way. All Gina knew was that she needed him in an interview room as soon as possible. She had to know why he had bloodied tissues in the bin at the cabin that had Jennifer's blood on them. She glanced back into the little wooden room and she recoiled at the smell of human waste. Traces of blood and dirt were everywhere.

Wyre stepped into the cabin. 'Ambulance is here, guv.' She let out a cough and held her nose before stepping just outside again.

Gina nodded at the steps and looked at Grant. 'Are you capable of getting out of the boat and down the ladder or do you need help?'

He waved his hand as if dismissing her. 'I can do it myself.' He stumbled out, cocked his leg over the barrier and stepped onto the ladder. PC Kapoor was ready and waiting to steady him, along with a paramedic who took him aside. From what Gina could see, Grant had only suffered from superficial injuries. They'd have him cleaned up in no time. She glanced into the boat. 'I wonder if Annabel was here. Call Bernard and the team. We need forensics to scale this place and cordon off the surrounding area, please?'

Wyre nodded. 'On it, guv.' She pulled her phone from her pocket and held it to her ear.

Gina stepped over the railing and onto the ladder. Once down, she headed over to where Grant was being tended to. 'How is he?' She pulled a few stray strands of her hair from the side of her mouth.

'We'll be taking him in as he's had a blow to the head but he's okay to speak if you want to follow.'

'I don't need to go to hospital.' He pushed the paramedic's hand out of the way as he reached for the wound on his head. 'I'm not going to hospital. There. I'll make it easy for you. I'm refusing treatment because I'm fine.' He scrunched his brow and swayed a little. 'Actually, I will get checked out but as soon as I'm done, I'm leaving. I'm not staying there. Can I see my daughter?'

Gina shook her head. 'Not yet. She's safe with your father-in-law.'

'Whatever.'

Turning to PC Kapoor, she said, 'Would you go with him in the ambulance? We'll meet you back at the station.'

'Yes, guv.'

Gina only hoped that Grant could tell them something that would lead them to Annabel. She glanced at the boat one more time. That's when she spotted the rough-looking symbol, written in the muck on the bottom of the boat with a full stop at the end. The perfect fingerprint. 'That's the pi symbol.' Gina pointed and Wyre ran over.

'Yes. Takes me back to geometry at school.'

'Annabel's left us a sign. She's telling us that she was here.' Her mind flitted back to Evan's pi fridge magnet, the one that Seth had given him. 'Have we contacted her brother-in-law, Seth Braddock, yet?'

'No, guv. Jacob said he didn't answer. He was trying to contact the university.'

Gina held her head with both hands. If only they'd known about the boat earlier. Whoever did this had now moved her, leaving Grant where Annabel once was.

FORTY-EIGHT

Grant sat upright on the plastic chair, opposite Gina and Wyre in the interview room. Evening was closing in. His clothes had been bagged and sent to the lab. The wound on his head had been dressed and cleaned at the hospital before he'd been discharged and brought to the station. His bald solicitor sat bolt upright, next to his client, his liver-spotted hand placed on a notebook.

Grant sipped from the can of pop that he'd been given and belched. 'I've never been so thirsty in my life but I gather that's not what you want to talk to me about.'

Gina shook her head. The tape had been rolling for a minute now. It was time to question Grant. 'Four thousand eight hundred pounds cash and fourteen small bags of amphetamine sulphate were found at your home. Were you supplying?'

'We're not having a warm-up then.'

'Your wife is missing, Mr Braddock, and your activities could be the connection we're looking for. We don't have time for small talk.'

'Touché. The drugs were for personal use.'

Gina shook her head. 'There was far too much to be classed as personal. Did the cash come from the sale of drugs?'

Grant shrugged. 'No comment.'

'Where is your burner phone?'

He shrugged again. 'The arsehole who locked me in the boat obviously took it if you didn't find it.'

Gina had called forensics and they had confirmed that no phone was found at the scene or in the surrounding area. 'Did you see who locked you in the boat?'

'No. I got hit and I think they injected me with something that sent me to sleep. At a guess and given the weird trippy dreams I had, I'd say it was ketamine. The next thing I knew, I'd woken up where you found me and I was tied up. All I could do was kick with both feet.'

'When did you get attacked?'

'Last night, about eleven.'

'What were you doing at the boat at that time?' Gina leaned forward, her gaze not leaving his. He would have had opportunity to murder Taylor.

'I got a message from Annabel.'

'Annabel had the number of your burner phone?'

He nodded. 'I told her it was my work phone. She called me on it when I didn't answer my other phone, as did a lot of people. My brother, my friends. It wasn't a secret number.'

'What did the message say?'

'It said that she was in huge trouble and she needed my help. I know we haven't had the best relationship but she's the mother of my child. There was no way I wouldn't meet her if she needed help. I had it in my head that someone was threatening her, someone who ran her and her friend over and I wanted to help her. It's obvious now. Whoever did this to me was waiting at the boat pretending to be her. The message came up from an unknown number. They knew I'd go.'

'Where have you been since we saw you at the café?' Gina knew the man had to have been staying somewhere local.

'Sleeping rough about five minutes from here, in a shed on Langley Road. I stayed there, not knowing what to do or where to go. I had Taylor calling me all the time on the burner and I knew you lot were after me. Taylor laid low too. I'm sure she mentioned that she'd been staying with one of her doped-up friends but I don't know who. She wouldn't have gone back to her aunt's place. She was always moaning that the woman was constantly on her back and letting herself into the annexe. I kept out of the way because I wanted to find a way of clearing my name before I came to you. I knew you'd find the drugs and I knew you'd blame me for Annabel going missing. When I got that message, I hoped that everything would get sorted; that Annabel would be okay and we could start thinking about getting back to whatever normal we could manage.'

'Do you have any enemies?'

'No.'

'Do you owe anyone any money? Maybe a drug dealer?'

'No.' He scrunched his brow. 'I only owe the boatyard. I was meant to pay for the storage on the boat. I'd been going through a bad period with money.'

'How so?' Gina placed her hands together on the table and Wyre leaned back in the chair.

'It was stupid. I wanted nice things like anyone else does. Nice clothes, good shoes. I wanted to go out, have a boat and get my Merc all done up.' He paused. 'That's not all true. I...' He blew out slowly and pressed his lips together for a few seconds. 'I have a drug problem. Most of our money went on drugs. One lie to my wife led to another, until it felt like my whole life was a lie. I take speed.' He began to tap his fingers on the table. 'It started off quite innocent. I just wanted to be able to perform better and run faster, feel less sluggish. A guy at the gym told me that he knew what would help. He introduced me to speed.

Fixed me up with his dealer and that was the start of it. Annabel and I had normal jobs, jobs that paid the mortgage, bought a few days out and an annual family holiday. We had our daughter to bring up. There was never much money left so I ended up drawing money with my credit card to buy drugs.'

'Did you deal to pay for the drugs?'

'No comment.' It was obvious to Gina that Grant was going no comment on all lines of questioning that opened up discussions as to whether he was dealing.

'What happened after that?'

'I got fitter and faster but I also craved more highs. That's when I really started to feel good about myself. I remember that Taylor had mentioned how fit I was looking. How pathetic does that sound? What a cliché.' He placed his head in his shaky hands. 'I enjoyed the attention. I mean, Taylor is fun, she's fit, she was my escape from the trappings of family life but she wants more than I can give her. I stupidly said that I'd leave Annabel for her, I promised her, but I didn't want to. Taylor was a fling, nothing more. I regret ever starting anything with her. She's become clingier and goes on about us moving in together. I'm going to have to let her down gently, I suppose. She's not a bad person. I know I'm the one to blame.'

Gina knew then that Grant had no idea that Taylor had been murdered. Either that or he was a brilliant actor. 'I'm really sorry to have to tell you this, but Taylor was murdered last night.'

He flung his torso back and held the palm of his hand on his forehead as he exhaled. 'It's all my fault. I should never have started anything with her. Whoever has Annabel and has killed Taylor, they're trying to get to me.' He gripped the edge of the table, his knuckles white.

'Which takes us back to the drugs. Who was supplying you?'

'No comment.'

'Mr Braddock, your wife is in serious danger. Who is your supplier?'

He remained silent.

'For the tape, Mr Braddock isn't replying. Where were you on the night that Annabel was taken?'

'At the cabin, with Taylor.'

'She couldn't verify that you were there all night. She said she was really drunk and went to bed and that you stayed in the living room.'

'I didn't go anywhere. I watched TV.'

'What did you watch?'

He stared blankly at the wall behind Gina with his mouth open before his attention came back to her. 'I can't remember. I was tired. Maybe I fell asleep.'

'Why did we find bloodied tissues in the bin on the decking?'

He swallowed. 'I cut myself on the cap of a beer bottle while I was unscrewing it.'

'The blood belonged to the victim of a hit-and-run. It belonged to Jennifer Bailey, the friend that Annabel was with on the night she disappeared. Those bloodied tissues place you at the scene. That's the only way they could have ended up in the bin at the cabin.' Gina leaned back, her stare intense. They had caught Grant Braddock out on a huge lie. His feet began to tap erratically on the floor. She wondered how long he'd last before his need for drugs would incapacitate him. They were racing against the clock for so many reasons now; the biggest being Annabel. 'We're looking at very serious charges here. Kidnapping and false imprisonment of your wife; attempted murder of Jennifer Bailey. I think you need to start telling the truth.'

'I feel sick. I need a break.'

Gina glanced at the solicitor, who spoke up. 'I request that my client has a break.'

'Granted. We'll take five minutes.' Gina tidied the case papers into a pile while Wyre spoke for the tape before stopping it.

She hurried out to Briggs who had been watching from behind the two-way mirror. A part of her wished that she didn't have to talk to him given that he wanted to speak to her. She didn't want to hear, not now. 'He left Jennifer in the road to die. Whatever happened, he's guilty of that and now he's lying through his teeth. If he's lying about that, what else is he lying about?' Keeping calm was going to be hard. She thought of what Jacob was going through, of him and Jennifer losing the baby they'd only just both found out they were having and Jennifer not knowing anything that had been happening while she lay in an induced coma, fighting for her life. Grant Braddock calling an ambulance straight away may have made all the difference but instead he'd left her there to die.

'We've had an update from forensics.' Briggs cleared his throat.

'What is it?'

'There was a keyring left at the hit-and-run scene, amongst all the fancy cocktail sticks. A print has been lifted but it doesn't belong to Annabel or Jennifer and we don't have a match on the system. This was dropped by someone else who was there at the time as it was on top of their items.'

FORTY-NINE

Annabel

It's a weird feeling, being drugged over and over. I have to keep thinking my name as if I'm saying it aloud in my head. Annabel – that's who I am.

As for my captor, it's not Grant. Grant didn't take me to the boat and leave me there. I wish it had been Grant. I could have reasoned with him. I heard Grant groaning in pain last night, just as I thought I might get my own freedom back but it wasn't meant to be.

Trying to get off a boat while in a woozy haze isn't easy. He cut the ties from my hands and feet so that I could get down but all the while, I felt the crowbar touching my shoulder. I knew I needed to leave a sign that I'd been at the boat and the only thing I had time to do was leave the pi symbol on the bottom as I climbed down the ladder, finishing it with a full fingerprint. My signature.

Throughout, he made sure I knew the knife was in his

pocket and he'd use either that or the crowbar. Grant is as good as dead. I know that now. He won't let Grant live and he even told me he was going to go back and finish him off. This man thinks he loves me, but this isn't love. He took me. He imprisoned me and now I'm once again bound and tied but in the boot of a car. I know where he's taking me. All this because I turned him down. My marriage is over, I know that, but I wanted the chance to find myself, to be on my own. I was going to give Grant the chance to get clean and come back to be the best father he could be and hope that the nasty things he said and did were just because of the drugs. Even though he's been an awful husband, I'm struggling to hate him. Maybe it's because I don't love him or maybe I pity him. He lied about so much. He thought I didn't know about his stash of drugs and money but I did. I also knew his other phone wasn't a work phone. He must have thought I was stupid. As if his company would have given him such an old basic phone. There's no way he could work on that.

Taylor thought I had no idea what was going on but I had my suspicions before I found that note. A part of me couldn't believe that the girl I once taught at high school was sleeping with my husband. The thought of them having sex turns my stomach, even now. I could smell her on his bedsheets in the spare room. They'd been in there together while I was at work. Talking to Jen had cleared my head. I was ready to confront him.

I now know that Taylor has been murdered. My captor told me. She hurt me deeply but there was no way she deserved what she got. Grant is trapped in *Freedom*. Taylor has been stabbed and now my captor wants Cally. That hurts more than anything else. My hands quiver as I struggle fruitlessly with my binds. Even if I was able to step out of the car boot and run, I know I'd fall. I'm weak and nauseous.

An image of my little girl fills my mind and the thought that the person who put me here is now going for her makes me sick to the stomach. I'm her mother. She grew in my womb. I stroked my belly and sang to her in the hope that she would know how loved and wanted she was. The thought of the little person I pushed from my body being scared, hurt, or worse is more than I can bear.

I try to kick again but this time, someone has heard me.

It's him. Now that I know who I'm up against, I feel worse. Everything about this is worse than I'd ever imagined it could be. Both mine and my little girl's lives are over.

FIFTY

The tape was rolling again. 'Feeling better?'

Grant kept sipping water from the paper cup in front of him, his twitchy fingers getting worse. 'Not really but I'm okay to go on. I just want this over with.'

'How did the tissues with Jennifer Bailey's blood get into your cabin bin?'

Shiny beads of perspiration formed at his forehead before dribbling down the side of his face. He wiped them away with his sleeve. 'I was there.'

'And you crashed into Jennifer Bailey and took your wife, Annabel Braddock.'

'No.' He slammed his hand on the desk.

'You had a tracker on your wife's phone. You'd know exactly where she was.'

'Of course. You know it all, don't you? I don't know why you're asking me if you know everything. I was there, okay? But I didn't take my wife and I didn't run anyone over. You have my car. It was left at the gym. I didn't crash into anyone.'

Gina stared at him, hoping a moment's silence would crack him further. His Mercedes had been parked near the boatyard and it did have a dent in it. He was lying again. That car was now with forensics and there had been signs of a struggle and blood in the boot. 'Tell me what happened then, from the beginning.'

He bit his lip and continued, 'I'd been with Taylor at the cabin all day. We were meant to stay for the weekend but something snapped in me. I felt like I shouldn't be there and I didn't want to be there with her. It was like hanging out with a teenager and all I wanted was the comfort of home. She was wasted and I was finding it annoying so we bickered a bit and she stormed off into the bedroom a bit worse for wear.'

'Worse for wear?'

'Plastered. Drunk. She'd thrown up a couple of times. Once on the other cabin's doorstep. The people staying there were really fed up with her and her music and I was getting embarrassed. It hit home when the woman said that my daughter was causing a nuisance. I knew I'd made the biggest mistake of my life by making her all those stupid promises about us being together, moving into a place of our own. I wanted out.' He played with his fingers, linking and unlinking them.

'And.'

'I got in my car and drove away. All I wanted was for all the noise and chaos to stop for a minute. I parked up on the roadside and sat there. Before long, I was drawn to my phone. I missed home and I knew Annabel was out with Jennifer so I checked Instagram. She hadn't put any photos up. It was then that I used the app. I wanted to know where she was and I know it was wrong but I could see that she was on Cleevesford High Street. I knew which route she'd take home, it was the one we'd taken on foot many times. I headed that way in the hope that I could give them a lift back to the house and go back home. Even though I was in the spare room, it was better than staying for a minute longer with Taylor. When I got there, I saw Jennifer in the road bleeding. I pulled up, ran out and began dabbing at her with some tissues I had in my car, then I panicked. I thought she was already dead so I got back in my car and drove away.'

'Which car were you driving?'

'My Volvo. I haven't used the Merc in ages.'

Gina felt her stomach clenching. 'You didn't think to call an ambulance?'

'I thought she was dead. I had blood on my hands. I'd had one beer at the cabin. I wasn't over the limit but still. It was stupid and I panicked.'

'And where did you go after that?'

'Back to the cabin. I went out on the decking, disposed of the tissues in the bin and cleaned myself in the hot tub. After about an hour, I left and stayed in my car. I thought and thought about what I should do, then I decided to act as if nothing had happened. I normally go to the gym on Sunday mornings and I had my gym bag in the car. I went to the gym. I...' He went silent and remained still with his mouth open.

'You what?'

Wyre sat back as they waited for him to continue.

'I heard on the news that Annabel was missing. I heard about the hit-and-run and I had to get out. That's when I knew you were looking for me too. I regretted being at the scene and not calling it in and I knew I was in trouble. After pacing the streets for a while, I then went to the café to grab a coffee and think. Then I saw you lot turn up so I ran. Eventually I escaped over the back gardens on Langley Road. That's when I found the open shed. I went in and I stayed there, too scared to come out.'

'How did you get back to the boatyard, to respond to the message that you thought was from Annabel?'

'I had cash on me so I called a taxi. The taxi dropped me off by Bidford Bridge. I walked the rest of the way. I didn't know whether the driver might recognise me at a later point and I didn't want him to know exactly where I was going. It took me about twenty minutes to walk the rest of the way, along the river. When I approached *Freedom*, my boat, I kept calling Annabel in the dark but she didn't answer. Next thing I know I'd been struck and then I woke up in that box. Everything after was a drugged-up haze.'

'Who knew you had a boat and who knew where it was?'

'Everyone. My friends, my brother. Annabel's friends, her family, all my colleagues, people at the pub. She probably told that teacher she was having it away with at the school. Her dad never approved of the boat but he knew where I kept it.'

'That's a long list. We found your car at the boatyard. It has a dent in the bonnet consistent with the injuries that Jennifer Bailey has received. There is a smear of blood on the car, we will soon know if it's a match to her blood. It's looking highly likely that the vehicle you kept in your garage was used to hit Jennifer. We also found traces of blood in the boot.'

'What! I told you, I haven't used that car for months. Someone else had to have been driving it. It wasn't me. Check with the taxi company. I got dropped off in a taxi. Wait. The driver asked me if I had a good night and he asked me where I'd been. I snapped at him, telling him to mind his own business. Rude, I know. But he'll remember me because of that.'

'What taxi firm did you use?'

'Cleevesford Private Hire. There was a sticker on the door. Check with them.'

Gina nodded to Wyre to make a note although she knew Briggs was behind the glass. He'd already have someone checking that out as they spoke. 'We will. Moving on to the night of Taylor's murder. Where were you between eight and nine on Monday night?'

'I was already in a taxi, heading to Bidford. Just check out the taxi. There has to be CCTV on the high street. I was around that area on and off for most of the evening. Taylor did call me. She said she was going to my house to see if I was there.

She was fed up of hiding out with her friend. She even had the nerve to accuse me of being guilty of the hit-and-run. I told her to stop being stupid and leave me alone to think, then I hung up. I should have met up with her, then all this wouldn't have happened.' He scratched his chin and began nervously tapping the side of his head, then he shivered. 'I swear on my little girl's life, I had no idea she had been murdered until you told me.'

'Would Taylor have had access to your other car and the keys?'

'She had keys and access to the whole house. She was our childminder, so, yes.'

'Could she have given them to someone else?' Gina knew Taylor hadn't driven the car on the night of Annabel's hit-and-run.

'I know she had the occasional friend over while looking after Cally. We never minded her doing that. None that I know offhand. My father-in-law had access to the whole house and he hates me. Have you wondered if he's setting me up? Maybe he and Annabel are having one big laugh at all of us right now as they frame me for her kidnapping.'

'What size shoes do you wear?'

'Eleven.'

'Do you recognise this?' Gina scrolled to the photo of the raspberry keyring that Briggs had forwarded to her.

'Nah.' He barely gave it a proper look.

Gina sighed. The whole line of questioning was getting bizarre with talks of Annabel setting him up. 'Do you recognise the name Thomas Whittle?'

Grant's face went white. 'I think I'm going to be sick.' He stood up and ran out the door.

'My client is clearly not up to answering any more questions. He's told you he has a drug problem and I'm requesting that he gets to speak to a doctor.'

'But we haven't finished.' Gina ran her hands through her

tangled hair and leaned back. 'Interview terminated at nineteen fourteen.'

Wyre stood. 'I'll go and see how he is.'

As the solicitor followed Wyre to find Grant, Briggs entered. 'We've checked with the taxi firm. They have cameras in their vehicles. When I sent them his description, they were able to confirm that he was indeed in a taxi when he said he was.'

'He didn't kill Taylor and he didn't drive his car to the boat-yard on that night. We need whoever is wearing those size tens. He was locked in that boat from the outside. He couldn't have locked himself in. He could have caused his own injuries. He could have left his car there but the container in the boat was locked from the outside. He's telling the truth about being placed there. Just to dot the i's and cross the t's, we need to find out which shed he's been hiding in on Langley Road.'

Briggs leaned against the door. 'Any news on Tom Whittle?'

Gina shook her head. 'No, and he's just become our number one suspect. He hasn't been back to his house. He hasn't used his cash cards or car. It's like he too has disappeared.' She flicked through the notes. 'After searching his house, we can also conclude that he wears size ten shoes.'

'We should get his face out there. I'll prepare a press release.'

'Maybe he was using Grant's other car. It's possible that he could have got the keys off Annabel. Maybe he visited their house at one point and swiped a spare set. We really need to put a rush on forensics. We need to do background checks on Annabel's father, the neighbour, and the rest of their families too. Everyone who had access to the Braddocks's house is a suspect, including Omar Abidar. He's been watching their home. If he hasn't taken Annabel there's a good chance he's seen something. We need him found. How hard can it be to find a kid? He's driving around in a stolen car, for heaven's sake.'

'Guv.' O'Connor burst through the door. 'We've found Nina Abidar's car. It's been badly parked, half-blocking delivery access to one of the businesses on the industrial estate.'

'That news couldn't have come at a better time. Let's hope that the lad isn't too far away from the car.'

FIFTY-ONE

Pulling up in the dark, Gina spotted Nina Abidar's silver Corsa parked badly, outside an electroplating company. PC Smith was parked on the opposite side of the road and Wyre had followed in her own car. Apart from the police team, it looked like all the workers had gone home as the road was empty.

'Guv.' Wyre tapped on the window and smiled.

Gina stepped out and straightened up her jacket. 'So this is where Omar left the vehicle. It's only a short walk away to Annabel's house.' She peered through the driver's window, the inside of the car fully lit up by the street light. The front was clean and tidy. She glanced into the back and saw two black shoes on the floor and a scrunched up uniform on the back seat. 'Looks like he changed out of his school clothes in the car.' She squinted to see the size on the bottom of one of the shoes but there was no size marked on it.

Wyre leaned in for a look.

'Hey, Smith,' Gina called.

The uniformed officer smiled. 'Guv?'

'Put an urgent call out for officers to head to the Braddocks's house. We know that Omar has been watching Annabel. He probably saw that we've been regularly driving by so left his mother's car here and walked. Actually, hold that. I don't want him scared off by lights and uniforms if he is loitering around there. Wyre and I will head over in a minute. We'll walk down. We're not in uniform so that shouldn't alarm him but be ready on standby with backup.'

'I'll get that sorted now.' Smith turned away and began to radio base.

'Will anyone be moving that thing, only it made one of our deliveries awkward earlier? The lorry had to come in through the front and load everything off in the visitor spaces. Not good. Is it stolen? It looks like someone has abandoned that car.' The short bald man loosened his tie.

She had to agree. It was parked halfway across the delivery entrance and half in the road. She pictured Omar driving with no license. Maybe he'd mastered his mum's automatic well enough to blend in on the roads but parking was another matter. 'Do you know when the car arrived?'

'No. All I do know is that whoever parked up came too late to get a safe space on the road. It gets busy here. There's talk of a park and ride system to stop idiots parking like this.' The man pointed his stubby index finger at the car.

'Do you have CCTV?'

'Only that which covers the perimeter of my units. It doesn't cover the road.'

In her mind, Gina knew that Omar could have been parked here all day.

'Will you be getting rid of it? I have more deliveries in the morning and I could do without a repeat of today.'

'Guv.' Wyre beckoned her over.

'Excuse me. Yes, we'll get the car towed away shortly.' The car was now evidence.

'Thank you. I'm working for the next hour if you need me. Just go to reception and ring the buzzer.' The man scurried off.

Gina nodded and smiled as she hurried over to Wyre. 'What have you found?'

Wyre bent down and shone her torch on the front of the car. 'Bumper damage and slight denting to the edge of the bonnet.'

'Smith, could you please get this car taken away for forensics to examine when you have a moment? It looks like it's been bumped.' She turned back to Wyre. 'It's looking likely that Grant Braddock's Mercedes was used to run Jennifer over but there's nothing like being certain. Let's go and look for the boy.'

Several minutes later they arrived at the road where the Braddocks lived. 'That line of hedges and trees on the opposite side of the road is perfect for hiding out.' Gina hurried across the road with Wyre close behind. She spotted an area of flattened grass and just behind it, layer upon layer of bike tracks were etched into the mud. She glanced into the darkness beyond then turned on her torch. A rabbit hopped in the middle of the field.

'It looks like someone's been here.'

'We'll get forensics to check this area out. Let's go around the back of the row. See if he's there.' They followed the frontage until they reached the dark path that led to the back gardens. Wyre held the torch as they walked on the uneven tarmac. Gina nearly tripped on a hunk of weeds that had burst through the pavement.

Wyre touched Gina's arm and whispered, 'Wait. I heard something.'

They turned left at the end of the back gardens, again they could only see trees and hedges and there was no street lighting. Wyre flashed the torch ahead.

'Omar,' Gina called, but there was no response. 'Your mum is worried about you.'

She could now see the back of the Braddocks's house. Something shiny caught her eye. 'What's that?'

Wyre stepped closer and held the light's beam still. 'Looks like Omar has been here.'

The keyring glinted again. They'd found Nina Abidar's car keys. Gina's gaze travelled to the bushes. She could see that a cut through had been trodden underfoot. She stepped a little closer. 'There's an open rucksack. I can see textbooks and exercise pads. They have Omar's name on the front. He has to be here. We must have scared him off.'

Wyre stood straight and wedged her body between the trees, onto the field. 'I can't see anyone. I know I heard someone though.'

'Message Smith for backup. We need this area cordoned off.'

Wyre stood dead still and held a finger up. 'I heard it again, guv.'

'What?'

She replied in a whisper. 'Someone is up ahead, just off the path. I'm calling backup.'

Gina crept off the grass and onto the path, frantically holding her torch out. 'Omar?'

No reply.

She took another step forward. A dark-dressed figure leaped out of the bushes so fast, she barely registered any details. Gina ran, jumping over every lump in the ground.

'He's heading that way, guv.'

She heard Wyre behind her and the woman overtook her, diverting onto the field. Gina pounded behind, seeing the figure fleeing towards the lane. If they didn't keep up, they'd lose him to the high street with all its little streets, making it perfect to get lost in. He'd do what Grant Braddock did and hide out in a garden or shed until they'd gone. With all she had, Gina forced her body into sprint mode, even though everything was beginning to hurt. As they reached the other end of the field, Wyre and their suspect were out of sight.

Stopping on the top of the lane, she glanced back at the area cordoned off by police tape and listened for any clue as to which direction her colleague may have taken. Then she heard the most sickening of screams. Wyre was at the back of the Angel Arms. Gathering pace, Gina pushed through the hedge and stood in the pub garden. Several smokers stared at her. 'Have two people just come this way?'

A woman nodded as she blew out a plume of smoke. 'The woman fell and hit her head on the bench but she got up and carried on chasing the man. She shouted police but it was too late for us to assist, the man had already gone. They went that way.' The woman pointed around the side of the pub.

Her phone rang. It was Wyre. 'I'm by the church, guv.'

'I'm coming.' She called it in immediately, hoping that uniform could now join in with their pursuit of the suspect. The church was all the way down the other end. Gina held her side as she panted and ran until she reached the church. Its large cross lit up the frontage. She saw a police car pulling up on the road. She waved and carried on, hoping to spot Wyre.

A flash of a torch lit up a gravestone around the back and a woman came out of the church wearing a dressing gown and her unlaced black heavy boots. Her dark hair stuck to the side of her face like she'd been asleep. Gina knew her to be the local vicar, Sally. 'There's something going on in the graveyard. I heard shouting a moment ago which is why I came out.' The sound of her dog barking from behind the kitchen door masked what Gina was trying to listen out for.

'Sally, keep back. We are in pursuit of a suspect and they could be dangerous.' The woman stood back and Gina hurried out the back. She could no longer see Wyre's torch.

'Paula,' she called, but her colleague didn't answer. She hurried forward, her own torch pointing ahead.

'Here, guv. I got him.' She peered up, over a grave. 'I've read him his rights.' Dragging the cuffed man to his feet, Wyre smiled proudly.

'We best get Mr Whittle to the station.'

'I haven't done anything,' he yelled as Wyre handed him over to Smith. They watched as Whittle yelled and struggled all the way over the graves.

'Good job.' Gina smiled at Wyre. 'We now get to find out what Whittle was doing hanging around the back of the Braddocks's house and we can get justice for the women he's assaulted. Did they make statements?'

Wyre smiled. 'Yes, I know Jacob interviewed the lunchtime superintendent and the cleaner. Miriam also came forward and made a full statement, as did Anita Teller.'

'That just leaves Annabel. We still need to find her, and where is the boy?'

They began walking towards their cars.

'I didn't kill Taylor. You have to believe me. I just looked after her.' Smith placed his hand on Whittle's head as he lowered him into the police car.

'We need to get back to the station, now. I'll meet you there.' Gina knew she had to be the one to interview Whittle. He knew something about Taylor and what was happening. There was a huge chance he'd taken Annabel and left her somewhere. If that was the case, Annabel was now alone. Unless they found her, she could die soon. Arresting Whittle could have cut off her lifeline so they had to act fast.

FIFTY-TWO

Annabel

I feel woozy but the softness my head leans on is most welcome. I was only just thinking about Cally and the time she dropped ice cream down my top when I lifted her up. Where am I? My chest is cold and damp and I seem to have been changed into a sweatshirt by the feel of it. Prising my eyes open I see that it's dark but there are round windows. I don't know how long I've been here but I do know this isn't *Freedom*. This is my brother-in-law's boat. We left *Freedom* and I remember I was in a car boot.

There is a length of material tied behind my head and it's dry in my mouth. There's a freshness about it. It's not the same filthy rag that he's been using as a gag. 'Help,' I try to half shout, but no one can hear me. The smell of fresh paint lingers in the air. Seth was meant to be in the Netherlands lecturing and I know he said his boat needed painting. I fidget, hoping that my restraints will come loose. I'm on my side, my hands are behind my back and my ankles are tied together. What I'm lacking is strength. This is how it must feel to be dying. The strength goes, the pain fails to be alleviated and a person lies there, hoping that death will come and take it all away. That is me, right now.

All I see is the light of the moon. I feel a slight swaying underneath. I hate boats. Memories of that day in the boat with Grant and Cally flood my mind. Grant always wanted what his brother had. The looks, the boat, the watch, the house; the job that took him to exciting places and the string of young women that he seemed to end up in brief relationships with. I chose to be with Grant after once dating Seth. Grant could never let me forget that I once went out with his brother.

Panic rises and I begin to pull at my binds again, tearing flesh on my wrists. Even though my hands are tied behind my back, I can feel that he's tied me up with rope. I wince as another tug stings, forcing tears from my eyes. If I don't do anything, he's going to take Cally. I have to get out and get to her before he does.

I pause and listen. I'm alone. Now that my eyes have adjusted, I can see a little. I've been on this boat before, only once when we all went out for a picnic. Cally was only a baby. That's how long ago it was. Later that day, Dad got drunk. He confessed to hurting my mother once and told me how much he hated himself. It took me a year to speak to him again. I know that my mother cheated on him but that was no excuse for what he did.

My heart pounds again as I think of Cally. If he's not here terrorising me, he's out there. Cally thinks the world of him. She trusts him. That thought sends a jolt of fear through me. I start fiddling with the rope again, my fingers barely reaching it. It's hopeless. Nothing I do is helping at all and everything hurts.

I need to get out. My heart pounds so hard, it feels like it's going to pack up. Maybe that's how I die. Heart attack. I breathe in through my nose and feel the slither of a tear slipping down my cheek.

Thinking of Grant, I wonder if he's dead. Left in that horrible old boat by this maniac. He's been a nasty husband but Cally loves him with all his faults. She doesn't deserve to lose her father and people can change. My dad changed. Maybe he can get help for his addiction and there might be a future for him. That doesn't mean I'll ever forgive him for how he's been with me.

I think of Taylor. Young and impressionable, taken in by my stupid husband. I should have nothing but hate in my heart, but I don't.

I think of Tom, of what happened that night at the party. It started on that boat. I wished I'd never gone for that walk with him. I know he put something in my drink but I could never prove it. Before that, I really liked him. Things were going downhill with Grant and I enjoyed being told that I was beautiful and interesting. I know some people didn't gel with him but he always said that when people were nice and kind, others wanted to bring them down. I believed him, until that night at the party. What he took from me can never be restored. I hate him.

I'm stuck. Yawning, I feel my eyelids begin to droop. *No, don't give up. You can do this*, I tell myself. I begin to wriggle like a worm until I fall off the end of the bed, wedged in next to the little door. My hands are still bound. That's when I hear a yapping noise and I know someone is out there with a dog. I bang and let out muffled screams, which are all that I can manage but then the yapping gets more distant and I want to cry.

A thud comes from the other end of the boat followed by the sound of dragging, then nothing. Shivering, I press my back against the end of the bed and I stare up at the door, waiting for it to open. As clouds cover the moon, taking away all my light, I hear a thud coming from the other side of the door and I flinch. I hold my breath as I wonder if he is there and whether he has my little girl. Maybe the thudding sound was Cally's body landing in the boat. Closing my eyes, I brace myself for the worst and hope that I misheard. Tears spill and I can't stop them. I don't care what happens to me anymore, I just want Cally to be safe. He can have me, I'll do anything, but the truth is, I know I'm not enough for him. He wants us both and now he has us both. What he does with us next is the question I can't answer.

FIFTY-THREE

Tom Whittle leaned over the table in the interview room. His clothes had been bagged and he was now wearing a standard issue tracksuit. Gina gave him a few seconds while he processed the rape, assault of a police officer and sexual assault charges. The tape was running and Annabel was still missing. The young solicitor representing him peered over her rimless glasses as she read the paperwork. Wyre sipped from her water bottle.

'Mr Whittle, where is Annabel?'

'My client has already told you, he doesn't know where Mrs Braddock is?'

'Why were you at the back of Annabel Braddock's house this evening?'

He whispered to his solicitor and she whispered back. 'I know when you went into my attic, you thought that it was me who took her and ran her friend over. After all, I'm the lover, well, I was the lover, which makes me a suspect. It was her husband, you know. He wanted to get rid of her so that he could take up with Taylor. I hoped to find Grant and get to the bottom of everything, I mean, the man has to come home at some point.'

Gina already knew Grant's side of the story and the information regarding his kidnapping hadn't been released to the press. Whittle was trying hard to divert attention from himself. 'Tell me about Taylor. I heard you mention her name when you were arrested. In front of PC Smith and DC Wyre, you said, "I didn't kill Taylor. You have to believe me. I just looked after her." Why did you say that?'

'Because I thought you'd try to blame her murder on me.'

'You wear size ten footwear?'

'So, it's a common size.'

'Size ten prints were found at the scene of Taylor's murder.'

'I didn't hurt anyone.'

Gina would beg to differ. She'd briefly read all the statements of the women he'd harassed and she knew that he had to have been doing the same to Annabel. Did he go too far this time? 'How did you look after Taylor?' She emphasised the words look after.

'The girl had no one to turn to and I saw her walking the streets. I used to teach her. I know her, which is why I couldn't see her walking the streets in such a state. She was crying so I took her in.'

'Where have you been staying?'

'When you lot came to mine, I went online using my dad's credit card and booked an apartment through a website in his name. I got the key out of the key safe and stayed there so no one saw me. When I saw Taylor, she told me what had happened and that she'd been with Grant. She said she couldn't go home as the police would be looking for her so I took her in. I told her how much time I'd spent with Annabel and how much I was missing her and needed to find her. I said that Grant was bad for her too, that she could do better than letting that player use her. We both agreed that we'd hide out in the apartment until things got sorted.'

'Got sorted?' Gina leaned forward.

He stared at her, his piercing blue eyes glinting in the strip light. 'Sorted as in you finding out who took Annabel and ran the woman over. We both realised that we could end up being blamed. Taylor told me that she heard Grant coming back to their cabin in the night. When she got up to see him, he had blood smeared on his arm. She said he then pushed her around and told her not to say anything or they'd both be in huge trouble. She told you she was too drunk to remember because she thought she'd end up in trouble with you lot or Grant. I mean she's twenty with the maturity of a fifteen-year-old. Anyway, at this point, she had no idea what had happened but she knew it was bad. Grant told her that if she went to the police, he'd say she was with him and with what he'd seen, they'd be in huge trouble. He kept going on about Annabel's phone not being trackable any more, that it must have been broken or switched off. That's what Taylor said. She thought that he'd hurt her. In the morning he was gone. Taylor had nothing to do with what happened. See, I didn't hurt Taylor, I tried to help her.'

Gina knew she would never find out the truth of what went on between Taylor and Whittle. Maybe Whittle had upset her or assaulted her, which is why she ran from the apartment and went looking for Grant. She pictured the girl scared to death of getting into trouble and even more scared of staying with Whittle. She looked into his eyes. He was the master of spin and she didn't believe anything he was saying. What he did to those women was unforgivable. 'Just like you tried to help Annabel?'

'What? I told you. I don't know where she is. I tried to help her by telling her that her husband was an idiot. That was all.'

'Did you see anyone else by Annabel's house?'

'No. I'd only been there about twenty minutes before you arrived.'

'Why did you run?'

'I've already told you. I thought you were going to pin Annabel and Taylor on me. You'd already come to my house and turned the place upside down and I know how it all looked.

I couldn't go back. I couldn't face any more questioning.' He scratched his head. 'So, I ran away.'

'Where were you staying?'

'Still staying. I'm at an apartment just behind the Cleevesford Cleaver bed and breakfast. They have two apartments that they let out through the site.'

'So all your stuff is there?'

He nodded. Gina saw that Wyre had noted the address down. A search of the rental property would be arranged. 'Does your dad know you used his credit card details?'

'Yes, I told him I was in trouble and he offered to help me. He's always looked after me when I've been short. He met up with me and handed it over. My dad's a good bloke. Will you tell him to get my cats and look after them? I can't see them out on the street.'

'I'll pass the message on.' Gina knew that they'd have to check out the claims that his father let him use the credit card so asking him about the cats wouldn't be a problem. The last thing she'd want was to see his cats being taken if there was another home they could go to. Finding Annabel was more important right now, so that would have to wait a while. 'What was your relationship with Annabel?'

'We've already been through this.' He shrugged and folded his arms.

'What really happened at the night of the party?'

He slammed his hand palm down on the table. 'If you really must know, we shagged against a tree. There you have it. Two colleagues, drunk at a Christmas party. We'd been flirting for ages and things just happened. Okay. Neither of us planned it, we got carried away in the heat of the moment.'

His solicitor whispered in his ear.

'All my answers will be no comment from now on. I will close by saying that I did not run over that woman. I did not take Annabel. I did not kill Taylor. I've just been in the wrong places at the wrong time. I confess to sexual assault. I know I have problems and I'm putting my hands up to them because I want to be a better person, to get better, which is why I'm going to get help and it starts with facing what I've done. I confess to all but I didn't rape Anita. She was up for sex as much as I was but I harassed her after when she didn't want to be with me. Okay?'

'I guess a jury will decide the outcome.' Gina knew with so many victims, it would go to trial.

'And that's all my client will be saying.' The solicitor sat up straight.

Wyre leaned toward the tape. 'Interview ended at twenty-two thirty hours.'

Someone tapped on the interview room door. O'Connor beckoned Gina out. She left Wyre to finish up before taking Whittle back to his cell. He'd be facing the magistrates' court with his charges the next morning, where there would later be a trial and sentencing at Crown Court in the near future. She followed him away from the room. 'Have you found the boy?'

He shook his head. 'Sorry. I wish we had. I've had Whittle's shoes examined and I've spoken to Bernard.'

'And?'

'Whittle's shoe is the same size as the prints we found at the scene of Taylor's murder. Our suspected perp walks with a limp and Whittle doesn't.'

Gina's shoulders dropped. 'That leaves Omar, and did the team look into the list of people that had been to the Braddocks's house? The ones who knew about the boat and where it was kept?'

'Yes, but one person did come up more than the others.'

'Who?'

'Annabel's father. He has previous. He has access to their life and would be able to use Grant's other car.'

'Go on.'

'When Annabel's mother was alive, in fact when Annabel was probably about five, he was convicted of hitting her mother. It was a one-off report and he pleaded guilty immediately and got a suspended sentence.'

'So, just theorising here. He didn't like who Annabel was married to and if he knew that Taylor was sleeping with Grant, maybe he wanted to make her pay too. I'm going over there now. If nothing else, he's looking after little Cally. We may need to involve social services so get them on hand.'

'On it right now, guv.'

Gina felt her fists clench. She liked Annabel's father. He'd come across as the perfect caring father and grandfather. To hear of his conviction had turned everything upside down.

FIFTY-FOUR

'Hey, sweetheart. We have to go. Get in the car.'

Cally rubbed her tired eyes and yawned. 'I need Olaf.'

'It's okay. He's in the boot. I'll give him to you when we get there.'

She looked up from the back of the car. It felt odd not sitting in her child's car seat. Her mum always told her she had to be strapped in, that it wasn't safe otherwise. 'Where are we going?'

'It's a surprise.'

'Are we seeing Mummy?'

'Yes. She's so excited to see you. She can't wait for you to arrive so that we can all go away together. She's been waiting for you.'

'Where are we going?'

'Somewhere amazing. We're going on a holiday.'

She pulled her pyjama top over her belly button. It had ridden up when she got in the car. She shivered. 'I'm cold.'

'It'll warm up in a minute, I promise.' He turned the fan on but it blew out cold air, making her shiver more.

'I need a wee.'

'You'll have to wait, sweetheart.'

'But I can't.'

'You can. It's easy. Just think of something else.' He drove for a while and Cally watched as they left Cleevesford and everything got darker. Something didn't feel right.

'Where's Daddy?'

The man slammed his hand on the steering wheel and Cally's wide stare rested on his angry-looking face. 'Your daddy is a bad man. He hurt your mother and for that, I can never forgive him. Only I can keep you and Mummy safe.'

'I want Mummy.' She began to cry and yell Mummy's name over and over again. He had to take her home. Her mummy had to be back from her trip and so did her daddy. They were at work. Mummy teaches children and Daddy makes sure buildings are nice and safe for people to live in.

'Cally, you have to shut up.'

'I want Mummy.'

'Shut the hell up.' He slammed on the brakes, propelling her little body forward. The seat belt snapped into place and she couldn't breathe for a few seconds as her little chest squeezed.

She caught her hand in the belt. 'My finger hurts.' Tears fell and her nose filled up. It wasn't because her finger hurt that much, it was because he'd never shouted at her like that.

He unbuckled his belt and hurried around the back. 'I'm sorry, so sorry. I shouldn't have yelled at you. Are you okay?'

Tears now flooded Cally's face, her mouth contorted into all shapes as she screamed and bawled. 'I want Mummy.' Her little hands hit his face and his shoulder. She unbuckled the seat belt and tried to escape him but he was too strong.

'You asked for this. Little girls that don't behave have to be punished.' He grabbed a length of rope from the front seat and effortlessly turned her over. 'I've been patient with you, all that crying and screaming, but now you have to be punished.'

She wriggled and wriggled until he tied her hands behind

her back. He lifted her over his shoulder. She glanced around at the grass and mud below. The air was cold and there were no street lights, only trees. There was a smell in the air, like when her mummy peeled boiled eggs for their sandwiches or like horrible water. His finger dug into the back of her leg. She started yelling and kicking until he flung her into the boot. 'Mummy,' she cried.

It was no good. Mummy wasn't coming. She was alone and scared, and he had hurt her. He'd never hurt her before and he'd never scared her either. As she yelled for Mummy and Daddy, the car began to move with a jerk and she was flung to the back of the boot, hitting her head. All she could do was weep and hope that he was telling the truth and she was going to see Mummy.

Mummy would know what to do.

Mummy always knew what to do.

FIFTY-FIVE

Gina slammed her brakes on outside Doug Latham's house and was closely followed by another two cars. Her heart banged as she thought of the sweet little girl that she'd spoken to only a few days ago. Wyre and O'Connor were close behind and PCs Smith and Kapoor stepped out of another car. Gina's attention was drawn to the barking lurcher in the upstairs window. Its nose kept catching on the bottom of the curtain and its paws spread out on the glass. She hurried to the door and knocked. There was no answer but the dog barked frantically.

'We'll go around the back, guv.' Wyre nodded and O'Connor followed her.

Gina left the front door and stepped onto the overgrown grass. Reaching out to part the shrubs, she pricked her finger on a rose bush. 'Damn.' She popped it in her mouth to soothe the sting. Standing on tiptoes to see through the living room window, she peered through the miniscule slit in the curtains but she couldn't quite see the settee through the nets. Hurrying back to the front door she knocked and lifted the letter box. 'Doug Latham, it's the police. Open up.'

She watched as a figure came into the hallway. All she

could see were legs wearing jeans. The dog barked continuously. 'Milo, shut up.' He opened the door, rubbing his eyes. 'What's going on?' He glanced upstairs. 'The dog must have got trapped in the bedroom.'

The stale smell of alcohol coming from Doug's mouth as he spoke made Gina recoil. She turned her head a little and inhaled the air outside. 'Where's Cally? We need to question you about your daughter's disappearance.' Gina saw that Wyre had reached the outside of the kitchen door. She gestured to tell Gina that she was heading back round the front.

'Cally,' Doug called with a gravelly voice. 'She's in bed, probably fast asleep. Come in.' He fully opened the door, turned on the upstairs lights and wandered upstairs. 'Milo, shut up. He's going to wake her.' With the opening of a door, the dog bounded down the stairs and straight into Gina's legs at the bottom.

She moved aside as Wyre stepped in, closing the door to prevent the dog escaping onto the street.

'She's not in bed. Cally?' The man opened and closed all the doors, calling his granddaughter.

Gina hurried upstairs.

'Cally?' The man was on his knees, checking under the bed. 'Where is she? What's happening?'

'We need to ask you the same thing. How can your granddaughter not be here?'

He ran his fingers through his grey hair, every line on his face emphasised by the stark lighting. 'I was asleep on the settee. I put her to bed about two hours ago and put the telly on. I don't know where she is.' His fingers began to tremble.

'Any sign of a break-in?'

'I don't know, I haven't checked. I was in such a deep sleep before you woke me up.' He began to hyperventilate. 'Cally.'

'Here, sit.' He balanced his bottom on the end of the single bed. The magnolia-painted room was bland except for the teddy bear on the chest of drawers.

Cally's iPad lay on the bed. 'She was watching her programmes when I put her to bed. Where is she? Where's my granddaughter?'

'Do you have a photo of Cally?'

He reached under the bed and pulled out a box. He threw a pile of photos onto the floor and continued to rummage. 'This one was taken last Christmas.' Gina took the photo of the little girl wearing a red dress and reindeer antlers, with a big smile on her face. She watched Doug, the man with the past, a man who could very well have been like her ex-husband, Terry. She wondered if people could change. The expressions he'd displayed seemed genuine but could he have done something with his granddaughter and then come back to the house. They needed one thing only and that was to establish where Cally was.

'Have you seen or heard anything out of the ordinary?'

'No.' He shook his head. 'I feel so alone at the moment with all that's going on. Where's Cally? I've lost her.'

'I'm really sorry, Mr Latham. We are doing all we can to get Cally back.'

'That's working really well for Annabel. I'm scared that I'll never see them again. I was looking after Cally and she's gone. That's on me. How could I sleep through whatever happened especially with the dog barking? I didn't shut the dog in the bedroom, which means someone was in my house. Cally wouldn't shut Milo in my bedroom, he's been sleeping in her room.' A puzzled look washed across his face. 'I've failed my daughter and granddaughter. I failed my wife too. I hit her once. I'm not a good person. Maybe this is karma.'

O'Connor poked his head into the room. Gina stepped back. 'Could you please sit with Mr Latham while we take a look downstairs? We have a missing child and I want to know how she got out. It appears that someone has been in the house. We need to minimise foot traffic through the house and get forensics to examine the scene. We need to know who came here and who took Cally.'

O'Connor gave Mr Latham a sympathetic smile and stood by the bed. Gina hurried back down. Wyre followed her into the kitchen. The back door was locked and the keys were in it. The windows were closed too. She headed to the dining room next door which was stuffed full of rubbish and old furniture. That too was well locked up. She headed to the lounge. 'That's why Mr Latham didn't hear anything.' She pointed to the almost empty bottle of whisky next to the empty glass. A stale smell hung in the air, one that only occurs when a drunken person has been festering in a room. She parted the curtains, already knowing that the window was closed. 'Cally walked out of here voluntarily. She had to have opened the door, which can only mean that she knew the person who took her. Could Mr Latham have taken her somewhere or have done something to her earlier this evening, then come back and got hammered? We still need to consider that. Who shut the dog in the bedroom? It's all so calculated. Alert the station that we have a missing child and get Cally's photo over to them.'

'Guv.' Kapoor leaned against the door frame as she got her breath back. 'We've found something. Hurry.'

Gina and Wyre followed Kapoor down the road, passing several houses until she stopped by a drain. Gina saw the white toy lying there, his happy snowman face looking up at the sky. 'Cally has a toy the same as this.' Gina avoided the temptation to pick it up, leaving it exactly where it was. 'We need to get this area cordoned off along with Mr Latham's house. Get him to the station and organise a search. A little girl's life is at risk. Something isn't adding up here.' She glanced up at all the houses. As they'd arrived, all the curtains had been shut but now, people were peering out and standing on their doorsteps.

A man came out of his house. 'What's happening?'

'We have a missing child.' Gina pulled the photo from her pocket. 'Have you seen her?'

He took the photo and held it closer to his face. 'Yes, that's Doug's granddaughter. I saw her with him earlier today.'

'How did they seem?'

'Okay, I guess.'

'You guess.'

'Cally was playing up, screaming for her mother and Doug was telling her off. I think looking after her is a lot for him. I saw the news. I know what's happening. He's under a lot of pressure at the moment.'

'How has Mr Latham seemed?'

The man shrugged. 'A bit sad, if I'm honest. He's alone all the time. His daughter hardly ever visits him. He's been quieter lately. Normally he drops into mine or one of the other neighbours for a chinwag and a cuppa, but lately, it's as if he's been preoccupied. I mean before his daughter went missing. We played bridge with a couple of other neighbours on Saturday evening and he was quiet then.'

'What time was he with you that night?'

'Until he received the call about his daughter. He came over about seven. When we have these nights, we normally have a takeaway first. I know it's all been hard on him so I said that if he needed me to help or keep an eye on Cally while he got his chores done, he'd only needed to ask. I have four children myself. All grown up but I'm used to having kids around. My wife loves them too.'

'Has he asked you to look after Cally at all?'

'I'm capable of looking after kids.'

'I wasn't suggesting otherwise. It's just important that we establish what has happened.'

He relaxed a little. 'Yes, we looked after both Cally and the dog on Monday evening. Doug needed to do a bit of shopping and he said that Cally was in bed. My wife and I went to his. He didn't want to wake Cally to take her or leave the dog. He's left Milo alone a couple of times and he's chewed the bottom of the door and barked nonstop.'

'How long was he gone?'

'Maybe an hour or longer. He said he was going to Sainsbury's. He needed petrol too. He came back with his shopping just after nine thirty. He even gave me a pack of beer even though I said he shouldn't have. Doug is a lovely man, one in a million. He'd do anything for his daughter or Cally.'

'Thank you.' Gina made a note to see if his whereabouts could be verified by the supermarket's CCTV.

'Have you seen Cally this evening?'

'I heard her talking about an hour ago. It sounded like she walked past my house. I was in the bedroom, drying off after having a shower. The place had steamed up so I opened the window, that's how I could hear her.'

'Did you hear Mr Latham?'

'No, only Cally. I didn't hear what she was saying, I just caught the ring of her high-pitched voice. She sounded okay, by that I mean not distressed. My thought was that they were taking the dog for a walk until I heard a car pulling away.'

'Did it sound like Mr Latham's car?'

'I don't know.' The man scratched his chin. 'Has someone taken her?'

'That's what we're trying to establish. Is there anything else you heard or saw that might help us?'

'I did see something but I don't know if it's related.'

Gina stood aside as PC Smith set the cordon up, looping the tape around a lamp post. 'What was that?'

'Someone was pacing around the path in the night, up and down. I was going to call the police but by the time I looked back, they were gone. I thought it was a burglar.'

'When was this?'

'Early hours this morning. Maybe about four or five.'

'Can you describe them?'

'As you can see, we all have a hedge separating our gardens from the path so I could only see the top half of this person from my bedroom. They were wearing dark clothing. I couldn't tell you whether it was a man or woman from what they were wearing as the jacket was padded. You can also see that there are no street lamps just outside my house so it was dark. This person was walking almost silently, like they had trainers on. They were wearing a hat, like a winter hat pulled over the ears. It wasn't Doug. Whoever it was moved a bit smoother than Doug. He doesn't move with speed as it makes his sciatica worse, this person seemed fitter.'

'Thank you. That's really helpful. An officer will come to take a statement in a short while.'

'Okay, you know where I am.' A woman wearing a dressing gown pulled the curtains apart, her dark hair up in a clip. 'Best get back in.' He waved at the woman.

Gina hurried over to Wyre.

'What was he saying, guv?'

'He saw someone loitering between four and five this morning. His description doesn't help us pinpoint anyone. He couldn't tell whether it was a man or woman. He was certain that it wasn't Mr Latham.'

'What are your thoughts on Annabel's father?' Wyre stepped back, placing her weight on the other foot.

'I don't know yet. He has a past that makes him a person of interest. He has a motive of sorts but would he really hurt his daughter and then his granddaughter, and why would he harm Jennifer? We know he's capable of violence even though the incident was many years ago. He's not had any police attention since but does a person change? He did go out to Sainsbury's on the night of Taylor's murder, which we still have to confirm, but he was playing bridge with his neighbours when Jennifer was hit and his daughter was taken. We still haven't found Omar. Could it have been him? He's fit and could easily sneak around. We know he's been watching Annabel's house. Maybe he'd taken to watching her father's house too. We only picked Whittle up a few hours ago. Maybe it was him looking for Annabel or Grant in the early hours. He's in custody now. He couldn't have been here this evening. The same goes for Grant.'

Gina's phone beeped and she relayed the message. 'We have word from officers at the Braddocks's house. They found Omar's phone with the battery removed and traces of blood on his bag. Also, word from the station. The damage to Nina Abidar's bonnet and bumper was done by hitting a lamp post. Ms Abidar even knew which lamp post it was. Forensics have confirmed that the damage matches her statement.' She closed the message. 'Who was driving Grant Braddock's Merc? Who did Cally see out of her bedroom window on the night that Annabel went missing? Who is the ghost Cally described coming into the garden in the dark? They had access to the garage and took the car.' Gina felt her muscles tensing. Whoever was pulling the strings had now put two kids in danger and after seeing how things worked out for Taylor, she knew that time was against them. She only hoped that they weren't too late. Her phone rang. 'Bernard?'

'I have some results for you. The paint that we found on the rag at the scene of Annabel's abduction is boat paint. To be more specific, it's topside paint. Its purpose is to protect the boat from the elements. We can also confirm that this paint doesn't match any of the paint samples that we took from *Freedom*. It's a popular make and colour used on barges. I don't know if that's any help.'

O'Connor hurried out and thrust a photo at Gina. 'He showed me some of his photos and this one was taken on Seth Braddock's boat. Cally was a baby when this was taken but there's Grant and Annabel Braddock, standing on the towpath.

You can tell that's Grant's brother, Seth, they look so alike, and that's Mr Latham holding the picnic basket.'

'I'll call you in a bit, Bernard.' She ended the call and looked slowly up at Wyre. 'The boat is called *Raspberry Pi*. We found a keyring at the scene where Jennifer was hit, a raspberry keyring. When Annabel left the pi symbol on the side of *Freedom*, it wasn't just a mark to say that she'd been there, it was a clue as to where she was being taken. Have you ever heard of a Raspberry Pi? The minicomputer about the size of a credit card?'

'Guv, you're a genius. The *Raspberry Pi*. It's the perfect name for a computer geek's boat.'

'Call Jacob now. He needs to urgently get in touch with the local boat navigation authorities, see if we can find out where Seth Braddock keeps his boat.' Gina bit her lip and scrunched her brow. 'I know who's behind this.' She filled Wyre in. 'With two children in immediate danger, we need to get a search warrant. It all makes sense. *Raspberry Pi* was right under our noses all the time.'

FIFTY-SIX

Omar

I think of my mum and how worried she must be. The police would be asking her all sorts by now, especially as I stole her car. They must have found my bag, the car or my phone. I know that his prints won't be on any of my things because he wore gloves. Maybe they'll find the car first. I'd parked badly. My head stings and my mouth is stuffed with a disgusting rag that makes me want to heave. I wriggle on the floor, rubbing my face on the carpet of the boat. I'm in what I think would be called the galley. I see the shine of the moon catching the oven door.

Another thud comes from the next room and I wonder if the person who's taken me has an accomplice. As I continue to rub my head on the floor, I manage to catch the rag on a coarse tuft of fibre and the gag comes loose and dangles at my chin. I gasp in the stagnant air, grateful that I can breathe easily again.

At least I'm not locked under the stairs any more. I can get out of this situation and I will find Annabel. I heard him whispering about her under his breath. The boat is called *Raspberry Pi*. I need the police. I have proof that I had nothing to do with Annabel's disappearance and I think she's on this boat. I wish I had my phone. In fact, I have nothing. He'd even taken my trainers when I tried to kick out at him.

I go to lift my head off the floor and a flash of pain stretches from back to front. He hit me hard and the pain is getting worse. 'Hello,' I call out, my throat just about croaking out this word.

A muffled cry comes from behind the door, then a succession of kicks. She's not saying a word but I recognise the tone in the nasally sound she's making. It's definitely Annabel.

'Mrs Braddock.'

Again, she makes that noise. Finally, I've found her. Actually, I didn't find her at all. He found me and he's taken me too. So much for being a hero and saving the day. I'm just another loser and both of us will die on this boat and everyone at school will know I messed up.

I'm sure he killed Taylor. What I don't know is why he hasn't killed me.

I call out as best I can. My throat is bone dry. 'It's me, Omar. I was trying to help. I'm really sorry but he caught me. I'm tied up. He's gone for your little girl.' A tear slips down my face. I wish I wasn't crying. If the kids at school saw me in such a mess, they'd have a field day. I am exactly what they say I am. A weedy loser who will never get a girlfriend. 'I'm sorry, Mrs Braddock. I tried to save you. I wanted to help.'

'Omar. What are you doing here?'

'I came to help you but he got me. Are you okay?'

'I've managed to dislodge the gag.'

'And me, but he's tied me up. My hands are behind my back and I'm on the floor. I can barely see. There's a little kitchen against one side and a bench seat and table the other. I'm wedged against the table.'

'Just keep trying to get free. Whatever it takes. We have to escape from here and get Cally before he takes her.'

'I'm trying but I really am stuck. Wait. It's just rope.' I lie on my belly and lift my head up slightly, pressing my face against a cupboard. With a struggle, I'm on my knees. There's a screwdriver wedged in the crevice of the seating. I hop towards it, on my knees, and press my lips into the crumby fabric. Open-mouthed, I try to bite the screwdriver. I miss and spit out a load of fluff and bits.

'Omar, what are you doing?'

'I see a screwdriver. I'm trying to bite it so that I can drop it onto the floor. If I can do that maybe I can weaken the rope and get us both out of here.' That little tool is my chance to save us. I lean in again. As I clasp my teeth around the metal, I fall forward, unable to get back up. I sit up and drop the screwdriver onto the floor to my left and take a few deep breaths. That tiny task had zapped all my energy.

'Did you get it?'

'I've got it onto the floor. I'm going to get free, then get us both out of here.' Sweating like a pig, I wriggle on my bottom until the screwdriver is behind me. In between both hands, I grab the tool and begin poking it at the rope. I yell as I stab the side of my wrist.

'What happened?' I hear Annabel shuffling behind the door.

I can't see but I feel my way around, getting a rhythm on as I poke and prod away at the rope, tightening it every time I go in. 'I stabbed myself.'

'How bad are you hurt?'

'It's nothing.' That's what I tell her but I can feel blood trickling down my wrist. As soon as we get free, I can get it looked at.

'Why did you come to help me?'

I swallow, not knowing if I should tell her that I love her.

I'm just a stupid kid. It's so clear now but that doesn't mean that I don't feel strongly. I do. Every day, I think about her. When she talks me through my schoolwork and gives me feedback, I hang on to her every word. She's incredibly clever and I like that in a girl. I pause my thoughts. A girl. Mrs Braddock is not a girl and I'm an idiot but we're stuck here alone so I'm going to be honest. When this is over, I'll probably be permanently put into Ms Law's class and she's not as good a teacher but I'll understand. 'I love you.' She pauses and now I feel awkward.

'Oh, Omar, I'm your teacher.'

I continue to prod at the rope, my head feeling woozy because I'm losing blood. The thought of blood always sickens me. I can't even watch horror films. Maybe this is how I die. I jolt forward. No, I can't die. Annabel's safety depends on me getting free and I'm scared of what will happen to Cally. She's just a little kid.

'I know you've been by my house, I saw you.'

'I'm really sorry, miss. I'm so stupid. When we get out of this, I won't do anything that stupid ever again. Please keep teaching me. I don't want to go into Ms Law's class. She's not as good as you. I've grown up a lot. And as for the things you told me not to say, I didn't tell anyone.'

I hear her weeping behind the door. 'It's okay, Omar, and thank you. Let's just get out of this. You're doing really well and I know you're going to go on to huge things in life. You're much cleverer than I was at your age. You're going to do your A Levels, you'll go to uni and I hope you'll study maths, then you'll graduate. It's there where you'll find out who you really are. You'll break hearts and you'll have your heart broken. Whatever happens now, I'm really proud of you and I thank you from the bottom of my heart for all that you've done to help me but if you get the chance, just run. Leave me and run. Go and get help. Don't look back for anything. Do you promise me you'll do that?'

My hands begin to shake. 'But I can't do that. I can't leave you.'

'Listen to me,' she shouts, 'you have to. My daughter's life will depend on your actions and getting the police here is the most important thing you can do and you're a child, I can't put you at risk any more than you already are. You are my responsibility...' She cries a little. 'I don't want anything to happen to you. Promise me.'

'Okay. I'll get free, get you free and run for help. Deal?'

'Deal. Now hurry up.'

As I go to speak, the rope loosens against my wrists and falls to the floor. Blood has pooled a little underneath me. A wave of dizziness sweeps through my body. I normally freak at the sight of blood. It scares me but I can't pass out, not yet. I grab a tea towel that is hanging from the handle on the front of the tiny oven and I use my teeth to tighten it around my wrist to stem the bleeding. Reaching down, I untie my feet and stretch out. My legs and arms are stiff. I reach for the table and use it to pull my body up.

'Omar, I can hear a car. Leave me and get out. Save Cally.'

I glance at the back of the boat and see that the main door is still closed. I have time to let Annabel out. I can't leave her. I know I promised. Staggering to the door, I reach for the handle and it's locked. I need something to smash it down with.

'I can hear him. Go.'

He jangles his keys from the other side of the door. I smash the little window above the cooker with a coffee jar and begin to push all the outer bits of glass out of the way. It's so small, I don't know if I'll fit. I push my head through and I'm thankful that it's pavement on the other side and not water. My shoulders are through. I'm nearly out.

'Where do you think you're going?'

I'm yanked back in. He pulls me that hard, I'm swept back

and I bash my chin on the table. The scared little girl cowers in the corner. I failed and now we're all going to die.

'Mummy,' Cally cries.

Annabel wails from the other side of the door. I've let her down. I've let her little girl down and I've let myself down. I feel as though the boat has tilted sideways as I fall onto the carpet. It's not the boat, it's me. I'm too weak to save anyone. He's won and I'm dead.

FIFTY-SEVEN

Annabel

My hair falls loose over my shoulders. He fluffed it up a little after he cleaned my face up. Cally is pressed against my side, her face pale and her eyes red and puffy. Then, I think of Omar, unconscious from the attack. At first, I thought our captor would kill us but instead, he threw Omar into the small bedroom where I'd originally been kept. I fear his injuries are serious and he's losing so much blood. If I could help, I would, but I'm trapped too.

As he tidied me up, my captor said, 'You look so beautiful, Annabel. I can't believe you're finally mine. In fact, I can't believe we're all together as a family.' He told me how he uses the same deodorant as Grant as he knows I buy it for him when I go shopping, therefore I must like it. I can smell it on him now that he's cleaned himself up a bit for dinner.

I swallow and try not to look alarmed so that I don't upset him. I try to listen above the gentle sounds of Chopin that he's playing but I can't hear Omar at all and I'm scared that he's dying. The smashed-in window that he tugged Omar back through has now been temporarily blocked off with a square of wood.

'When we get up the canal a bit, we'll dispose of him. Can't have him stinking the boat up when he starts to decompose. Eat.'

He holds a forkful of packet mash potatoes to my face. Grimacing at the thought of Omar's body in the bedroom, I force myself to bite and swish it around my mouth. A big glob of dried potato hits my tongue and I want to spit it out. Now all I can think is that Omar is dead in that cabin. I wished that he'd done as I asked. He should have run earlier instead of trying to free me. I can't help feeling like I should have done more or maybe I should have been a bit crueller to stop him hanging around me and my classroom. I knew his father had died and I wanted to offer him support, make sure that his academic gift didn't get wasted in a bubble of grief. The mash is still in my mouth. I swallow, forcing it down. It feels like a big lump that is sticking all the way down. If my child wasn't next to me, I'd spit it in his face and take my chances, but for her sake, I won't antagonise him.

'I'm scared, Mummy.' Cally snuggles closer to me. I can't hug her with my hands tied at the front of me now. 'Mummy.' I can tell she is about to cry. Her eyes shine like they're filling with water.

He smashes his fist onto the table and the bowl of mash jumps. My little girl begins to cry and all I want to do is hold her tightly and take her out of all this. 'Shut up with the whinging.' He turns the music off.

'Cally, it's okay. I'm okay. Just be a good girl and eat your potatoes.'

'I don't want them. I want Daddy.' She throws her spoon onto the table and the boat is soon filled with her sobs.

'Shut up. I am your daddy now.' He stares at her hard, and she buries herself into my side. She stops crying and sucks her thumb, something she hasn't done for years. She knows not to say another word. 'Eat.' He presses the fork to my lips again and I take his offering even though I know it is going to cloy in my throat. We have to play along if we are to survive.

My heart goes out to Omar. He risked everything to help me and he's bleeding, battered and bruised and from what my captor is insinuating, dying or dead. I'm scared he won't make it unless I can get him an ambulance, pronto. 'Omar needs help. Please can you leave him somewhere where someone will find him and help him? You have me. You don't need him.'

He grins. 'You think it's that easy. I just drop him off in a busy area and all will be okay?'

'He'll die. I don't want him to die.'

He shakes his head. 'You'll come to realise that's the best outcome. He'll ruin everything. He knows who I am. The police are closing in on me and I know that we're meant to be together. He dies and we get out of here and start a new life on this boat. One day we'll have a home. Somewhere where no one will know us. Cally can go to a new school. You can stay at home all day while I go to work. I love you, Annabel, and I love Cally too. That is why the boy has to go.'

I don't know how to respond. Omar is as good as dead. I think of the geeky kid who stayed and asked me all those questions after class. He'd then begin to enquire into my private sphere. *What's your favourite film, miss? Do you like pizza? I can cook pizza really well. I've been on holiday to Menorca. It's my favourite place too. I love dogs. Lurchers and greyhounds are my favourite. They're so... so fast.* Of course, he'd been making everything up to please me and to engage in further conversation. If I wasn't in this situation, I'd smile. At the time, I found him demanding of my time and annoying, but I loved teaching him.

'He's a kid. You don't need to hurt a child. That's not you.' My daughter presses her head against my arm and I feel her trembling. She's cold too. My wrists are tied at the front of me but my fingers are free. I use them to stroke her head. Her sobs are now little hiccups. The wetness from her eyes and nose is seeping through my sleeve. I want nothing more than to hug her.

'Child? You make me laugh, you only have to look at him to know he wants you. He's an obsessed little prick who has basically been stalking you.'

'Obsessed!' I don't know how he has the nerve to talk about Omar like that when he has me tied up on a boat and is about to take me away from the life I've built. My job, my friends, my dad, Cally's father. 'He's obsessed?'

He knows exactly what I mean by that and he shakes his head. 'I don't lurk around your house. I've been a part of your life as long as you've been with Grant. I knew as soon as you and he moved in together that you'd chosen the wrong man to settle down with. He's a liar and a cheat. He walks around, constantly peacocking when another woman passes him. You would never be enough for him but for me, you're more than enough. I will literally worship the ground you walk on. Only, you couldn't see that. I was always there and I love Cally too.' He stares at Cally with his head tilted but she buries her head into me, not looking. 'She'll grow to love me as time passes. It'll be Dad before we know it. Children of this age soon forget things.'

Cally slips under the table and I see her dodge under him and run for the door. I already know that he locked it but that doesn't stop her from trying the handle. 'Cally, come back to Mummy.'

He doesn't even get off the stool opposite me. He knows he can overpower Cally anytime he wants to. 'Kid, get back on the chair, now.'

She sits on the step by the door, her bottom lip wobbling. I can see the whites of his knuckles. He's getting angry.

'Cally, sweetie, please come back to Mummy.' I know she can see the fear in me and coming back goes against every instinct she has right now.

'I want to go home.'

'You are home.' He grabs a knife from the drawer and stabs it into the table. My daughter's eyes are wide and she gets up, her legs visibly trembling and she runs past him and back to me. 'Good girl. I know this is confusing for you but things are going to change in your life. Mummy and I love each other, which is why we're all going away to start a new life. I have something for you and I know it will make you a very happy little girl. Do you want to see your present?'

She nods slowly.

'That's better.' He smiles. 'It's in the car. I kept it in the footwell of the front seat because I didn't want to ruin the surprise. I'll go and get it, then we'll be on our way. Can I trust you to be good and look after Mummy while I go to the car?'

With her knuckle in her mouth, she nods. I'm so proud of her for being so calm at what must be the most terrifying time of her life.

'I'm going to unlock the door then I will go to my car. If you run away, I will take Mummy and you'll never see her again. Do you understand?' He grabs the knife from the kitchen table and tucks it in his belt. 'I'll take this with me, just in case I see a scary fox. If that fox runs, I will catch it and I will kill it.'

I know exactly what he's saying. There's no way I can risk Cally getting hurt. He's taken Cally because she's part of me and he knows that I'd never leave her but it's me he wants. He will hurt her, I'm sure he will.

He unlocks the door and glances back giving me a sinister smile, letting me know that he won't be taking his eyes off me. 'It's okay, baby.' Cally is crying on my arm again.

'Omar,' I call.

Omar doesn't answer and not a sound comes from the bedroom. All my captor has to do is drop him into the canal and his life will be over. If there is any life left in him, the cold water would soon take him. Cally begins to fiddle with the binds on my hands, trying to loosen them. 'Keep doing that, Cally, but don't let him see.'

She sniffs and wipes her nose on her sleeve then continues. 'He's the ghost, Mummy.'

'The ghost?'

'I saw someone in our garden when you went out with Jennifer. He moved his arms the same when he climbed out of the boat, just like the ghost. I thought it was a ghost because I was watching ghosty things.' She paused. 'He was locking Daddy's garage.'

He walked back in. 'Come here, kid.'

I glance down at my scared child and nod. 'It's okay.' I kiss her on the head and she reluctantly leaves my side.

He opens the box and my little girl stands there, open-mouthed. 'Right, let's get this boat moving. Cally, back on the seat. If you're good, you can play with your present later. I can't trust you yet I'm going to have to pop this on your wrist.' He grabs a coil of rope and uses the knife to cut a length. He grips Cally's wrists and holds them in front of her. 'Keep them like that.' He wraps the rope around her skinny wrists several times and then ties it in knots over and over again. 'Now for your feet.' He does the same with her feet.

Cally does exactly as she is told. She now fully understands the situation and it breaks my heart that she has to at five years old. She is literally complying for her life, just like me.

'There, now be good girls. Any problems and this one will go overboard,' he says as he points at Cally, making a diving action with his hand. 'Understand?' We both nod. 'One more thing, have a drink.' He holds the cup to Cally's mouth. She recoils. 'It's just juice. Drink.' She drinks from the cup as he pours it into her mouth then he leaves through the back door, locking it behind him.

'That drink tasted funny, Mummy.'

I saw him bring the juice with him, already made up.

'Mummy, I feel a bit funny.' She yawns.

Every muscle in my body is tense. He's drugged my child and I hate him. We are now moving up the canal. I start fiddling with the binds around my hands. Cally has barely touched them but I do feel a weakness in the knot. 'It's okay, baby girl. Go to sleep. When you wake up, it will all be over.'

Seconds later, the rhythmic chugging begins and the faint smell of fuel enters the galley. We're moving closer to Omar's death and potentially our own. I can't let him hurt Cally and the same goes for Grant. Mrs Abidar has already lost her husband, I won't let her lose Omar and I won't lose Cally.

The box begins to move as something is scratching to escape.

She mumbles like she's drunk. 'Mummy, Thumper is scared.' Then her head falls heavy on my shoulder and her breathing deepens. I've never felt so terrified and alone.

FIFTY-EIGHT

WEDNESDAY, 6 APRIL

'With Cally and Annabel's life in danger, we need this door down now.' They had knocked and shouted 'police' but Evan Bryson had not answered. It was obvious that he wasn't in.

O'Connor came from around the back, leaving PC Smith watching the garden. 'No sign of him or of anyone being in.'

'Right. We're going in.'

PC Smith moved to the front and held the enforcer before giving all he had to get the door open. On the second slam, the door gave way and bounced against the wall. 'We're in, guv.'

Gina twisted her stab vest a little so that it was comfortable and led the way. 'Police, we have a warrant to search the property.' There wasn't a sound. 'Cally, Annabel?' Again, no reply. 'Omar?' She reached out and turned on the hall light. Nodding back, Wyre, PC Kapoor and O'Connor stepped in. She nodded to O'Connor and Kapoor to head upstairs and they nodded their reply. Gina shifted past the sideboard in the hall but there was hardly any room. The whole area felt cramped. She peered into the living room, which was a mirror of Annabel's next door. The old leather settee was opposite the fireplace and the TV was tucked on a brick-built stand in the corner. She glanced in every corner. 'Clear.'

'Ouch.' Wyre walked into the sideboard, nudging it slightly.

Gina followed her into the kitchen, turning the light on as she brushed past the switch. A plastic cup sat on the side. Gina put on a pair of latex gloves and opened the top. It smelled like juice and the cup was almost empty. Next to it was a plate containing a sandwich with a missing bite. 'Looks like someone never finished their food.'

'Guv?' O'Connor shouted to her from the landing. 'Get up here, now.'

'Keep looking through the kitchen. Open the drawers, open everything.'

'Yes, guv.' Wyre began searching as Gina ran up the stairs. 'What have you found?'

'His laptop and some paperwork. It's not password protected. Check out his emails.'

Gina stood in front of O'Connor and began reading the one that was on the screen.

Hiya mate,

I'm loving Amsterdam. The boats here are awesome which is why I've rented one to stay in while I work here. You'd love it. Maybe soon we can organise a boys' break, you, me and Grant. It's the best place ever. If I wasn't working so hard, I'd have a chance to enjoy it more but hey, it pays for my bills and boat.

Thanks again for looking after the Raspberry and I'll pay you for the paint job when I see you next. If you want to take her for a run up the canal, just do it. Stratford is the best, you can head on to the Stratford-upon-Avon Canal. Don't know why I'm telling you that as you probably did this route with your boat when it was at Bidford. I guess I'm just saying, you can take her for a substantial run. Take your fishing gear and have a good time. I like her to have a run out and I know how much you miss your boat. Grant never appreciated the one he bought off you which is why it's knackered. So sad to see. I know it needed some work but it could have been restored. Not anymore.

Anyhow, I'll give you a bell next week. Keep an eye on my gorgeous little niece and if you see her, tell Cally that Uncle Seth will bring her something nice back.

'Call ahead, see if local police at Stratford will check to see if the *Raspberry Pi* is still moored up.'

O'Connor nodded and pulled out his phone. 'Check these out while I call.' He pointed to the paperwork on the bed and left the room to make the call.

Gina spread the statements and letters out. The first thing she spotted was the notice to repossess his house. She glanced at the statement underneath showing that his main account was overdrawn. She lifted that up and saw a savings account statement with another bank.

O'Connor stepped back in. 'They're heading over there now. I've brought them up to date and I said we'd head over too.'

'Have you seen this?' She held the savings statement up.

He nodded. 'It looks like he withdrew twenty thousand pounds in cash over the past month in smaller chunks.'

'And he hasn't paid any bills. He's been planning a new life for a while.' Gina exhaled. 'Have you searched everything?'

'No, not yet. I found the laptop and paperwork and called you up straight away.'

Gina opened the louvre doors to the built-in cupboard and it was mostly stuffed with old clothes that were about to topple out. She removed them, dropping jumpers, coats and jeans all over the floor. She closed that door then opened the next one. It was empty except for a shabby looking photo album. She turned open the first page. Behind the plastic protector sheets were photos of Annabel.

Annabel getting into her car. Annabel eating lunch with a friend. Annabel at the Christmas party with her colleagues on the boat. Annabel in the bushes being pinned to a tree by Whittle. Gina saw the teary shine on Annabel's cheek and the tired, glazed-over look in her eyes, his hands pinning hers above her head.

She turned to the next few photo sleeves.

Grant and Taylor kissing in his garage. Grant at dinner with another woman, holding her hand over a table. Grant and Annabel arguing. As she turned the next page, she shivered at the photo in front of her. Annabel asleep in her bed and Grant next to her. Annabel in the bath, eyes closed and surrounded by candles. A close-up of her breasts. Then there was the photo of Cally fast asleep. He had access to their house, had keys cut. He came and went as he pleased. He must have kept a spare key to *Freedom*. She'd bet everything that the fingerprints on the raspberry keyring matched his.

O'Connor leaned in. 'Shit.'

'Looking at all this, I'd say Evan Bryson probably drugged Cally with something mild and left her in bed. He took Grant's car from the garage. He ran over Jennifer and took Annabel. He parked the car up close by and came back to lock up the garage, and Cally thought he was a ghost. He dealt with us then he took Annabel to *Freedom* and left the car hidden out the way by the boat. I don't know how he got back from *Freedom* yet.' Gina's brow furrowed. 'Maybe we can check with the local taxi firms, Uber, buses, to see if anyone remembers him. After that – Taylor was getting in the way, coming back and looking for Grant so he killed her. He then took Grant using his own car and swapped him for Annabel after he finished painting *Raspberry Pi*. I think he'd intended to come back later and kill Grant but we found Grant and the Mercedes.' Gina paused. 'What about Omar? Did he see the boy hanging around?'

'He'd have no need for the kid.'

'Guv, you've got to see this,' Wyre called from below.

Gina slightly knocked into O'Connor as she rushed out of the small room and down the stairs. 'What?'

Wyre had pushed the sideboard out of the way to reveal a small understairs cupboard door. Gina kneeled on the wooden floor and pulled her pencil torch from her pocket. The smell of stale body odour and urine hit her. She held her breath as she shone it to reveal everything. A smelly grey blanket was scrunched up one end and a length of rope. Scratched in the plaster of one wall were the words, "Tell my mum I love her and I'm sorry. Omar." Gina could just about read them. She grabbed her phone and took a photo. 'He has Omar, too. We need uniform to check the grounds, the shed. Check everything and everywhere. We have to get to Stratford, that's where the boat is based. We'll need dogs and a helicopter on standby. The lives of two children are in danger and Annabel's is too. I fear we're too late. He has them and he has nothing to lose. That scares me.'

FIFTY-NINE

Annabel

'Why him and not me?' Evan's hair was now slick with sweat even though it's cold. He placed Cally on the couch when he came back into the boat and she remains in a slumber. She has stirred and spoken a couple of times. Whatever he gave her wasn't strong acting, not like what he gave me when I was left on *Freedom*. It sickens me to know that he probably bought that drug from Grant.

I don't know where we are or where he's stopped the boat. We could be anywhere. I know Seth kept his boat at Stratford, just opposite McDonald's. 'Answer me. Why him?'

'Grant is my husband.'

He stares at me and scrunches his nose. 'I didn't mean that jerk, I meant the stuffy geography teacher who smells of cat. I tell you I like you and you joke it away and we carry on like I never said anything. That hurt. We both agreed that Grant was no good. I told you about the woman he had dinner with too, that it didn't stop there. They got a hotel room after and we can guess what happened. Then there was Taylor. Young, fresh and exciting, she perked him up. All the while you played the dutiful little wife until *he* came along. Let me remind you. The boat party.'

My head hurts with all that runs through it. He's bringing up something I've tried so hard to forget. 'He's nothing.' I really can't go there. This has to stop.

'It didn't look like nothing when you were pissed out of your head and shagging him against a tree.'

A tear trickles down my chin.

'No good being all regretful now. Let me get this straight, I have been a good friend, in fact the best friend ever. I do jobs for you, for Grant, for his brother, and I ask for nothing. I look after your daughter. I take in your dog when you go on holiday. When you've been a bit down and drunk, I've been there, I've listened to you. I've been a part of your lives since you moved in and what do I get in return? Nothing. People like you and Grant use people like me and give nothing back. All I wanted was your love and I get that you rejected me. I get that you wanted to try to save your marriage but when I saw you with him, I knew it was nothing but a lie.'

'It's not what it looked like.' I have to explain in order to get him back on side or I fear he will have no use for me.

'I could play this another way. Maybe I dispose of you and Omar and I keep Cally. I get to be her dad and look after her. I'll be a great dad, better than Grant, so you won't have to worry.'

I shake my head and for a second, I can't breathe. The thought of him taking my child and me never seeing her again – it's like the air has been sucked out of me. I try to gasp but I feel as though I'm being gripped around the throat.

'Oh calm down, for heaven's sake.'

I manage to take in some air. It wasn't my first panic attack,

I've had a few since that night of the party but each time it happens, it still feels like I'm about to die. Slowly, my breaths begin to regulate but now I shake erratically. 'You saw me that night, while he was raping me. He drugged me and you did nothing and now you sit there and blame me.'

He stares, unsure of what he saw. I can tell he's thinking about that night as his brow scrunches and he looks beyond me. 'You weren't screaming.'

Tom Whittle raped me and my neighbour takes me and my child. Why would I expect him of all people to understand? I had been seeing Tom. I'd met him for a few dates and I'd even kissed him but after that night, school had become hard. I'd suddenly see him everywhere. After a particularly bad day, he cornered me by the gym block. I know I couldn't prove that he raped me but I still wanted him to know that I knew what had happened. I stood up to him and said those words "you drugged me and you raped me," but he denied it all, said it was me who lured him into the woods and that I assaulted him, taking advantage because he was drunk. All the time I had a witness and it sickens me to know that that witness was stalking me. I feel double violated. Tom left me shaking in that corridor, so sure that he'd got away with it, and he has. I still haven't told but there was one person who knew. Omar. He asked me if I was okay and I made him swear not to tell a soul, which then led him to feel that we were closer than we were. Everything is such a mess. No child should have to hear that conversation.

I jolt back into the present and inhale sharply. 'No, I wasn't screaming.' Comments like this is why I didn't say a word, why I got home to Grant and told him that the evening had been fine even though I staggered up the path and fell through the door, and it's why I went to school on the Monday and carried on as normal, even though I had the sickest hangover ever on the Sunday from whatever he'd given me.

'I'm prepared to put all that behind us. Let's start again.' He walks to the fridge and pulls out a bottle of Prosecco. After popping the cork, he pours some into two tin mugs and comes back. He places one into my tied-up hands and I manage to loop a finger through the handle. 'Let's make a toast to family.'

He bangs his cup against mine and drinks. I sip the liquid, but only a little. The last thing I need is to be even remotely tipsy or worse, get drugged. I saw him pour it straight out of the bottle but I don't know if he put anything in the cup earlier. Muffled murmuring comes from the bedroom and I feel adrenaline coursing through me. Omar is alive.

'Before we start our new life, there's something we have to do.' He opens the door to the bedroom. 'Wakey, wakey.'

He's alive but I know Evan is going to kill him now.

SIXTY

Gina pulled up outside McDonald's in Stratford-upon-Avon and she ran across the pavement, towards the boats where three officers stood next to a restaurant barge and another moored up boat. Every vessel looked far more luxurious than *Freedom* which still stood in the boatyard, surrounded by police tape until it could be removed for evidence. A woman peered out of the door in a yellow nightshirt, watching the commotion unfold. Gina went over to one of the uniformed officers. 'DI Harte from Cleevesford.'

'PC Blake,' the young man replied. '*Raspberry Pi*, the boat your colleague was looking for is registered here. It is owned by a Seth Braddock. As you can see, it is missing. I've taken the liberty of contacting the council and checking CCTV. This boat left on Monday morning. Although it's not brilliant, I have a screenshot.' The officer held his phone up to Gina.

'That's Evan Bryson, our suspect. Have you watched the footage?'

'Yes.'

'Was there anyone else on the boat?'

'No. No, only your suspect got on that boat, here.'

'Thank you, that's really helpful. Did you see which way it went?'

He nodded. 'Yes, we have it on camera two more times. It travelled on the Stratford Canal not on the Avon. It runs around twenty-five miles to Kings Norton. We don't have it on camera after it left Stratford.'

'Are there any other routes off this canal?'

'Yes, the Kingswinford Junction leads to the Grand Union Canal. I think that's about halfway.'

'Sorry to ask so much so fast.' Gina hated that her knowledge on boating was so poor but she'd barely had any downtime to research further and neither had her team. 'How fast do these boats go?'

'Around three miles an hour, I think. They're not the fastest.'

'Thank you.' She left the officer and hurried to Wyre who had just turned up. 'The boat has left.'

'Damn.' Wyre hurried beside her and they went back to the marina.

'Hey, DI Harte.'

'Yes.' She turned back to the officer. 'The woman in that boat has been in hers for the past week with her partner. They saw and spoke to your suspect.'

'I know where he was heading,' she called.

SIXTY-ONE

The woman who'd introduced herself as Deanna grabbed a coat and buttoned it up, covering her nightshirt. The middle of the night air pinched with a chill. Her partner, a more petite woman, came out of the boat joining Deanna and Gina on the pavement.

'Where was he heading?' Gina and Wyre were poised to go.

'I don't know exactly but he said that when he had a boat of his own, he enjoyed taking the Stratford to Kings Norton route and he said how beautiful Wootton Wawen was and the aqueduct. I had a little conversation with him as I know who the boat belongs to and the boat community look out for each other.'

O'Connor headed across the road. 'Bear with me.' Gina left Wyre holding the fort for a moment and hurried over to her colleague knowing that time was of the essence. 'He's on the Stratford to Kings Norton route and has a particular liking of Wootton Wawen. Get the chopper out. Find that boat.'

He ran over to uniform, leaving Gina to go back to the two women and Wyre.

'When did you last see him?'

'Monday. He said he was taking the boat for a ride out. I got worried and checked with the boat's owner, Seth. He's working in Amsterdam and I know that boat is his pride and joy. He confirmed that his friend, Evan, was okay to use the boat, that he'd asked him to paint it and said that he could take it out. I saw Evan working on the boat and assumed he was doing a job for Seth, but I didn't know they were friends. After that I didn't take much notice of him. He's come and gone over the past three weeks, painting the top and the top front of the boat in blue. I even thought to ask him if he wanted to paint our boat after.'

'Did he bring anyone to the boat at any time?'

The woman wrapped her arm in front of her body and her friend left. Gina heard the kettle boiling.

'No. He said he was going to take the boat out and that his wife was working. He said she'd join him in a day or two. He seemed lovely and even showed us a picture of her and a child. What's happened to them all?'

Gina pulled up photos of Cally and Annabel on her phone. 'Is this them?'

Deanna scrunched her brow. Her partner came out with a tray of hot milky coffees and offered them around. Gina and Wyre took one as they thanked her.

'Yes. I remember saying how cute that little girl was and I could tell how much he loved them. I've never seen a person grin so much with pride. He told me how they'd been married a few years, that she was a teacher and how much he loved his little girl.'

'So, you haven't seen him since Monday?'

'No, we left the boat on Monday and came back this afternoon. Thought we'd spend the night on it while we gave it a clean out. We don't live far so we're here a lot.' The woman drank her coffee down.

Her partner piped up. 'Is everything okay? He seemed so nice? He's not hurt, is he?'

Gina drank the warm coffee down, grateful of the perk that the caffeine would give her. They were all going to need to be on their best form. 'We are concerned. If you see him or if he comes back here, call me immediately. Do not approach him.'

Arching her brows, Deanna gave her partner her empty cup. 'So he's dangerous.'

'I can't discuss the investigation with you but here's my card. It has my number on it. Have you seen the news this week?'

Deanna shook her head. 'No, I've been so busy.'

'The woman you just identified is missing and we're worried about her safety.'

The woman went to speak and then stopped as she furrowed her brow as everything clicked into place.

'As I said, if you see him, call us immediately.'

'I will, thank you for the warning.' She gave her partner a worried glance.

O'Connor ran over and Gina stepped away not wanting the women to hear whatever it was that he had to say. Any gossip on social media could hinder the case. She left them with Wyre and knew her colleague would be wrapping up their conversation. 'Guv, the eye in the sky has spotted three boats close to the area of investigation. There are also several moored up at Wootton Wawen.'

'Where are the three?'

'One is just past Wootton Wawen as if it was cruising from Stratford, one is before Wootton Wawen and the other is a little further on. I have the exact locations messaged to me.'

'Forward that info to me. Let's hope that he's a little nostalgic when it comes to Wootton Wawen and he's not further away. Let's concentrate on or before Wootton Wawen but we need someone to head to the third location too, the one a little further up. I'll head over now. We can't waste any more time. We need to bring those children and Annabel home and we can't lose them.' Gina swallowed as she ran to her car knowing that O'Connor would fill Wyre in. As she turned her engine on, she almost trembled at what they might be walking in to. Two dead children and a dead woman? A hostage situation? Or maybe Evan Bryson isn't on any of those boats. He might already be on another route that could take their search much further out, giving him an opportunity to slip away.

SIXTY-TWO

Gina pulled up behind PC Smith. Wyre would join them in a moment. Uniformed officers were already on the scene of the first boat, just before Wootton Wawen. She ran, phone in hand, stab vest making her sweat like mad. Although chilly, she was boiling as she ran along the slim path until it reached the canal. The landscape was in pitch darkness. In the distance she could see street lights flickering as the gentle breeze caught the branches on the opposite side of the road.

'Here, guv.' PC Smith shone his torch in her face.

She closed one eye and squinted before moving out of his light beam. She held a sleeve over her nose for a few seconds to dampen the smell of stagnant water. 'Where's the boat?'

'There's one just back there. See.' He pointed. In the darkness, she could just make out the shape of it. She pointed her torch in its direction. It was blue on the top. 'Is it *Raspberry Pi*?'

'Let's go and check.'

A uniformed officer reached the boat, treading carefully so as not to alarm Evan Bryson, knowing that the situation could easily get out of hand. The officer shook his head. 'This is old chipped paint.'

'Damn.'

A white-haired man opened the back of the boat and could just about see Gina. 'What's going on? Clear off or I'll call the police.'

Gina ran forward and the uniformed officer stepped into view. 'We are the police, sir.'

'Oh.' He stepped out. 'What do you want?'

'Have you seen a boat called *Raspberry Pi* at all? Maybe it passed you at some point.'

'Oh yes. It's hard to miss the big raspberry next to its name. That arsehole nearly wrecked my boat earlier. I've come back from Kings Norton and I was a bit tired but he woke me up. He looked distracted and almost crashed into my side as we passed. Probably drunk. People try it on the canals. They think it's okay but it's not. More should be done about drunk boating.'

Gina exhaled. She didn't have time to discuss anything other than where the boat was. 'How long ago was that?'

'Only 'bout an hour or so. His kid was having a bit of a tantrum too. I could hear crying. No wonder with the way her dad was steering that boat.'

'Thank you.' She turned and ran back, almost bumping into Wyre. 'It has to be the boat on the other side of the village and Cally's with him.' Her phone went. 'Hello.'

She ran as fast as she could until she stood at her car, panting and out of breath.

Wyre hurried past. 'Meet you there.'

Her caller had told her that the boats moored up at Wootton Wawen had been checked. *Raspberry Pi* was not there, but Evan's car had been found. The witness that she'd just spoken to had seen Evan within the last hour. He had to be no more than four miles away. Gina suspected he had to be at the far end of Wootton Wawen. The last boat the helicopter saw was too far away for the speed the boats could travel. They had him.

She grabbed her phone and spoke to the officer who had

just called. 'Don't approach him. Everyone on board could be in danger and I don't want this to turn into a hostage situation. Children's lives are at stake. Stay back until I arrive and we'll take it slowly. We need an ambulance on standby. Do not approach him until I give you further instruction.' She took a deep breath and started up her engine, ready to step into the unknown.

SIXTY-THREE

Annabel

Cally starts to fuss and I begin to shake. 'Mummy.' With one eye open, she tries to stand but stumbles like she's half sleep-walking.

'Baby, stay there and pretend to be asleep.'

Her bottom lip quivers and the rope at her ankles falls away. She cries as she staggers across the boat, holding on to anything to get to me, her little wrists bound together loosely. There's no use me trying to tell her what to do. She's confused and half drugged. She plonks her little bottom next to me on the bench and leans her head on my shoulder, yawning.

Evan bursts through the bedroom door, dragging Omar under the arms. I place my arm over Cally's eyes, trying to nestle her in my armpit, which is all my tied hands allow me to do. 'Don't look.' I kiss her on the head and hope that she can't see what's happening right in front of us. Under the table, Cally has managed to get free of the rope around her wrists. In haste,

Evan hadn't tied them properly, relying on the drug to control her.

'Please,' Omar says, his wavering voice sounding drunk. The blood on his wrist has partially crusted. It would be a relief if I knew that Evan wasn't about to throw him overboard to his death. I wonder if Omar would have the strength to float or swim.

Evan dropped him on the floor and repositioned the kitchen knife that he'd been keeping in his belt, then he grabbed the boy again. 'What are you doing there?' He stares at Cally.

'It's okay. She woke up and came to me. She's scared. Please leave her with me.' I pause. 'You don't have to do this. Please, Omar is just a child. He hasn't done anything. If you leave him out there it will be hours before help arrives and he's too weak to get far. You have me. Do what you like to me. I'll come willingly. None of this is needed.'

He looks at me and then at Omar.

'I'm all my mum has. She needs me.' Tears slip down his cheek and little bubbles form under his nose as he cries like the child he is.

'Evan, you are not this person. I know you, you've been a brilliant neighbour and friend. Cally thinks the world of you and I don't want her to be scared of you. If you hurt him, she will be. She's a child too and she needs to feel safe with you.'

Evan shakes his head and runs his fingers through his hair. As he focuses on Omar, I begin to prod and pull at the rope around my wrists and it becomes even looser. Cally begins to play with it under the table. In my mind, I could lunge at him and simply hope that Omar could escape with my petrified child. I'd fight him to the bitter end, not caring if I die. My daughter is everything to me and I'm prepared for what may come.

'No,' Omar shouts as Evan grabs him again. Just for a moment,

I thought we had a breakthrough. I was wrong. 'One move from you and I'll plunge this knife straight into him. Hear me?' He's looking at Cally now and I can tell she's now peering at him. How could I have ever trusted this man with my home and my child? Omar tries to kick out but he's no threat to the strong, fully grown man who is pulling him along like he weighs nothing. Evan drags him up the steps at the back of the boat that I know will lead to the cruiser deck, and he bounces on each one with a sickening thud.

'Evan, please.'

'Shut up, bitch.' I know things have worsened and he is determined to carry out his plan. He's never called me a name before. As he leaves, he disappears out of view. Thuds, bangs and grunts fill the air. I can't tell who is making the noises but what I do know is that Omar is probably fighting for his life with the little bit of energy he has. That will only leave him with less when he hits the water. The initial plunge will take his breath away, then he'll likely ingest mouthfuls of the rancid water. He'll fight for a short while but it's hard when your breath has been taken away, and you're wounded and spent. Omar is both of those.

Cally stops teasing the ropes. I know she saw Omar being dragged and heard everything. 'Mummy, is he going to kill the boy?'

I can't believe my child has even got to ask that question. Tears trickle down my face. He is going to kill him but I can't say yes, it would break her to know that our once friendly neighbour is about to commit murder. A loud bang makes us flinch. Cally sits up, looking more alert now.

Omar screams. 'Don't throw me in. Please don't kill me.'

Cally slips from my underarm and runs along the boat.

'Cally, no.' It's too late, my child sidesteps the rabbit that is loose on the floor before hurrying up those stairs, and there's nothing I can do. Panicking, I yank the ropes over and over. I go to hop off the bench and fall flat on my face, right next to where Omar bled.

A piercing scream reverberates through the boat, sending a shiver through my body and I hear a loud splash. 'Cally,' I cry, but she does not answer. It's as if time stands still. I'm not breathing and everything runs through my head at lightning speed. I shake my head and my legs tremble. The only thing I hear are Omar's sobs. I've never had a more uncontrollable reaction in my whole life. To know my daughter is drowning in that freezing cold water and there's not a thing I can do, is the worst. I let her die. It should have been me. Then I hear another splash and I can no longer hear Omar.

Cally can barely swim. She can manage half a width doing the doggy paddle but the water is warm in the pool where I take her.

Evan runs back in, pacing up and down, hands tapping his temple as he speaks incoherently to himself. He's panicking too.

'You killed my child.' I can't contain my tears and heartache and I can't breathe for sobs. This is unreal. I want to die. I have nothing to live for. He has ruined my life. Right now, I'd do anything to be back at home with my pathetic excuse of a marriage with all its problems and my cruel husband. I'd have my daughter. But it's too late. How a couple of minutes can change a person's life. Mine is changed forever.

'I'm sorry, she slipped. She ran for me and I couldn't get her off me. It was an accident.'

'Get out there and save her. If you love me, you'll bring her to me.'

He kneels on the floor and walks towards me on his knees, kissing me on the head. 'She's gone. We'll get through this, I promise you. We can have a baby; our baby.'

This is too sick. The rope has loosened and I unravel it. I have to get out and find her. I know how to do CPR. I'll do whatever. I bring my fist around and strike him in the nose. He falls to the side, tears spilling from his eyes. I reach out and dig a nail in his right eyeball and that confuses him. Reaching down, I untie my leg binds. He pulls himself onto me, squashing and restraining me. With no effort he brings his fist to my kidney and the pain renders me senseless. With that, he stumbles to his feet, using the table and the cooker to pull his body up. His vision is back and I see the anger on his face and I know that I have no chance of saving Cally now. It's been too long. She's dead and I'm going to die too.

'You made me do this. You only have yourself to blame. All you had to do was control the child and stay put. You couldn't do it so you killed Cally. Blame yourself.' My breath is taken away as he kicks me in the stomach. 'I didn't want it to end up like this but one more sound out of you and you're going the same way.'

I gasp and heave as he locks the door. All I hear is the boat starting up. We're moving again. I don't even know where we are. My daughter and Omar have died in this water and I'll never know where that was.

Chug, chug, chug. It's like the boat is laughing at me. The rabbit hops towards my face and lies next to me.

My baby; I want my baby. I've never felt so hollow.

SIXTY-FOUR

'Guv,' O'Connor called. Officers were at the boat. It was heading this way but it had stopped one lock down on this side. There was nowhere to park any closer so on foot it was. She jogged alongside O'Connor, both of them slowing down. The gravelled towpath tapered into mud and undergrowth. Wyre hurried past them, kicking all trailing brambles out of the way.

The helicopter headed back their way, lighting up the area. Gina popped her torch back in her pockets, needing the swing of both arms to keep going. O'Connor slipped back. Wyre held out a hand and stopped, bending over to get her breath back. Within a few seconds Gina caught up with her. She panted and grimaced as she held her side.

'That's the boat, guv. We've found them.'

She heard chugging and the small police boat pulled up alongside them. 'Hop in,' the operator said. With a leap, Gina landed in the boat and was quickly followed by Wyre. It swayed as they got their balance. 'Here, you might need this.' She took the megaphone off him and the boat chugged forward. Now they were in a position to follow the boat if their perp decided to keep going.

'Stop the boat, here.'

O'Connor and uniform took various positions, trying to keep out of view unless instructed. Their only objective was to bring everyone out alive and unharmed.

'Mr Bryson, please come out so that we can talk.' She resisted using the megaphone, not wanting to alarm him. There was no answer. An officer was sneaking around the side of the boat, trying to peer in. A message caused her phone to light up.

He's in the cabin and he has a woman. He's holding a knife to her throat.

She held her hand up to acknowledge that she'd received the officer's message. Gina gripped the megaphone handle so hard she feared she might break it. She then spoke, the sound of her amplified voice getting everyone's attention. 'Mr Bryson, please come out. Police, you are surrounded. We can talk if you come out.'

The back door made a click sound and the worst-case scenario was staring her in the face. She swallowed knowing her chances of helping Annabel were slim. She had one crack at this and he was the one holding the knife.

SIXTY-FIVE

Annabel

'Damn!' He holds the point of the knife to my jugular vein. 'It's over.'

We can both hear the helicopter now. It's circling again and it must be low. The police have us surrounded. 'Please, you're hurting me.' My face is cold and wet with fallen tears. Fallen for my daughter and Omar.

'Nothing matters any more. You know that this is the end for both of us. All I ever wanted was you. I didn't want to lose you to him.' He pauses. His hands are shaking so much, I fear he will slip soon and slit my throat before he's planned to.

'Police, you are surrounded. Come out slowly and drop your weapon.'

He shakes his head, perspiration from him dripping down my cleavage. I'm not getting out of this one. I can see his reflection in an old mirror at the back of the boat. His eye is swollen and there's blood smeared under his nose and on his cheek. I did that. It wasn't enough. If I could go back a few minutes, I'd have left my feet tied and used the rope from my hands to throttle him first. That's what I should have done, then, maybe, I might have still had time to save Cally. I swallow. Could I really have killed a man?

My gaze meets his in the reflection. I could kill him. This primal emotion that sweeps through me is like nothing I've ever felt. He killed my child. Too right, I want to kill him. I want him to suffer and die for all that he's done to me and taken from me. For once in my life, I allow myself to feel the rage I so deserve to feel and I jab him in the ribs as hard as I can as I scream.

His grip is temporarily loosened. I'm a fighter and I will fight my way out of this. I will get justice for Cally and so will Ms Abidar for Omar. He will not win. If I die, he is coming with me. This man can't be left to walk the earth. He'll do time and maybe thirty years down the line, he'll probably get out. Even the worst of killers seem to walk eventually.

There is a toaster on the side. It's small and light but still, it's a weapon. I grab it and bring it down on his head but this time he isn't dazed. He grabs me, twists me around and I'm back where I started. 'Time to face what's out there, then we die. There's nowhere to go, no moves left to take.'

My rage has been replaced by the shakes. I'm angry, I'm bereaved; I'm enraged and terrified. He's homicidal, maybe suicidal. Most of all, he has nothing to lose.

He pushes me along the boat and up the steps.

'Drop your weapon.' The sound of the policewoman rings through my ear.

He's not moving. I feel the blade pierce the delicate skin on my neck and I know the end has come.

SIXTY-SIX

'Evan.' Gina gets the man's attention. He stares in her direction, his trembling fingers on the knife, then he glances at Wyre. A trail of blood trickles down Annabel's neck. 'Please let Annabel and the children go. You don't have to do this.' Gina was now looking at the man who mowed Jennifer down, leaving her for dead. That alone told her what he was capable of doing now.

'I have nothing. I love her. All I ever wanted was her and she chose him. She had sex with that prick.'

'Look, put the knife down and we can talk about this. No one needs to get hurt. Can we see the children?'

Annabel's fists are clenched and she looks weak and tired.

'The children have gone.'

Gina swallowed. 'Gone? Where?'

'It was an accident. I didn't mean for them to get hurt. Cally ran out of the boat and fell overboard. Omar then fell in. I couldn't save them.'

Gina swallowed. Finding the children dead was one of the things she'd dreaded the most but seeing what he did to Taylor showed them that he had it in him. Out of the corner of her eye, she saw a team heading up the canal on foot, flashing torches at the water as they searched for the bodies. The bodies – thinking it made her struggle to swallow.

Annabel's eyes were streaming now and she wriggled at the mention of her daughter's name. He pressed the tip in further and she let out a slight squeal.

'If it was an accident then there was nothing you could do, but you can help Annabel. If you love her like you say you do, let us help her. There's an ambulance waiting.' Gina paused. He was still and she hoped that she had him, but in these situations, she knew how things could turn in an instant. 'Your eye is badly hurt. You need help. We can get it seen to.'

'You think I give a toss about my eye!' He began to clench his teeth and stared at Gina.

'Please put the knife down. We don't want either of you to get hurt.'

He shook his head. 'For you lot to pounce on me and throw me into a cell for the rest of my life. No way. You must think I'm stupid. There is only one way out of this and it's not your way.'

He went to cut Annabel's throat and the woman desperately cried out.

'No, stop.' The man wasn't listening. She'd lost him. She gave the nod to the officer on the towpath and he gently crept onboard at the back end. 'Annabel is scared. You're scaring her. I know how much you love her. You don't want this.'

He used his knife to scratch a clump of dried blood from his nose. Gina saw the fire in Annabel's eyes as she punched him in the throat. He gasped for breath and stumbled back. She ran from where they'd been standing, straight into the hiding officer who'd just reached them. Evan turned the knife to his own throat. 'Please forgive me, Annabel.' He paused and stared at Gina. 'Tell everyone, I didn't kill the children. I've never killed anyone.' He stepped back around the other side of the boat, the knife still on his own throat with the dark murky water behind him. A slight breeze caught his hair. 'I didn't kill

Taylor. Tell everyone that too. I never went anywhere near her.'

Gina scrunched her brows. That statement wasn't expected. 'We can help you, Evan. Please step away from the edge.'

He shook his head. 'No one can help me. I've crossed that line. What I've done was unforgivable. It all got out of hand. She was meant to love me, that was all. I was going to kill Grant. He treated her appallingly. The ketamine I used on him and Annabel, to shut them up, I got that from him. He's a bloody drug dealer. How many people has he killed? There's another confession for you. Nothing matters.' He leaned over the top of the boat, his demeanour that of someone who'd given up.

Annabel broke free from the officer and ran along the towpath. 'I hate you. You killed my little girl.'

'I'm sorry. Please forgive me.' Evan's eyes glassed over and with a swift plunge, the knife pierced his throat. He fell backwards with a splash into the water.

Annabel fell to the floor on her knees. 'I will never forgive you.'

The police boat chugged over to Evan and both Gina and the officer panted as they pulled Evan's body onto the boat. The knife had slipped out into the canal and blood began to gush from his wound. He cracked a few half words that Gina couldn't understand. She removed her coat and pressed it to the wound but it was no good. He was gone. The officer manoeuvred the boat to the side where the paramedics took over but Gina knew it was too late for him. The gash he'd made to his own throat was done with a purpose and that was to kill himself. She left him and hurried over to Annabel.

'Annabel, I'm DI Harte.' She took a foil blanket from PC Smith and she sat on the muddy path. Throwing the blanket over Annabel's shoulders, she tilted her head. 'Annabel.'

'He killed my child. He killed her. He was going to kill

Omar too. All that on the boat, it was lies. He's a killer.' She went to stand but fell.

'Annabel, let's get you to the ambulance. You need to get checked over.'

'No, I need to find Cally. She's in there, somewhere.' She pointed at the water. 'I am going to find her. I want to hold her.' She stood and went to jump in.

Gina held her back. 'Please let our officers do that. A dive team should be here shortly. You need help.'

'She needs help, my Cally.' Annabel's bottom lip began to quiver. 'She's dead. They're dead.' Annabel leaned into Gina's arm and she allowed the woman to sob on her shoulder. Gina's eyes began to well up slightly. If she could take Annabel's pain away, she would.

'Guv.' O'Connor ran down the towpath. 'We've found the girl.'

Annabel broke away from Gina. In the distance PC Smith was carefully walking through brambles and entangled undergrowth, carrying the small child. The woman wiped the trickle of blood from her neck. 'Cally.'

'Mummy, Omar saved me,' Cally said through chattering teeth. Her hair and clothes wet and dotted with grass and twigs.

Annabel half-hopped to reach her child and she took her off Smith and fell to the ground, hugging her closely and kissing her head. 'It's okay, baby girl. It's all going to be fine. I love you so much. I thought...' She burst into tears. 'Omar saved you. Where is he?'

Evan's body had now been taken and another paramedic ran over.

'Look after them.' Gina left them to get treated and hurried over to O'Connor. 'Have you found Omar?'

O'Connor wiped his eye. 'Yes.'

PC Smith cleared his throat and removed his police hat. 'Cally said he saved her. He held her under the water so that the horrible man couldn't see her. They held their breath and then hid in the reeds. When he'd gone, he pushed Cally to the side and told her to run and hide in the bushes. She said he was breathing funny and then he went to sleep in the water.' PC Smith turned away for a moment. 'Sorry.'

Gina felt herself welling up but she had to be strong. She wanted to hit something and cry. That boy had saved Annabel's child instead of himself. Mrs Abidar had lost her son.

'His body is trapped in the reeds which is why we probably didn't spot it when we first looked.'

'First Mrs Abidar loses her husband, a firefighter, killed in the line of duty, and now her teenage son. I don't know how we're going to tell her.' Gina closed her eyes for a second. 'We should have got here earlier. If only. That famous statement. We've caught our killer but we've failed.' She bit her lip and wiped her nose with her sleeve. Undoing her stab vest, she left it flapping open and inhaled.

'We did all we could, guv.' O'Connor looked at his feet.

Smith left them to be with the other officers. 'I'll be back in a minute. I'm just going to help out.'

Gina let out a snort and shook her head in disbelief at all that had gone down. 'How's Jennifer?'

'Jacob left earlier. They were bringing her round and he wanted to be there. It's going to be a long recovery but she's out of the danger zone. Treatment has worked and the swelling to her brain has gone down. She'll be out of intensive care tomorrow but she'll need a lot of physio.'

Gina smiled. 'That's really good to hear.' She paused. 'Most of it fits into place now. Evan had access to the Braddocks's home. He took the car in their garage. Cally saw him loitering in the garden even though he was meant to be looking after her. She fell asleep. He left her alone, knowing the route that Annabel would walk and he waited for her to leave the pub. Once they stepped onto that quiet road, he took his chance, running Jennifer over and taking Annabel. Of course, Grant got there too late and saw the aftermath.'

'His car has been found too, guv. In the next car park up.'

'And.'

'There's a fold-up bike wedged in it.'

'So he takes Annabel and leaves the car hidden until later in the night when he sneaks out, cycles to where he left it and takes Annabel to *Freedom*. He then takes the long cycle back, leaving the car by the boat. He'd have known we'd be looking for it. Then Taylor and Grant vanish but he sees Taylor.' She paused. 'We know he took Grant but he said he didn't kill Taylor.'

'And you believe him?' O'Connor bit his lip.

'Yes, I do. He had nothing to lose in saying that. He knew he was going to kill himself. It was something Bernard also said about the footprints in the ground by the field. Evan Bryson is guilty of everything we see before us but not that. I guess some people can't change even if they look as though they've turned their life around. Taylor was immature, she was a lot of things but she was young. Grant had promised her the earth and not delivered. She was totally played by him but seeing Taylor and Grant acting in this manner, had him triggered. Get on the phone. We need to make an arrest.'

SIXTY-SEVEN

'Have you found her?' Gina walked into the family room at the station and stared at the man. He stood and walked over with a slight limp, his sciatica obviously playing up.

'Doug Latham, I'm arresting you on suspicion of the murder of Taylor Caldwell. You do not have to say anything, but it may harm your defence if you do not mention when questioned something which you later rely on in court. Anything you do say may be given in evidence. Do you understand?'

He slowly nodded and sat down again. 'Just tell me my daughter's okay and you can do what you like with me.'

'Your daughter and granddaughter are safe. They're being checked over in the hospital at the moment.'

He paused and leaned back on the couch. 'I'm ready. Is this where you take me to one of those horrid little interview rooms and interrogate me?'

Gina nodded and led the way.

A short while later, Gina and Wyre were sitting opposite Doug and the tape had been rolling for a couple of minutes. He'd declined a solicitor.

'I did it. She was sleeping with Grant and you know what? I know how it feels to be cheated on. That one time, I hurt my wife, I found out she was sleeping with my married friend. Taylor reminded me of her. I was over theirs one day and Taylor was looking after Cally. I don't know whether it was half term or whether Cally wasn't well but I turned up with some sweets for her. They weren't expecting me. I peered through the window and saw Cally watching the TV. I then went around the back. That's when I saw Taylor and Grant with their tongues down each other's throats. After, he left her and I stepped behind the garage. When she came out, I said to her, "Hurt my daughter and I promise, I will hurt you." She just called me old man and told me to get lost. That was it. When I popped to Sainsbury's, I thought I'd check on Annabel's house. I let myself in, picked the post up but before turning on the lights, I saw someone in the garden. I thought they were going to burgle the place, until I saw it was Taylor. I grabbed one of Annabel's knives from the drawer and I ran on the inside of the field, then I stabbed her. I struggled to keep up but I did. After, I hurried back to my car and went. I knew the boy was close behind. I'd watched him staring in shock from behind the trees, and then a woman came. That was my cue to leave. It was all over in what seemed like hours, but it was only about fifteen minutes from start to end.'

Gina sipped her coffee and let him continue.

'Then, I went home, relieved my neighbours from babysitting and dog watching duties.' He paused. 'I'm too old and tired to run, lie or hide. I did what I did for my daughter. She's never hurt anyone and people always let her down. I'm her father. That's what fathers do.'

Gina exhaled. That's not what fathers did. Fathers did not murder the woman that their daughter's husband was sleeping with.

'I saw my wife in her and I don't know what came over me.

That red mist had stayed within me for years but... I just couldn't control it.' He placed his head in his hands.

It was lunchtime. The CPS had been spoken to. Grant Braddock and Tom Whittle would face their charges. For now, Gina was going to go home, take a long hot shower and head to the hospital. As she tidied up her desk and went to leave, she bumped straight into Briggs. 'I need to speak to you,' he said.

'Okay.' She looked down.

'Not here. At yours, later.'

'Look, I don't need to hear it.'

'You do. I need my chance to tell you what's going on. You deserve that much.'

She checked her watch. 'I have to get to the hospital.' Pushing past him, she hurried towards the exit.

'I'll see you about seven,' he called. She didn't answer.

As Gina left, she caught sight of Nina Abidar sitting on the wall, a cigarette dangling from her lips. Gina sat beside her.

'Want one?' She held the cigarette packet up to Gina.

'No, thank you. I'm really sorry about Omar.'

'You should have saved my son.' She wiped her glassy eyes with her hand.

Gina looked down at her muddy boots. Nina was right. They were too slow, the clues to solve the case were complicated. If everyone hadn't run and hidden, they'd have got to the bottom of everything sooner, but that's what some people do. When in trouble, some people face it, others hide until they can make sense of it, prove their innocence or they have other crimes that they're hiding.

'You know?' Nina sucked on the cigarette and exhaled a plume of smoke. 'I told my boss what had happened and my friend, all they can use is the word hero for my son. Hero! My husband was classed as a hero for saving someone from a burning building at his own expense. My son saves someone else and he dies. Hero. What is a hero? Maybe they are but I wish they'd both been cowards. They'd still be alive. I wish my son had looked after himself, first.' Nina let out a yowling scream and tears dripped onto her cigarette. 'I would swap all of them, including the good people, for my husband and son. I miss them and he was still my baby boy. He was always my baby even though he was growing up. Do you have children?'

'A grown-up daughter and a young granddaughter.'

'Imagine if you lost one of them tomorrow.'

Gina couldn't. There was no way she could comprehend the pain this woman was going through.

Nina threw her damp cigarette to the floor and stamped on it. 'I hope he rots in hell for what he did to my son.' She held a hand up and walked off.

SIXTY-EIGHT

After hurrying to intensive care, Gina was told that Jennifer had been transferred to a recovery ward. On the way she hoped that the rabbit they'd found on the boat wasn't chewing her chair legs to pieces. Her cat had vanished out of the cat door, clearly upset by their new addition. It was temporary though. She would find a home for the tiny animal.

Box of chocolates in hand, she entered the ward and could see that one bed had the curtains pulled. It had to be Jennifer's.

Creeping closer, she passed a woman with earphones in and one who was snoring, and she waited and listened.

'I love you,' Jacob said.

In a crackly voice, Jennifer replied. 'I was going to tell you... about the baby.' She paused and sobbed a little, 'I didn't think you would be—'

'You mean everything to me. When they told me you were pregnant, I was so scared I'd lose you.' He smirked. 'I went home that night and I allowed myself to imagine being a dad—'

Gina felt like she was intruding. What she should have done was walk away and come back in a few minutes, but she couldn't.

Jennifer's voice was laboured as if she was grasping for her words and elongating them. 'And I wanted to be a mum.'

They both cried together for a few seconds.

'I lost our baby.'

'Shh, it's all going to be okay.' He paused. 'These past few days have made me think about life, about us, about everything. I don't care what colours you want to paint the house. I'm sorry for going on about something so stupid. I... I...'

'What?'

'I know you're not big into the idea, but will you marry me?'

Gina couldn't make out what Jennifer was trying to say.

'Here, your throat's still dry from that horrible breathing tube. I'll get some fresh water.'

Gina moved backwards towards the entrance just as the curtain swished open.

She held the chocolates up and Jacob took her aside. 'Were you here, listening?'

She shrugged her shoulders. 'I've only just arrived.'

He stared at her for a moment as he stood there with the jug. 'Jennifer's going to need a lot of help for a while but she might be home in a few days. Depends on what the doctors and physio say. Go and say hello. You can keep her company while I go and take a leak.'

Gina smiled and waved at Jennifer. She smiled back, too weak to respond. A huge cannula stuck out of her hand and a bag of something was being dripped into her. The monitor beeped away. The young crime scene assistant's mouth was dry and sore, with redness where the tube had been resting in the corner. Her plum-coloured hair greasy on one side and shaved on the other where the medical staff had treated her. 'These are for you.' She popped the chocolates on the bedside cabinet.

'Thanks.' Every word was hard for her. Gina appreciated the effort it was taking. 'What happened?'

'The person who ran you over killed himself in the early

hours. I'm so sorry that I wasn't able to bring him properly to justice for you.'

Jennifer placed a shaky hand on Gina's. 'Annabel?'

'She's fine. In fact, she's being treated for a few minor injuries as we speak. They kept her in overnight and her daughter stayed with her.'

'So, she's here?'

Gina nodded. 'How are you?'

'Pained.' She paused. 'Can I tell you something?'

Gina smiled. She hoped it was the answer to Jacob's proposal.

'We're getting married.'

'Congratulations. You deserve every happiness. You and Jacob are perfect together.'

A twinge of sadness washed over her ashen face and a tear slid down her cheek. 'Our baby died.'

'I'm so sorry, sweetheart.' Gina leaned forward and gently held Jennifer like she would her own daughter. Jennifer's tears dampened her sleeve. The poor woman had been through the wars.

'Jen.' Annabel held Cally's hand in hers and they both hurried over, gently hugging and kissing Jennifer.

'I'll leave you to it. You all have a lot of catching up to do.'

Jennifer gripped her hand. 'Thank you.'

Cally smiled at Gina. Annabel had given a statement in the night. For now, Gina would let the friends be together before asking her any more questions. They all needed time to be together and Gina was going to respect that. Annabel had lost her father, her husband, and she'd told them everything about Whittle, adding weight to the case against him too. She'd done enough for now. She needed her strength for the court case.

As Gina left she passed Jacob in the main corridor. 'Call me if you need anything at all, okay?'

''Course, guv.'

'It's Gina when we're not on duty. Now, go and be with Jennifer.' They had been through so much over the past few days and Gina knew that the healing would be tough. They would mourn the loss of their baby, they'd have their work to do with Jennifer's recovery and they would carry the burden of never getting justice. Evan had determined his own end.

As she reached the main entrance and left the hospital, the April sun shone golden rays across the car park, little glints of it bouncing off all the windows. She checked her watch and for a second hoped that Briggs would forget to come over for their talk. She knew he wouldn't. He had something to say and he was going to say it.

EPILOGUE

'Do you want a drink?'

Briggs shook his head and sat at her kitchen table under the stark main light. She'd put the rabbit in the living room.

'Well?' There was no point in prolonging this agony any longer. She could tell from the worry lines across his forehead that the news wasn't going to be good. He wasn't going to shout, "Surprise, she's my long-lost sister."

He fidgeted a little and went to speak but then stopped.

'How long?' They'd spent the night together two weeks ago. Had he been cheating on her?

'Not long. I met up with her several days ago. Things have moved fast. I've known her a long time.'

Gina poured herself a brandy and sat at the opposite end of the table. Her cat sensed an atmosphere and fled out of the cat flap. 'Okay.'

'I knew her a long time ago. She's just moved back to the area.'

'So you rekindled a school romance?'

He shrugged. 'We were close back then, not romantically but that was because she moved away. I always wondered why we never kept in touch. After my divorce, I wondered if we'd ever meet again and I saw her in the supermarket. She lives locally now.' He paused. 'I never meant to hurt you.'

A tear slid down Gina's cheek. 'I don't know what I expected from you and I always thought if you met someone, I could handle it.'

He pressed his eyes closed for a second. 'She had a child and she's a widow.'

'Okay.'

'It sounds stupid but I've never experienced being a father and let's face it, I'm past it and I'm never going to get the opportunity to be a dad, and I want that so badly, you can't imagine.'

'You never said.'

'I never said because I never thought I'd get the chance. This yearning right in my core is like nothing I've ever experienced. I can't let this go.'

Gina drank the brandy down in one. 'Do you love her, I mean really love her?'

He shrugged.

'Or do you like the idea of being a husband and father?'

'All I know is I can't stop thinking about having a normal family life when all we experience is horror on a daily basis. I want a reason to exist. I want someone to look after, to nurture. I'm human, Gina. What more can I say? This is my chance to be happy.'

'Will she make you happy? This seems rushed.' She hoped that he'd change his mind. Everything seemed too rushed. She loved him immensely and she'd never try to ruin any genuine happiness that would come his way but she could tell that he didn't love this woman; he loved the fantasy that he'd created in his head. 'It's not real.'

'You're a fine one to talk.'

'What does that mean?' Her hands gripped the empty glass.

'What we have, had... I wanted it to be real but it's like a weird dream. No one knows about us. It's not a relationship.'

'Well, what is it then?' Her head was aching with tension.

He didn't reply.

'What about all the secrets we share?'

He sighed. 'Is that all you care about?'

'No.'

He remained silent for a few seconds. 'They'll go to the grave with me.'

Gina imagined him getting closer to his new partner, eventually he'd tell. Couples always do. Then what? She had no choice but to trust him. 'You didn't answer me. Do you love her?' He remained silent. 'If you don't love her, you'll not only be messing around with her feelings, you'll have the child to consider.'

He scraped the chair on the floor and walked out, slamming her front door behind him without answering her question. She threw the glass against the wall and it shattered, just like she had. Laying her head on her hands at the table, she sobbed so loud she thought she might literally sob her broken heart out of her mouth. This woman had something to offer that Gina could never give him. A child. Love was irrelevant when the yearning to have a child was so strong.

Just when she thought that this week couldn't get any worse, it had. She leaned over and grabbed the bottle of brandy. Taking it into the lounge, she poured herself another glass. It was going to be a long lonely night and one which she'd never forget.

Once a loner, always a loner.

A LETTER FROM CARLA

Dear Reader,

I'd like to thank you massively for reading *One Girl Missing*. I loved exploring obsession as a theme. The way Annabel had been pursued and stalked gave me the shivers as I wrote her story. Without a doubt, what I put her character through has to be everyone's nightmare.

If you enjoyed *One Girl Missing* and would like to keep up to date with all my latest releases, just sign up at the following link. Your email address will never be shared and you can unsubscribe at any time.

www.bookouture.com/carla-kovach

Whether you are a reader, tweeter, blogger, Facebooker, TikTok user or reviewer, I really am grateful for all that you do and as a writer, this is where I hope you'll leave me a review or say a few words about my book.

Again, thank you so much. I'm active on social media so please feel free to contact me on Twitter, Instagram or through my Facebook page.

Thank you, Carla Kovach

KEEP IN TOUCH WITH CARLA

 facebook.com/CarlaKovachAuthor

 twitter.com/CKovachAuthor

 instagram.com/carla_kovach

ACKNOWLEDGEMENTS

I have a few words of gratitude to everyone who's helped bring *One Girl Missing* to life. Without a doubt, creating a finished book is a team effort.

My editor, Helen Jenner, has given me so much help and encouragement through the writing journey so thank you. Without her wisdom and notes, my book definitely wouldn't be what it is.

The whole Bookouture team are brilliant. Peta Nightingale, Saidah Graham and Richard King all keep me updated and informed in every way. I'm truly grateful, thank you.

The first thing everyone sees when the book is out there is the cover and I love what Lisa Brewster did with this one. It's fantastic, so many thanks to her.

A book is nothing if no one knows that it exists and I have the fabulous Bookouture publicity team to thank. Noelle Holten, Kim Nash, Jess Readett and Sarah Hardy all work incredibly hard and they make publication day special. It's both exciting and heart-warming to see them sharing the news of my book on what is a hugely special day to me.

Bloggers and readers are the best. There are so many books to choose and some of these lovely people chose mine. For that I'm hugely appreciative. I know how long it takes to prepare a review or blog post, so here's a great big thank you.

I love the Fiction Café Book Club. They've invited me to do Facebook lives in the past and I love posting into their group. I really feel as though I'm part of the friendliest, most supportive, book loving community. While I'm mentioning community, I'm grateful to be a member of the supportive Bookouture family. Thank you.

Beta readers, Derek Coleman, Su Biela, Brooke Venables, Anna Wallace and Vanessa Morgan, all gave so much time to read my earlier draft and for that, I'm so thankful. I need to add in a special note of gratitude here again to Brooke Venables who writes under the name Jamie-Lee Brooke, and Phil Price who are both authors. We are in a mini word count/motivation support group and it's fantastic how the three of us spur each other on. Long live the Writing Buddies group.

I need to say a gigantic thank you to Stuart Gibbon of Gib Consultancy for answering my policing questions. Without his expertise, I'd be lost. As I've barely even stepped into a police station, it's fantastic to know he's got my back when it comes to procedure and charges. Any inaccuracies are definitely my own.

The last and biggest thank you goes to my husband, Nigel Buckley, for the endless coffees and encouragement. He sends me up to do my work and keeps me hydrated and for that, I'm eternally grateful.

Made in the USA
Las Vegas, NV
06 March 2022

45117208R00194